THE ISLAND OF THE FIN PEOPLE

I

T he shaft of the arrow was black and fletched with crow feathers, but Hylas couldn't see the head because it was buried in his arm.

Clutching it to stop it wobbling, he scrambled down the slope. No time to pull it out. The black warriors could be anywhere.

He was ragingly thirsty and so tired he couldn't think straight. The Sun beat down on him and the thorn scrub gave no cover; he felt horribly exposed. But even worse was the worry over Issi, and the aching disbelief about Scram.

He found the trail that led down the Mountain and halted, gasping for breath. The rasp of the crickets was loud in his ears. The cry of a falcon echoed through the gorge. No sound of pursuit. Had he really shaken them off?

He still couldn't take it in. Last night he and Issi had made camp in a cave below the western peak. Now his sister was missing, his dog was dead, and he was running for his life: a skinny boy with no clothes and no knife; all he had was a grimy little amulet on a thong round his neck.

His arm hurt savagely. Holding the arrowshaft steady, he staggered to the edge of the trail. Pebbles rattled down to the river, dizzyingly far below. The gorge was so steep that his toes were level with the heads of pine trees. Before him the Lykonian mountains marched off into the distance, and behind him loomed the mightiest of them all: Mount Lykas, its peaks ablaze with snow.

He thought of the village further down the gorge, and of his friend Telamon, in the Chieftain's stronghold on the other side of the Mountain. Had the black warriors burnt the village and attacked Lapithos? But then why couldn't he see smoke, or hear the rams' horns sounding the alarm? Why weren't the Chieftain and his men fighting back?

The pain in his arm was all-consuming. He couldn't put it off any longer. He picked a handful of thyme, then snapped off a furry grey leaf of giant mullein for a bandage. The leaf was as thick and soft as a dog's ears. He scowled. *Don't* think about Scram.

They'd been together just before the attack. Scram had leant against him, his shaggy coat matted with burrs. Hylas had picked out a couple, then pushed Scram's muzzle aside and told him to watch the goats. Scram had ambled off, swinging his tail and glancing back at him as if to say, *I know what to do. I'm a goathound, that's what I'm for.*

Don't think about him, Hylas told himself fiercely.

Setting his teeth, he gripped the arrowshaft. He sucked in his breath. He pulled.

The pain was so bad he nearly passed out. Biting his lips, he rocked back and forth, fighting the sickening red waves. Scram, where are you? Why can't you come and lick it better?

Grimacing, he crushed the thyme and clamped it to the wound. It was a struggle to bandage it with the mullein leaf one-handed, but at last he managed, tying it in place with a twist of grass that he tightened with his teeth.

The arrowhead lay in the dust where he'd dropped it. It was shaped like a poplar leaf, with a vicious, tapered point. He'd never seen one like it. In the mountains, people made arrowheads of flint – or if they were rich, of bronze. This was different. It was shiny black obsidian. Hylas only recognized it because the village wisewoman possessed a shard. She said it was the blood of the Mother, spewed from the earth's fiery guts and turned to stone. She said it came from islands far across the Sea.

Who *were* the black warriors? Why were they after him? He hadn't done anything.

And had they found Issi?

Behind him, rock doves exploded into the sky with a whirring of wings.

He spun round.

From where he stood, the trail descended steeply, then disappeared round a spur. Behind the spur, a cloud of red dust was rising. Hylas caught the thud of many feet and the rattle of arrows in quivers. His belly turned over.

They were back.

He scrambled over the edge of the trail, grabbed a sapling and clung like a bat.

The pounding feet came nearer.

Scrabbling with his toes, he found a ledge. He edged sideways beneath an overhang. His face was jammed against a tree root. He glanced down – and wished he hadn't. All he could see was a dizzying view of treetops.

The warriors came on at a punishing run. He caught the creak of leather and the rank smell of sweat – and a strange bitter tang that was horribly familiar. He'd smelt it last night. The warriors' skin was smeared with ash.

The overhang hid him from view, but to his left the trail curved round and jutted over the gorge. He heard them run past. Then they rounded the bend, and through a haze of red dust he saw them: a nightmare of stiff black rawhide armour, a thicket of spears and daggers and bows. Their long black cloaks flew behind them like the wings of crows, and beneath their helmets their faces were grey with ash.

A man called out, terrifyingly close.

Hylas stopped breathing. The warrior who'd shouted was directly above him.

Further up the trail, the others wheeled round and moved down again. Towards him.

He heard the crunch of pebbles as a man came walking back. His pace was unhurried – Hylas guessed this was the leader – and his armour made a strange, hard clink.

'Look,' said the first man. 'Blood.'

Hylas went cold. *Blood.* You left blood on the trail.

He waited.

The leader made no reply.

This seemed to rattle the first man. 'Probably just the goatherd's,' he said hastily. 'Sorry. You wanted him alive.'

Still no reply.

Sweat streamed down Hylas' flanks. With a jolt, he remembered the arrowhead, left lying in the dust. He prayed they wouldn't spot it.

Craning his neck, he saw a man's hand grasp a boulder on the edge of the trail.

It was a strong hand, but it didn't look alive. The flesh was smeared with ash, the fingernails stained black. The wrist-guard that covered the forearm was the dark red of an angry sunset, and so bright that it hurt to look. Hylas knew what it was, though he'd never seen it this close. Bronze.

Dust trickled into his eyes. He hardly dared blink. The two men were so near he could hear them breathe.

'Get rid of it,' said the leader. His voice sounded hollow. It made Hylas think of cold places beyond the reach of the Sun.

Something heavy pitched over the edge, narrowly missing him. It crashed into a thorn tree an arm's length away and swayed to rest. Hylas saw what it was and nearly threw up.

It had once been a boy, but now it was a terrible thing of black blood and burst blue innards like a nest of worms. Hylas knew him. Skiros. Not a friend, but a goatherd like him: a few years older, and ruthless in a fight.

The corpse was too close; he could almost touch it. He sensed the angry ghost fighting to break free. If it found him, if it slipped down his throat . . .

'That's the last of them,' said the first man.

'What about the girl?' said the leader.

Hylas' belly tightened.

'She doesn't matter, does she?' said the other man. 'She's only a –'

'And the other boy. The one who ran off.'

'I winged him. He won't get far –'

'Then this is not the last of them,' the leader said coldly. 'Not while that other boy remains alive.'

'No,' said the other man. He sounded scared.

Pebbles crunched as they started up the trail. Hylas willed them to keep going.

At the bend where the trail jutted, the leader stopped. He put his foot on a rock. He leant over to take another look.

What Hylas saw did not resemble a man, but a monster of darkness and bronze. Bronze greaves covered his powerful shins, and a carapace of bronze overlaid his short black rawhide kilt. His breast was hammered bronze, surmounted by bronze shoulder-guards of fearsome breadth. He had no face: just an eye-slit between a high bronze throat-guard masking nose and mouth, and a black-painted helmet made of scales sliced from the tusks of boars, with bronze cheek-guards and a crest of black horsetail. Only his hair showed that he was human. It hung below his shoulders, braided in the snake-like locks of a warrior, each one thick enough to turn a blade.

Hylas knew the leader might sense his gaze, but he couldn't look away. He just had to keep watching the slit in that armoured head, knowing those unseen eyes were raking the slopes to find him.

For a moment, the head turned to scan upriver.

Do something, Hylas told himself. Distract him. If he looks back and sees you . . .

Bracing himself on the ledge, Hylas silently let go of the sapling with one hand, and reached for the thorn tree where the body of Skiros hung. He gave it a push. The corpse shuddered, as if it didn't like being touched.

The armoured head was turning back.

At full stretch, Hylas gave another push. Skiros fell, rolling and bouncing down the gorge.

'Look,' chuckled one of the warriors, 'it's getting away.'

A ripple of laughter from the others; nothing from the leader. The helmeted head watched the boy's body crash to the bottom – and then withdrew.

Blinking sweat from his eyes, Hylas listened to their footsteps recede as they headed up the trail.

The sapling was beginning to give under his weight. He grabbed a tree root.

He missed.

2

Hylas half slid, half fell all the way to the river. Pebbles rained down on him – but no arrows.

He'd landed face down in a gorse bush, but forced himself to stay still, knowing that a hunter spots movement quicker than anything. He felt bruised and scratched, but he didn't think he'd broken any bones, and he still had his amulet.

Flies buzzed in his ears and the Sun scorched his back. At last he raised his head and scanned the gorge. The black warriors were gone.

Skiros, however, had come to rest a short way up the slope. At least, most of him had. His guts were strewn over the rocks, like a fishing net spread out to dry. Vultures were already circling, and his head was twisted round, as if he was trying to take a look.

His ghost would need help to ease its passing, but Hylas couldn't risk burying him or doing the rites. 'Sorry, Skiros,' he muttered. 'Rules of survival. Don't help someone if they can't help you.'

Willows and chestnut trees overhung the river; it was a relief to be under cover. Stumbling into the shallows, Hylas fell to his knees and drank. He splashed himself, hissing at the cold on his hot, scraped flesh. He glimpsed his broken image in the water. Narrow eyes, mouth taut with strain; long hair hanging down.

The drink steadied him, and for the first time since the attack, he could think. He needed food, clothes and a knife. Above all, he needed to reach the village. Issi would know it was the safest place to be, and she must have got there by now. She *must* have, he told himself fiercely.

The gorge rang with the squawks of vultures; Skiros had disappeared beneath a heaving mound of snaky necks and dusty wings. To stop the ghost from following him, Hylas hurriedly picked wood garlic leaves and scattered them behind him; ghosts feed on the scent of food, the smellier the better. Then he set off at a run, following the river through the gorge.

He felt the trees and the rocks watching him. Would they give him away? He'd grown up in these mountains. He knew their secret trails and the ways of the wild creatures: the cry of that hawk, the distant *ugh! ugh!* of that lion. He knew the charred gullies you had to avoid because of the Angry Ones. But now everything had changed.

This is not the last of them, the warrior had said. He knew that Hylas was still alive. But what had he meant by 'them'?

With a shock, it occurred to Hylas that Skiros hadn't only been a goatherd. He'd been an Outsider.

Hylas was an Outsider. So was Issi. They'd been born outside the village; Neleos the headman had found them on the Mountain when they were little and set them to work. In summer they herded his goats on the peaks, and in winter they tended them down in the gorge.

But why were the black warriors after Outsiders? It didn't make sense. Nobody cares about Outsiders; they're the lowest of the low.

The Sun rode west, and shadows crept up the sides of the gorge. Somewhere far off, a dog was barking. It sounded anxious. Hylas wished it would stop.

He came to a little three-legged clay offering-table set under a tree for the god of the Mountain. It was covered with a mouldy hareskin; he grabbed the skin and tied it round his hips. A lizard watched him coldly, and he mumbled an apology in case it was a spirit in disguise.

It was good not to be naked, but he was dizzy with hunger. Too early in summer for figs, but as he ran he snatched a few mouse-bitten strawberries. He spotted a thorn bush where a shrike kept its food: on the thorns the bird had impaled three crickets and a sparrow. With a quick 'sorry' to the shrike, he gobbled the lot, spitting out feathers and bits of cricket shell.

He began to pass olive trees and patches of flat ground cut into the slopes. The barley was ready for harvest, but there was no one about. Everyone must have fled to the village – unless the black warriors had burnt it to the ground.

To his relief, it was still standing, although eerily quiet. Like frightened sheep, the mudbrick huts huddled behind their palisade of thorns. Hylas smelt woodsmoke, but heard no voices. Outside there should have been donkeys, and pigs nosing for scraps. Nothing. And the spirit gates were shut.

They were daubed with red ochre and, from the wild bull's horns lashed to the crossbeam, the Ancestor peered down. It had taken the body of a magpie, but it was an Ancestor all right – although not one of his.

Hylas scattered the barley he'd stolen on the way, but the Ancestor ignored his offering. It knew he didn't belong. The spirit gates were there to protect the village – and keep Outsiders out.

The gates creaked open a crack, and grimy faces peered through. Hylas had known the villagers all his life, but they glared at him as if he were a stranger. Some held sputtering torches of giant fennel stalks; all gripped axes and sickles and spears.

In a frenzy of barking, the dogs burst through and hurtled towards him. Their leader was a sheephound called Dart, as big as a boar and trained to rip open a man's throat at a command. He came to a bristling halt before Hylas and fixed his eyes on him, his head menacingly low. He knew Hylas wasn't allowed in-village.

Hylas stood his ground. If he took a step back, Dart would attack. 'Let me in!' he shouted.

'What do you want?' growled Neleos, the headman. 'You're supposed to be on the Mountain, watching my goats!'

'Let me in! I want my sister.'

'She's not here. Why would you think she was?'

Hylas blinked. 'But – where is she?'

'Dead, for all I care.'

'You're lying,' said Hylas. But inside he was panicking.

'*You left my goats!*' roared Neleos. 'She wouldn't dare come back without them – and neither would you unless you want a red skin!'

'She'll be here soon. Let me in! They're after me!'

Neleos narrowed his eyes and scratched his beard with one horny hand. He had a peasant's bent legs and lumpy shoulders from hefting a yoke, but he was sharper than a weasel, always scheming to get more for less. Hylas knew he was torn between the urge to punish him for leaving the goats, and the desire to keep him alive so that he could do more work.

'They killed Skiros,' said Hylas. 'They'll kill me too. You've got to break the rules and let me in!'

'Send him away, Neleos!' shrilled a woman. 'He's been nothing but trouble since the day you found him!'

'Set the dogs on him!' shouted another. 'If they catch him here, we're all in danger!'

'She's right, set the dogs on him! He must've done something or they wouldn't be after him.'

'But who *are* they?' cried Hylas. 'Why are they after Outsiders?'

'I don't know and I don't care,' snarled Neleos; but Hylas could see the fear in his eyes. 'All I know is they're from somewhere out east and they're hunting Outsiders. Well, *let* them! They can do what they like as long as they leave us alone!'

Shouts of agreement from the villagers.

Hylas licked his lips. 'What about the law of sanctuary? If someone's in danger, you've *got* to let them in!'

For a moment, Neleos hesitated. Then his face hardened. 'That doesn't work for Outsiders,' he spat. 'Now get moving or I'll set the dogs on you!'

Dark soon, and nowhere to go.

Well then, all *right*, Hylas raged at the villagers in his head, if you won't help me, I'll help myself.

Doubling back through the pines, he made his way to the rear of the village. It was deserted: everyone was still at the spirit gates.

If they thought he'd never been in-village, they were wrong. When you're an Outsider, you steal to survive.

Slipping through a gap in the thorns, he crept to the nearest hut, which belonged to a sly old widow named Tyro. The fire was banked up, and in the smoky red gloom he upset a little dish of milk that had been set down for the house-snake. On a cot in the corner, a bundle of rags grunted.

Hylas froze. Silently, he lifted a haunch of smoked pig off a hook.

Tyro shifted on her cot and snored.

He took a tunic slung over the rafters, but left the sandals, as he always went barefoot in summer. Another grunt from Tyro. He fled, righting the house-snake's bowl as he went; snakes talk to each other, and if you annoy one, you annoy them all.

The next hut belonged to Neleos, and it was empty. Hylas grabbed a waterskin, some rawhide rope for a belt, and a wovengrass sack into which he crammed a coil of blood sausage, a ewe's-milk cheese, a flatbread and handfuls of olives. He also stole a drink from the old man's wine jar, then flung ash in what was left, to pay him back for all the thrashings over the years.

Voices were coming closer; the spirit gates creaked shut. He slipped out the way he'd come – and realized too late that he'd forgotten to steal a knife.

The Moon had risen and the night crickets were starting up as he reached the shadowy grove of almond trees beyond the village. Hastily, he pulled on the tunic and tied the rope round his waist.

A few late bees hummed about the hives, and he spotted an offering-table in the grass. Hoping it had been there long enough for any creatures sent by the gods to have eaten their fill, he gobbled two honey cakes and a chickpea pancake crammed with a delicious mush of lentils, dried perch and crumbled cheese. He left a scrap for the bees and begged them to look after Issi. They hummed a reply; he couldn't tell if it meant yes or no.

It occurred to him that Issi couldn't have been this way, or she'd have eaten that pancake. Should he wait for her here, or try to find his way to Lapithos, and hope she'd gone there to find Telamon? But Lapithos was somewhere on the other side of the Mountain, and neither Hylas nor Issi had ever been there. All they knew about it was from Telamon's vague descriptions.

Somewhere in the distance, that dog he'd heard earlier was still barking. It sounded dispirited, as if it no longer believed anyone would come. Hylas wished it would stop. It reminded him of Scram.

He didn't want to think about Scram. There was a wall in his mind, and behind it were bad things waiting to be remembered.

In the mountains the heat goes fast once the Sun is down, and despite the coarse woollen tunic, he shivered. He was exhausted. He decided to get clear of the village and find somewhere to sleep.

He hadn't gone far when he realized that the dog had stopped barking. Now it was uttering long, outraged yowls.

These grew abruptly louder as Hylas rounded a bend.

The dog wasn't as big as Scram, but just as shaggy. Its owner had tied it to a tree outside his pine-bough shelter and left it a bowl of water, which it had drunk dry. It was young and frightened, and when it saw Hylas it went wild, rising on its hind legs at the end of its rope and flailing its forepaws in an ecstasy of welcome.

Hylas felt as if a hand had reached inside his chest and squeezed his heart. An image of Scram flashed before his eyes: Scram lying dead with an arrow in his flank.

The dog barked at him eagerly and waggled its hind-quarters.

'Shut up!' he told it.

The dog cocked its head and whined.

Quickly, Hylas untied his waterskin and sloshed water in its bowl, then threw it the sausage. The dog slurped the water and inhaled the sausage, then knocked him over and licked his cheek. Grief twisted inside him. He buried his face in the dog's fur, breathing in its warm doggy smell. With a cry, he pushed it away and scrambled out of reach.

The dog swung its tail and made imploring *oo-woo-woo* noises.

'I can't untie you,' said Hylas. 'You'd only follow me and I'd get caught!'

The dog gazed at him beseechingly.

'You'll be all right,' he told it. 'Whoever tied you up cared enough to leave water; they'll be back soon.'

That was right, wasn't it? Because he couldn't take it with him, not with the black warriors on his trail. Dogs don't understand about hiding. You can't tell a dog not to give you away.

But what if they killed it, like they'd killed Scram?

Before he could change his mind, he snatched the water bowl, untied the dog, and dragged it after him. When they were within sight of the village, he tied it to a tree, refilled its bowl, and checked that the rope round its neck wasn't too tight.

'You'll be all right,' he muttered. 'Someone will come.'

He left the dog sitting on its haunches, whining softly and watching him go. When he glanced back, it sprang to its feet and gave a hopeful *oo-woo*.

Hylas clenched his teeth and ran off into the night.

Clouds hid the Moon, and he lost his way. The waterskin and food sack weighed him down. At last he found a stone hut built into a wooded hillside. He could tell from the silence that it had stood empty a long time.

He crawled through the low doorway, crunching over bits of broken pot and inhaling a dank breath of earth. It was cold, and it smelt as if something had slunk in here to die – but it was shelter.

He huddled in the dark with his back against the wall. He could smell the dog on him. He thought of the last time he'd been with Scram. He'd pushed his muzzle away – but had he stroked his ears, or scratched him under his front leg, the way he liked?

He couldn't believe that he would never see Scram again. No big, warm, furry body leaning against him. No whiskery muzzle snuffling under his chin to wake him up.

Wrenching open the waterskin, he gulped a drink. He opened his food sack and groped for olives. His hands began to shake. He dropped the olives. He scrabbled on the ground. He couldn't find them.

The wall in his mind broke apart. Everything flooded back.

He and Issi had made camp in a cave on the western peak. Issi had wandered off to dig up asphodel roots, and he'd skinned the squirrel and set it to roast over the fire.

'I'm going to the stream to cool off,' he'd called to Issi. 'Don't let that squirrel burn.'

'When have I ever done that?' she'd shouted indignantly.

'Day before yesterday.'

'I did not!'

Ignoring her, he'd started down the track.

'It wasn't *burnt*!' Issi had yelled after him.

At the stream he'd left his knife and slingshot on a rock, pulled his tunic over his head, and eased himself into the water. The cry of a hawk had echoed from the peak: *Hy hy hy*. Vaguely, he'd wondered if it was an omen.

Suddenly Scram was barking furiously: *Come quick! Bad trouble! Come quick!*

Then Issi had screamed.

Hylas hadn't stopped to fling on his tunic. Grabbing his knife, he'd raced up the trail. Bear? Wolf? Lion? It had to be bad for her to scream like that.

As he neared camp, he'd heard men's voices, low and intent, and caught a strange bitter stink of ash. Ducking behind a juniper bush, he'd peered through the branches.

He'd seen four goats lying slaughtered; the rest had fled. He'd seen warriors – *warriors* – searching the camp. He'd seen Scram. In one appalling heartbeat, he'd taken in the shaggy fur matted with burrs, and the big tough paws. The arrow jutting from Scram's flank.

Then he'd glimpsed Issi hiding in the cave, her sharp little face white with shock. He had to do something or they'd find her.

His slingshot was back at the stream. All he had was his flint knife – but what good was that? A boy of twelve summers against seven men bristling with weapons.

Stepping into plain sight, he'd shouted, 'Over here!'

Seven ash-grey faces turned towards him.

Zigzagging through the trees, he'd led them away from his sister. He couldn't risk calling to her, but she was clever; she'd grab her chance and get out of that cave.

Arrows whined. One struck him in the arm. With a cry, he dropped his knife . . .

Huddled in the hut, Hylas hugged his knees and rocked back and forth. He wanted to rage and shout and howl. *Why* had the black warriors attacked? What had he and Issi and Scram ever done to them?

His eyes stung. A lump rose in his throat. Angrily, he choked it down. Crying wouldn't bring back Scram. Or find Issi.

'I won't cry,' he said out loud. 'I won't *let* them do that to me.'

Baring his teeth, he ground his fist against the wall to keep back the tears.

Moonlight woke him, shining through the doorway, and for a moment he didn't know where he was. He lay on his side, fighting panic. Then it all came back, and that was worse.

Soon as it's dawn, he told himself, you're off to Lapithos to find Telamon. Issi's bound to be with him. If not, you'll find her. She's tough and she knows the mountains, she can survive until then.

He shut his mind to the possibility that she might be dead.

As his eyes adjusted to the gloom, he made out what looked like a clay brazier near the doorway, mounded with charred bones. Beside it lay a broken knife and a row of arrows, each one neatly snapped in two.

With a prickle of alarm, Hylas sat up. There was only one reason for a row of broken arrows.

The dead man lay on his back against the opposite wall. His face was covered with a cloth, but Hylas could tell from his undyed tunic and calloused feet that he'd been a peasant.

His kin must have been torn between terror of the black warriors and the need to placate their kinsman's angry ghost; but they hadn't neglected the rites. They'd laid him on a reed mat with his sickle and spear, having killed both weapons by breaking them in two, so that his spirit could make use of them. For the same reason they'd smashed his cup and bowl and strangled his dog – which lay nearby, ready to pad at his heels into the afterlife. And this must have been one of the richer peasants, because in the far corner huddled a dead slave. Like the dog, the slave had been killed so that he could attend his master.

A *tomb*, thought Hylas. You've taken shelter in a tomb.

He couldn't believe he'd missed the signs. This was why the villagers had left that offering at the hives: so that the bees could share in the funeral feast. This was why the tomb had been standing open: to let the spirit pass.

And he'd broken all the rules. He hadn't approached from the west with his fist to his forehead, or asked the Ancestors if he could come in.

Not daring to breathe, Hylas reached for his gear.

In the corner, the dead slave opened his eyes and stared at him.

3

The corpse had the waxy pallor of the newly dead, and its eyes glinted in the moonlight.

Hylas shrank against the wall of the tomb. He watched the grey lips part. He heard it speak.

A voice as distant as death. Speech like the cry of hawks in a high, cold sky – in a tongue that he couldn't understand.

No, he thought. This can't be.

The corpse gave a long, rattling sigh. 'Ah . . . *Stay* . . .'

Hylas gasped. He saw how its speech stirred the dusty moonlight. *Breath.* This corpse had breath. 'You – you're *alive*,' he whispered.

The corpse bared its teeth in a terrible grin. 'Not – for much longer . . .'

Shrinking inside, Hylas edged closer. Beneath his hands the ground turned sticky. He smelt fresh blood.

The dying man was young: he had no beard. He wasn't a slave as Hylas had thought; his dark hair wasn't cropped, but long, it lay twisted beneath him. And he wasn't a peasant; his feet were too smooth. He wore a knee-length kilt of fine linen sewn with spirals round the hem, and a wide leather belt cinched tight about his slender waist. From the belt hung a dagger in a richly tooled sheath, and from his neck a beautifully carved amulet of white bone: a tiny, leaping fish with a mysterious smile. The fish swam on his chest in one black glistening slick of blood.

'*Hide me . . .*' he breathed.

Hylas tried to draw back, but the young man's icy fingers clutched his.

'I am from Keftiu.' He spoke haltingly, in a tongue not his own. 'A great island . . . far across the Sea . . .' His face worked. 'Dawn. They'll come to shut the tomb. They'll find me – fling my body to the vultures.' His agonized gaze sought Hylas. 'Help my spirit find peace.'

'I can't,' said Hylas. 'I've got to get away – if they catch me –'

'You need a knife,' gasped the Keftian. 'Take mine. I stole it. It's precious. Keep it *hidden*.'

The hairs on the back of Hylas' neck rose. 'How did you know I needed a knife?'

Again that terrible grin. 'A man crawls into a tomb to die. A boy crawls in to live. You think that's chance?'

Hylas didn't know what to do. The Moon was setting, and the night crickets were changing their song. He had to get out of here before the villagers came.

'Hide me . . .' pleaded the Keftian.

A dying wish is a powerful thing. Hylas couldn't bring himself to ignore it.

Quickly, he searched for somewhere to hide the man. The tomb was bigger than he'd thought, and in the gloom he blundered against piles of clay coffins. Some were for children, as small as cooking-pots, but others were bigger. He found one in the darkest corner and heaved back the lid, releasing a musty smell of bones.

Nothing would have made him touch them with his bare hands. Grabbing one of the broken arrowshafts, he shoved the skull and the larger bones aside, to make room. 'I can't carry you,' he told the Keftian. 'You'll have to climb in yourself.'

It was horrible, dragging the dying man across the floor and half-pushing him into the high-sided coffin, then folding his limbs till he lay curled like a baby in an earthenware womb. It must have been torture, but the Keftian barely moaned.

'How did you get here?' panted Hylas when it was done. 'And who killed you?'

The Keftian closed his eyes. 'They come from the east – from Mycenae. They're . . . I can't say it in your tongue. Birds that make a noise . . .' He gave a feeble caw.

'Crows?'

'Yes. We call them the Crows. Because they're so greedy and they feed on death.'

Hylas thought of the black warriors. He saw their dark cloaks flapping like wings.

Again the Keftian bared his teeth. 'It was night . . . To disguise myself I wore a poor man's cloak of rough hare-skin. They mistook me for a – an Out-sider. What does this mean, Out-sider?'

'It means someone who wasn't born in a village,' Hylas said curtly. 'It means you've got no Ancestors to protect you, and you've got to live out-village. You're not allowed to take part in sacrifices so you don't get any meat unless you can snatch time to hunt, or kill a sheep on the Mountain and fake its death in a landslide. Everyone looks down on you. That's an Outsider.'

'You're an Out-sider,' said the Keftian, watching him. 'Yes, you look different, your hair . . . you belong to the Wild. Are there many Out-siders in Lykonia?'

Hylas shook his head. 'Far as I know, only a handful.'

'And – you have kin?'

Hylas didn't reply. When Neleos had found him and Issi on the Mountain, they'd had nothing but the bearskin on which they lay, and Neleos had told them their mother had abandoned them. Hylas had never believed that: partly because he never believed anything Neleos said, and partly because it didn't fit his one memory of his mother. She'd loved him and Issi, he felt sure of it. She would never have abandoned them.

'On my island,' murmured the Keftian, 'we call such as you the People of the Wild. They paint patterns on their skin. You don't . . . How can they tell what you are?'

Hylas touched his left earlobe. 'We've got a nick cut out here. Neleos did it when he found us.' He swallowed. He'd never forgotten Issi's screams when it was her turn.

'Do you worship the Goddess?' breathed the Keftian.

'What?' Hylas was startled. 'We – we worship the god

of the Mountain, and the Lady of the Wild Things. But what's that got to do with –'

'Ah, that's *good* . . .'

'Tell me about the Crows,' Hylas cut in impatiently. 'Who are they? Why are they after Outsiders?'

'The Goddess . . . She has many names, in many different lands – but She is always the same Goddess . . .'

Hylas opened his mouth to reply, but just then a hoopoe called from the hillside: *oopu-pu-pu-pu*. Dawn soon. 'I've got to get out of here,' he said.

'No! Stay! I don't want to die alone!'

'I can't.'

'I'm scared!' begged the Keftian. 'At home we bury our dead in sight of the Sea – but I have *nothing* of the Sea – I'll never get home!'

'You've got that fish on your chest –'

'It's not a fish – it's a *dolphin* – but it's made of *ivory*, that's not of the *Sea*! Please . . .'

Hardening his heart, Hylas gathered his gear. Then, with a snarl, he crawled back to the coffin.

'Here,' he muttered, wrenching off his amulet and pressing the little pouch into the young man's palm. 'It hasn't done me much good, but you're dying anyway. It's got a bit of rock crystal I found on the peak, that's for strength, and some hairs from a lion's tail, that's for courage, I found a dead one in a cave. And a shell. I don't know what that's for, but it's from the Sea.'

'The *Sea*!' The Keftian's face lit up. 'So you've been there!'

'No, never. Someone gave it to me, but I haven't –'

'The *Sea* will give you the answers you seek! Yes, and the Fin People will find you . . .' Suddenly he grabbed Hylas' wrist and pulled him closer, his dark gaze piercing Hylas with alarming intensity. '*They know you're coming,*' he breathed. 'They are seeking you through their deep blue world . . . They will find you . . .'

With a cry, Hylas wrenched himself free.

'The Fin People will take you to their island . . . the fish that fly and the caves that sing . . . the hills that walk . . . the trees of bronze . . .'

He was raving. And grey light was stealing into the tomb. Hylas slung his waterskin over his shoulder and reached for his food sack.

'And when you reach the Sea –' the Keftian went on.

'I'm not *going* to the Sea –'

'– you must give it a lock of my hair.'

'I can't, I just told you!'

'Take it, take it now . . .'

Grinding his teeth, Hylas grabbed an arrowhead and cut a lock of the crinkly black hair, then crammed it in his belt. 'There! See? That's the last thing I do!'

The Keftian smiled up at him: no longer a ghastly grin, but a true smile that transfigured his face. 'And when you reach the Sea, you will ask the Fin People to fetch my spirit . . . You will see them coming . . . leaping together over the waves – so strong – so beautiful . . . and they will take me to the Shining One – and with Her I shall know peace, as a drop of water becomes one with the Sea . . .'

'For the last time, I'm not *going* to the Sea!'

The Keftian didn't answer.

Something about his silence made Hylas turn back and peer into the coffin.

The Keftian stared up at him with eyes that would never see again.

Without knowing why he did it, Hylas reached in and touched the lean cheek with his finger. He felt the warmth draining from the flesh as fast as water sinking into dust. A moment before, this had been a man. Now all that remained was an empty husk.

Again the hoopoe called from the hillside.

As quick as he could, Hylas slid the heavy coffin lid in place and muttered a swift prayer.

In the strengthening light he made out the coffins stacked against the walls, painted with red and yellow people dancing and making sacrifice. He spotted the Keftian's hare-skin cloak in a corner, and hid it behind a coffin. Where the dead man had lain was a big dark stain. He scuffed earth over it. That was the best he could do.

A distant music of reed pipes floated in from outside. The villagers were coming. Despite the terror of the black warriors, they had to bring gifts of wine and honey for the kinsman who'd become an Ancestor.

No time to lose. Hylas headed for the doorway.

The dagger. The Keftian had said he could take his dagger, but he'd gone and left it on the body, inside the coffin. He glanced back – and was startled to see the dagger lying right there on the ground in plain sight, *beside* the coffin.

He told himself that the Keftian must have slipped it from

its sheath and let it fall just before he'd climbed into the coffin. He must have done. Because there it lay.

Take it . . . Keep it hidden . . .

It was made of bronze, very plain and unadorned. It had broad square shoulders and three smooth rivets on the hilt; a tapered blade twice the length of Hylas' hand, with a strong straight spine sweeping down to a lethal point. The edges gleamed faintly red in the morning light. He had never seen anything so beautiful.

He picked it up. It was heavy, and though its hilt felt cool to the touch, in a heartbeat it acquired the heat of his hand.

The song of the flutes was coming closer.

Clutching the dagger, Hylas fled.

4

Hylas had scarcely taken cover on the hillside before the villagers reached the tomb.

To his relief, they hadn't noticed anything wrong: already they were piling rocks in front of the entrance. In the throng he spotted the dog from the night before, standing close to one of the village boys. Hylas was glad it was all right, but it hurt to see it snuffling the boy's palm. Scram used to do that.

He started over the hill at a run, picking buckthorn leaves to keep the Keftian's ghost away, and stuffing the lock of hair in his food sack, along with the dagger. He would make a sheath for it later; for now it had to stay hidden. Bronze wasn't for Outsiders. If he was seen with it, it'd be like shouting 'thief'.

Trying to remember everything Telamon had ever said about Lapithos, he headed east into the foothills. Straggling pines gave no cover, and man-high thistles scratched him with spikes as long as boars' tusks; but he saw no sign of the black warriors, or anyone else. He was thinking about this when he rounded a spur and nearly fell over a chariot.

In one horrified instant he took in two horses and a warrior in a rawhide helmet. The warrior had his back to him, but when the horses whinnied, he turned. Hylas didn't wait to see any more, he was off like a hare, racing up a ridge where the chariot couldn't follow.

Scrambling over the top, he skittered down the other side and made for the stream at the bottom. The chariot came thundering round the base of the hill in clouds of dust, the warrior yelling above the din. Hylas splashed into the stream, the waterskin and food sack bumping at his back.

Behind him a crash and the squeals of horses, then the warrior was coming after him on foot. Hylas zigzagged. The warrior zigzagged. A hand grabbed Hylas' shoulder, yanked him back, and they both went down with a splash. The warrior got him in an armlock, but Hylas flipped him over and held his head underwater. Wildly, the warrior lashed out with his fist, catching Hylas on his wounded arm. Hylas snarled and jerked aside. The warrior twisted out of his grip and came up spluttering. Hylas kneed him in the groin. The warrior fell back with a howl – but was up before Hylas and kicked him on the jaw. Hylas swayed. The warrior knocked him over and knelt on his chest, grabbed his hair with both hands, and shook him till his teeth rattled.

'Hylas it's *me*! Telamon! Your *friend*!'

30

'I can't believe you didn't recognize me,' gasped Telamon.

'I told you,' panted Hylas, 'I couldn't *see* you with that thing on your head.'

They sat by the stream, splashing cold water on their bruises. The horses were tethered nearby, quietly drinking.

'Sorry I kicked you,' mumbled Telamon.

'Sorry I nearly drowned you,' Hylas replied.

Telamon snorted a laugh. 'What happened to your arm?'

'I got shot,' said Hylas. His makeshift bandage had come off, and the wound was throbbing viciously.

'Does it hurt?' said Telamon.

Hylas splashed him in the face. 'What do you think?'

Telamon grinned and splashed him back. Then he jumped to his feet. 'Come on. We have to get out of here.' He seemed to take it for granted that they were in this together. Hylas wanted to thank him, but couldn't find the words.

They'd been friends for four summers, but always in secret, because Telamon's father had forbidden his son to befriend an Outsider. Despite that, Telamon sometimes managed to slip away to see Hylas and Issi without anyone knowing, although he went through agonies of remorse about deceiving his father.

At first, Hylas had been suspicious. What did this rich boy want with him? He'd soon perceived that Telamon didn't want anything, except to be friends. They were very different, but maybe that was why it worked. If Telamon needed to make a decision, he considered the outcomes carefully before he did anything, while Hylas thought fast and acted faster; he had to, or he wouldn't survive. Telamon lived by the warrior code of honour, which Hylas only laughed at, although he secretly found it intriguing. Above all, Telamon had a father whom he loved and revered. Hylas couldn't imagine what that was like. He'd never known his own father, and he'd never revered anyone.

For four years they'd been friends without anyone knowing – except of course for Issi, who adored Telamon. Together they'd built their first raft, and learnt to swim. Telamon had saved Hylas from an angry bull, and Hylas had hauled Telamon out of the cave of an irritated lioness. Telamon was a year older, and bigger because he got more meat, but Hylas knew more tricks in a fight. Telamon hated the fact that Hylas stole, he said it wasn't honourable; and yet he never betrayed Hylas and he never let him down.

But now, as Hylas watched Telamon inspecting the chariot for damage, he was struck afresh by the gulf between them.

Telamon was the son of the Chieftain, and he looked it. His tunic was banded with scarlet at the sleeves and hem, and his calf-high boots gleamed with oil, as did the sheath at his belt that held his knife. His long dark hair was braided like a warrior's, with little discs of clay at the ends to stop them unravelling, and on his wrist hung his sealstone of polished red jasper, carved with a tiny boar with bristles down its spine. His father had given it to him that spring, when he'd turned thirteen and started hunting boar. He had to collect enough tusks to make his own helmet, which meant killing twelve. So far he'd only got one, but he wouldn't let Hylas help, because to become a warrior you had to do it yourself.

'Telamon, what's going on?' Hylas said abruptly. 'Why are the Crows after Outsiders?'

'The Crows?' Telamon looked startled.

'The raiders, the black warriors! Why are they after Outsiders and no one else?'

Telamon frowned. 'I don't know. Soon as I heard what was happening, I went to warn you. I – I found your camp.'

'They killed Scram.'

'I know. I buried him. It was horrible. I thought they'd killed you too. Then I found your tracks. I lost them but I picked up Issi's –'

'She got away?' cried Hylas.

'She was heading west, but I lost her trail too.'

'*West!* And I've been going east! I thought she'd be bound to make for the village, or try to find you.'

'We'll find her, Hylas. She'll be all right.'

'She's only nine summers old.'

'They won't bother going after a girl.'

'But why hunt us at all?'

'I told you, I don't know!'

'What d'you mean you don't know?' exploded Hylas. 'Your father's the most powerful man in the whole of Lykonia!'

'Hylas –'

'He's the Chieftain! He's supposed to *fight* raiders! How can he *let* them hunt his own people?'

Telamon's dark eyes narrowed. 'Are you questioning my father's decisions?'

'Or does he only protect villagers, and leave Outsiders to fend for themselves?'

'Are you questioning my father?' demanded Telamon. His handsome face had gone stiff, and he was gripping the hilt of his knife.

The thing about Telamon was that to him honour was everything. He wouldn't hesitate to punish the least slur on his kin.

'No,' snapped Hylas. 'I'm not questioning your father.'

'Good,' Telamon said curtly.

There was an angry silence. Telamon went to check the horses' hooves for stones, and Hylas stayed where he was, by the stream. He knew his friend's capacity to brood. Telamon would not be the first to break the silence. Hylas thought about showing him the bronze dagger; but then he'd have to explain about its being stolen, and hiding a dead stranger in a tomb, and Telamon would be horrified.

Instead he called out to Telamon to lend him his knife. Without a word, Telamon chucked it over, and Hylas cut a strip from his tunic for a new bandage for his injured arm. He found some woundwort and chewed a few leaves for a poultice, then bound it in place with the bandage. Walking over to the chariot, he handed back the knife. Telamon took it, still without speaking.

When the silence had gone on long enough, Hylas said, 'So these are horses.'

Telamon grunted.

There weren't any horses on the Mountain, and Hylas had only ever seen them at a distance. The one nearest him was a towering monster with a glossy chestnut hide and a mane as black as pine pitch. He made to stroke it, but it set back its ears and tried to bite.

The other horse was friendlier, rubbing its nose against his chest and whiffling into his ear. Its great dark eyes were soft as plums, but the neck beneath his hand was solid muscle. 'Are they yours?' he asked Telamon.

'Not likely,' snorted Telamon. 'They're Father's. I'm not allowed to take them out.'

Hylas whistled. 'Don't tell me you *stole* them,' he said drily.

Telamon flushed. 'Borrowed.'

Telamon was fiddling with his sealstone, as he sometimes did when he was thinking through a problem. 'They're not raiders, Hylas. They're from the east, from the High Chieftain of Mycenae. And they're not called "Crows". They're a great clan: the House of Koronos. They have many warriors who fight for them. It's only ignorant peasants who lump the clan and their warriors together, and call them all Crows.'

Hylas gave him a sharp glance. 'You seem to know a lot about them.'

'I'm a Chieftain's son,' retorted Telamon. 'Of course I know something about them.'

'Well, as far as I'm concerned, Crows are Crows. They killed Scram and they tried to kill me and Issi.'

'I know, but . . .' Telamon's flush deepened. 'My father – he has no quarrel with them.'

Hylas stared at him. 'No *quarrel*? With raiders who come on his land and hunt his people?'

'Hylas . . .' Telamon hesitated. 'He's a Chieftain. That

means he can't always choose who he – who he has dealings with.'

Hylas brushed that aside. 'What about you?' he demanded. 'Do you have "no quarrel" with them?'

Telamon knitted his brows. 'I don't *know* why they're after Outsiders – but I'll do my best to find out.' He looked Hylas straight in the eye. 'I'm your friend,' he said distinctly. 'We will find Issi. I will get you out of this. I swear it on my honour. Now shut up and let's go.'

Gathering the reins, he jumped into the chariot. The horses reared, and he struggled to calm them.

'Do you know how to drive this?' said Hylas as he leapt in beside him.

'Hold on tight,' muttered Telamon, 'and keep your knees bent.'

The horses sprang away, the chariot lurched, and Hylas nearly went flying.

'I said hold on!' yelled Telamon.

As they went rattling over the stones, the flimsy wicker frame bucked so violently that Hylas thought it was going to break apart. The rawhide webbing sagged alarmingly under his feet, and he had to narrow his eyes against the grit thrown up by the flying hooves. But the horses were *fast*, faster than anything he'd ever known. As the land rushed past, the hot wind streamed through his hair and he laughed aloud.

Telamon threw him a glance and grinned.

With a jolt, Hylas realized they were going the wrong

way. Grabbing the reins, he hauled the horses to a skittering halt. 'We've got to turn round! We've got to go *west*!'

Telamon was furious. 'Why'd you do that?' he fumed as he battled to bring the horses under control. 'We can't take a chariot into the mountains! Besides, they're guarding the pass, we'd never make it! We have to go *round* the mountains! I've got it all worked out. We'll head south to the Sea, then we'll –'

'The *Sea*?' cried Hylas.

'We'll find a boat and row up the coast, then make land on the other side of the mountains and head in from there. It's not that far. We'll find Issi. I promise.'

The Sea, thought Hylas.

And when you reach the Sea, the Keftian had said . . . *When*. He'd been so sure.

'Which way d'you want to go?' demanded Telamon. 'Hurry up, Hylas, I can't hold them much longer.'

Hylas chewed his lip. 'You're right,' he said. 'We'll have to head south, and go round by the Sea.'

'*Thank* you,' said Telamon. He slapped the reins on the horses' rumps and they were off, clattering down the trail in billows of dust.

Hylas didn't have time to change his mind. Suddenly they were sweeping round a bend and the plains were opening out before him: a vast, flat, forested land dotted with patches of golden barley and silver olive trees – and beyond that, frighteningly far away – *more* mountains: peak upon peak, holding up the sky.

Hylas had never been so far east, and for a moment his spirit quailed. Mount Lykas was all he'd ever known: the peaks, the gorge, the village. He had only a hazy idea of what lay beyond.

He knew that Telamon's father got his wealth from the rich crops of the plains, and that Lykonia was the southern-most chieftaincy in a vast land called Akea. He was vaguely aware that somewhere far away there were other Akean chieftaincies – Messenia, Arkadia, Mycenae – and that across the Sea lay distant lands peopled by monsters; but he'd never really thought about them. Until now. The outside world was unimaginably huge. It made him feel as insignificant as an ant, and as easily crushed.

They reached a stream overhung by giant reeds, and Telamon hauled the horses to a halt to let them drink. He and Hylas jumped down. Telamon slumped on a rock, groaning and kneading his shoulders. Even on the ground, Hylas still felt the swaying of the chariot. The reeds were three times the height of a man and gave good cover, but he didn't like them. He pictured black warriors creeping up on him unawares.

Telamon took a calfhide bag from the chariot and tossed him a chunk of dried sheep's liver and a cowhorn flask with a wooden stopper.

'What's this?' said Hylas.

'Walnut juice. Your hair, Hylas. No one has yellow hair, you stand out like a beacon. You've got to look like everyone else or you'll be caught.'

After gulping his meat, Hylas smeared the walnut juice

on his hair, and it turned from the colour of wet sand to a streaky dark brown.

'Better,' said Telamon. He went to spy out the land, while Hylas stayed with the horses.

The friendly one was called Smoke; the vicious one was Jinx. Smoke stood quietly with one hind hoof tilted, but Jinx snorted and tossed his head. He wasn't as beautiful as Smoke – he had a bony nose and angry eyes – but Hylas guessed he was cleverer. It made sense to be angry. He probably hated having to pull a chariot.

Hylas told him so, and Jinx swivelled his ears to listen, then tried to bite his hand. Hylas grinned. 'Trust no one. Clever horse.'

Just then, both horses pricked their ears and uttered piercing whinnies.

Answering whinnies in the distance.

Telamon came crashing through the reeds. 'It's them!' he panted. 'Quick! There's a trail up ahead!'

Hylas jumped into the chariot and reached down to give Telamon a hand up, but to his astonishment his friend tossed him the provisions and thrust the reins at him. 'Go south,' he told Hylas. 'Follow the river and find a boat –'

'*What?* But you're coming too!'

'I'll head them off in the wrong direction, then go over the pass and meet you the other side –'

'Telamon, I'm not leaving you!'

'You've got to, it's your only chance!'

'I don't care!'

'They're not after me, they're after you! Now *go*!'

5

The horses were unbelievably strong. It was all Hylas could do to hang on to the reins and stay in the chariot.

A glance over his shoulder told him this wasn't going to work: he was trailing a cloud of dust a blind man could have followed. Then he saw a fork up ahead. The track on the right was wide enough to take the chariot, but the one on the left was narrow and plunged into reeds; he guessed it led to the river.

Tugging at the reins with all his might, he yanked the horses' heads to one side and brought them to a squealing halt, then leapt down and started frantically unhitching Jinx. Jinx stamped and tried to bite, but somehow Hylas got him free of the yoke without tangling up the reins. That left Smoke hitched to the chariot. A slap on the rump sent him thundering down the wider trail with the chariot bouncing behind him. With luck the Crows would follow its dust, and only discover the trick when it was too late.

Hylas scrambled on to Jinx's back, and the horse was so startled he shot off at a gallop. Hylas had ridden donkeys before, but never a horse – and Jinx *hated* being ridden. Clutching fistfuls of mane, Hylas clung on grimly. Reeds whipped his face and his food sack thumped against his back. Jinx tried to scrape him off under a willow. Hylas ducked, bashing his cheek on the horse's bony withers.

After a battle that went on forever, Jinx jolted to a halt and refused to go on. With a snarl, Hylas slid off and hauled him down the riverbank to drink.

The reeds made a stifling green tunnel, and the rasp of the crickets was so loud that if the Crows came after him he'd never hear them. He was worried about Telamon. *I'll head them off in the wrong direction . . .* How would he manage that without getting killed?

Watching Jinx munch giant fennel, Hylas realized he was ravenous. He'd left Telamon's provisions in the chariot, but he still had his food sack. Grabbing olives and a hunk of cheese, he ate some and offered a bit to Jinx. The horse flattened his ears and bared his teeth.

His flanks were dark with sweat and criss-crossed with fine black scars. Hylas had scars too, from Neleos' beatings. 'Poor Jinx,' he said.

Jinx shot him a wary look.

Hylas put the cheese and a couple of olives on the ground. Jinx snuffled up the olives and stamped on the cheese.

Hylas moved to stroke the steaming neck. 'You're not so bad, are you? You just don't like being beaten.'

Jinx reared, lashing out with his front hooves. Hylas

jumped out of the way – the reins whipped through his hands – and Jinx went crashing off into the reeds.

Hylas raced after him, but Jinx was gone.

First Issi and Scram, then that dog, then Telamon, and now Jinx. Some malevolent spirit didn't want him to have any friends.

'Well then all *right*,' he muttered. 'I'll go it alone.'

All day he followed the river down through the foothills. He quickly came to loathe the reeds. They were full of secret rustlings, and they wouldn't let him see where he was going – or what was in front.

Then he reached a gap, and that was worse.

The Sun was a bloody, burning globe, sinking behind the black mountains. The triple fangs of Mount Lykas were terrifyingly far away. Hylas thought of the trails he'd wandered with Issi and Scram, and the Ancestor Peak which he and Telamon had dared each other to climb. Above the peaks the sky was an ominous grey, and he caught a growl of thunder. The Sky Father was grinding the clouds together to make a storm. Hylas pictured Issi in the wind and the rain.

Until now, he hadn't even thought he *liked* her that much; she was just his annoying little sister, always asking questions and getting in the way. For the first time ever, he missed her.

On the lower slopes of Mount Lykas, he made out a tiny red flicker. Was that Lapithos, and were they lighting the beacons? Was Telamon safe in his father's stronghold? Or were the Crows burning it to the ground?

Suddenly Hylas had a terrible feeling that he would never see Issi or Telamon again.

'*Stealing* my chariot!' roared Telamon's father. '*Laming* my horses! Haven't I got enough trouble without you making it worse?'

Telamon leant against the wall to keep from falling over. He was exhausted, and he knew he was in for a beating: his father was gripping his oxhide whip. Telamon only hoped he could take it without making a sound.

But even worse was the fact that his father had discovered that he'd been friends with Hylas behind his back. One of his shepherds had glimpsed them in the chariot.

'*Lying* to me,' growled his father, pacing like an angry lion. 'Lying for *years*! Was this *honourable*?'

'No,' muttered Telamon.

'Then why?'

Telamon took a breath. 'He's my friend.'

'He's an Outsider and a thief!'

'But – *why* are they after Outsiders? It's not right!'

'Don't you tell me what's not right!' exploded his father. 'Just tell me where he went!'

Telamon raised his chin. 'I – I can't.'

'Can't or won't?'

'Won't.'

The Chieftain gave him a searching look. Then he threw up his hands. Telamon watched him prowl to the far wall and fling himself on to his green marble seat. On either side of it, painted lions greeted him with silent roars.

Apart from Telamon and his father, the great hall of Lapithos was deserted. It smelt of stale incense and rage. Even the mice in the rafters had fallen silent. Now and then the slap of sandals echoed in the courtyard, but no one dared come any closer. Thestor was a kindly man who rarely raised his voice. When he did, it meant something.

Telamon stood facing his father across the huge round central hearth: a throbbing sea of embers two paces wide, guarded by four massive pillars carved with black and yellow zigzags, like angry wasps.

The fire had been burning for generations without ever being allowed to die. The hearth was ringed with a circle of painted flames, and when he was little, Telamon had loved to crawl around it while Thestor sat drinking with his men, and the women in the upper chamber chatted over their weaving, and the big dogs lazily thumped their tails.

He'd loved the floor too, and he'd explored every one of its red and green patterns that warded off evil spirits. Those patterns now whirled sickeningly before his eyes.

'Someone get the boy a stool before he passes out,' bellowed Thestor.

A slave scuttled in, set one before Telamon, and fled.

Proudly, he ignored it. 'I did what I had to do,' he said.

His father glared at him.

But it was true. He *had* helped Hylas escape and he *had* decoyed the warriors away. He'd even recovered the chariot – what was left of it – along with poor Smoke, whom he'd found standing forlornly under a tamarisk tree with a stone in his hoof. Jinx was still missing. Telamon hoped this meant that Hylas was on his way to the Sea.

'Why are they after Outsiders?' he said again.

'Why is he your friend?' his father flung back. 'Does he matter more than your own kin?'

'Of course not!'

'Then why?'

Telamon bit his lip. Perhaps it was because he and Hylas were so different. He himself could brood for days over an insult, but Hylas simply didn't care what anyone thought of him; why should he, when they looked down on him anyway? Hylas was ruthless and self-reliant, two qualities that Telamon secretly feared he lacked. And Hylas had no father to live up to.

But it was impossible to explain any of this to Thestor.

Telamon watched the Chieftain put his forearms on his knees and rub his hands over his face. His scarlet tunic was covered in dust, and he looked tired and careworn.

Telamon felt a flash of love for him, and a twinge of anger at Hylas for coming between them. Hylas was his friend, but he would never understand that being the Chieftain's son meant you were torn between friendship and blood.

Hylas knew nothing of Telamon's world. He'd never seen painted walls where the Ancestors speared boars and conquered enemies. He'd never seen doors studded with bronze, or marble cups, or gold. He'd never even seen stairs, or a bath. And he had no idea that when Telamon was with

45

him, he only ever brought his second-best knife, because his bronze one would have been showing off.

His father was scowling and tugging at his beard. 'Things are worse than you know,' he said suddenly. Then he heaved a sigh. 'If you're a peasant, you can live your whole life without ever going out of earshot of your village; but we can't, Telamon. We're leaders.' His scowl deepened. 'For years I've kept Lykonia separate from what's been happening in the rest of Akea. But now this. I can't keep us apart any longer.'

'What do you mean?' said Telamon.

His father met his eyes for a moment, then glanced away.

Telamon felt a stab of alarm. He'd seen something in his father's eyes that he'd never seen there before. Fear.

'Father, I'm sorry,' he blurted out. 'But whatever's going on, I'll help you!'

Thestor rose to his feet and hefted the whip in his hand. Then he told his son to bare his back. 'I'm sorry too,' he said.

As dusk fell, Hylas found a fisherman's raft drawn up on the bank. *Much* better. Now the river could carry him all the way to the Sea.

Lying on his belly on the raft, he paddled with his hands. To his relief he saw no people, although once he glimpsed the fires of a village through the reeds. He pictured everyone huddled inside with the spirit gates shut against the Crows. But did they have spirit gates on the plains? In the mountains they said that plains people grew black barley and had no toes . . .

On impulse, he drew the bronze dagger from his food sack. Holding it made him feel stronger. It was too dark to make a sheath for it now, so instead he cut strips of willow bark and twisted them into twine, then strapped the dagger to his thigh, under his tunic, where it wouldn't show.

With more reluctance, he tied the Keftian's hair securely to his belt. He hated touching the dead man's hair, but if his food sack fell in the river with it inside, that would be worse: then he'd have an angry ghost at his heels.

Gripping the edge of the raft, he peered into the darkness, while the gurgling river swept him ever closer to the Sea.

The Sea will give you the answers you seek, the Keftian had said.

Hylas had never even seen the Sea except from the mountains as a distant blue-grey blur, but when he was small, Neleos' mate, Paria, had enjoyed scaring him with tales of the monsters of the deep. He had no desire to get any closer.

Night wore on, and the creatures of the wild came out. A viper swam past, its tapered head glinting in the moonlight. On the bank a lioness raised her dripping muzzle to watch him pass. In the reeds he caught the shadowy flicker of a water spirit. Her eyes were silver and inhuman, and she looked through him as if he didn't exist.

What power, he wondered, had chased him from the mountains?

Until now, he'd never thought much about the Great Gods. They were too far away and they didn't care about goatherds. But what if he'd offended one of them? The

Sky Father or the Earthshaker, or the Lady of the Wild Things? Or the shadowy immortals whose true names may not be spoken out loud: the Angry Ones, who hunt those who have murdered their kin; or the Grey Sisters, who crouch in their cave like ancient spiders, spinning their vast web which contains one thread for every living creature?

Which of these had decided that Skiros should die and he, Hylas, should live?

And what about Issi?

Fireflies flashed past, trailing threads of burning gold. On a reed he spotted a frog which had eaten so many of them that its belly glowed green.

Frogs were Issi's favourite animal. Once he'd caught a frog for her like this one and put it in a cage of twigs. She'd watched it till it stopped glowing, then carried it carefully back to the river and set it free.

She was always trying to make friends with wild creatures: with weasels and badgers and once, to her cost, a porcupine. And she adored Scram. When she was four and Scram was a puppy, Hylas could always make her laugh by shouting 'Scram! Scram!' – and instead of scramming, Scram would come racing towards them, his ears flying and his tongue hanging out. Issi never got tired of it. She'd clap her hands and yell 'Scram! Scram!', laughing so hard that she fell over.

Thinking of her made Hylas feel lonelier than ever.

From the moment Neleos had found them on the Mountain wrapped in a bearskin, it had been him and Issi against the world. Hylas had been about five; Issi about two. The old man had tried to take the bearskin, and Hylas had bitten him. And Issi had laughed . . .

The Sun woke him, shining in his eyes. The raft was stuck on a sandbank. The voice of the river had changed into a distant sighing, as of some vast creature breathing in its sleep.

Scrambling off the raft, Hylas found himself on a shore of glaring white pebbles. The river was gone. Before him shimmered water of astonishing blue that stretched all the way to the sky. Wavelets rimmed with white lapped his feet. The shallows were so clear that he could see right down to the bottom, where the waterweeds weren't green but *purple*, and among them he glimpsed weird little round creatures that bristled with black spines, like underwater hedgehogs.

Stooping, he touched the water with one finger. He licked it. He tasted salt.

They know you're coming, the Keftian had said. *They are seeking you through their deep blue world . . .*

Hylas swallowed.

He had reached the Sea.

6

The dolphin was restless.

For some time he'd had a feeling that he was meant to do something, but he didn't know what. The odd thing was, the rest of his pod didn't feel the same.

Usually if he felt something, so did the others. That was what it was to *be* a dolphin: you swam through a shimmering web of clicks and whistles and flickering dolphin thoughts – so that often it felt as if there weren't many dolphins but *one*, all leaping and diving together.

But not this time. When he tried to tell them, none of them understood, not even his mother. So now he decided to leave them for a while and see if he could find out for himself.

At first he kept to the Edge, where the Sea was noisy and bright. He heard the spiky cries of seabirds and the hiss and fizz of foam on the shore. He sped through a forest of seaweed because he liked its slippery tickle, and listened to a shoal of bream nosing for worms in the shallows. To take a look at the island that jutted from his range, he leapt out of the Sea, and for the flick of a flipper he was in the Above, where sounds were jagged and the Sun was yellow instead of green. But whatever he was supposed to do, it wasn't here.

Splashing back into the Sea, he left the restless clamour of the Edge and dived down into the beautiful Blue Deep, where the light was soft and cool, and he could hear himself click. He caught the suck and slither of an octopus, and was tempted to go after it, as octopus were his favourite prey and he enjoyed nosing them out of their holes. But the feeling of something he had to do stuck like a barnacle, and wouldn't let go.

As he swam deeper, the Sea grew darker and colder. He clicked faster, listening to the craggy rocks crusted with coral. Mullets fled from him in panic, and groupers grunted warnings to each other. He ignored them. Down he swam, clicking faster and faster till he reached the Black Beneath, where he couldn't see at all, but he could hear the peaks and valleys and the blind creatures moving in the dark. Here the Sea surged heavy and slow, which was a relief after the crashing, uneasy Edge. But whatever he was supposed to find, it wasn't here either.

As he sped back to the Edge for air, the dolphin wondered what to do next. It never took him long to decide things, even though he sometimes made mistakes, and now, in a splash, he knew. Telling the pod that he'd be back soon, he turned tail on them and struck out bravely for the open Sea.

For a while he was busy sorting the tangled noises, and

tasting the currents. The swell was bigger here, and he had fun racing up and down inside the waves. The whistles of the pod were growing fainter, but he wasn't scared; he was excited. He was the most adventurous young dolphin in the pod, and he loved exploring.

He also liked meeting new creatures, even if most of them didn't enjoy meeting him. After several failed attempts, he'd learnt that jellyfish stung and crabs pinched, and that it was no good playing with fish, because he always forgot and ate them. The best time he'd ever had was an amazing game with a seal, until it had remembered it was a seal, and swum away. The worst was when he'd tried to make friends with a dolphin from another pod; she'd butted him in the belly, then raked her teeth across his nose, which had hurt a lot.

Suddenly he heard a large, lumbering body wallowing on the Edge.

At first he thought it was a whale, but as he swam closer he heard that it didn't have a tail, and was made of trees. Humans!

The dolphin liked humans. They were so odd. They had no blowholes, and they talked through their mouths; and as they couldn't really swim, they just splashed about on the Edge. He also felt sorry for them, because they had to live in the Above, on horrible little dry scraps of land.

But humans were brave too, and almost as clever as dolphins; and the best thing about them was that if you swam just in front of one of their piles of floating trees, it pushed the Sea at your tail, so that you could go faster without even trying. It was exactly like riding the nose-wave of a whale, but without the danger of annoying the whale.

For a while the dolphin wove happily in and out of the waves in front of the humans, while they leant over the side, calling to him and flailing their flippers. Although he couldn't understand their strange, muffled speech, he felt that they were friendly and glad to see him.

It came to him that he was getting too far from his pod and ought to turn back; but at that moment he sensed that one of the humans wasn't happy.

He couldn't see her, she was hidden deep inside, but he sensed that she was half-grown and scared, and *angry*. He was sorry for her and he wanted to help, but he didn't know how.

Faint and far away, the pod was calling his name-whistle.

The dolphin felt a tug of regret. He wanted to stay with the humans. He hadn't found what he was seeking, and he felt in his fins that it was still out there waiting for him – and that it had something to do with humans.

But the pull of the pod was strong.

To say goodbye, the dolphin leapt out of the Sea and flicked his tail flukes, while the humans waved at him and bared their teeth.

Then he splashed down again into his beautiful Blue Deep, and raced off to find his pod.

7

Pirra heard the splash on the other side of the hull and pictured the dolphin plunging back into the Sea.

She knew it was a dolphin because she'd heard the sailors shouting, but she couldn't see it. She wasn't allowed.

It was hot in the hold and it stank of almonds and sick. She couldn't move. The cargo was crammed in around her and the deck was only a hand's breadth above her face.

Her throat tightened with panic. She gulped air, but couldn't get enough. If the ship went down, she'd drown.

Don't think about it. The Sea is calm. We're not going to sink.

Clutching her sealstone, she lay listening to the slap of rigging and the creak of timbers. They'd been sailing forever, the ship rolling nauseatingly from side to side. She'd been sick over a bale of linen. It was too dark to make sure, but she hoped it was her mother's best. Serve her right for shutting her in the hold.

Until yesterday Pirra had never even seen the Sea, and if the High Priestess had had her way, she still wouldn't have, because as part of her punishment she'd been blindfolded when Userref had carried her on board. But just before they'd put her in the hold, he'd broken the rules and unbound her eyes, to give her a glimpse.

She'd grown up with pictures of the Sea. It was painted on the walls of her room: neat blue waves zigzagged with yellow sunlight, and smiling dolphins nosing tidy little fishes, while big-eyed octopuses clambered about on the bottom, among sea urchins and crinkly green weeds.

The real Sea was nothing like that. Pirra had never imagined it would be so restless and so huge.

All her life she'd heard stories of the world outside, but she'd never been there. She'd grown up in the House of the Goddess: an entire hillside covered in chambers, courtyards, storerooms, cookhouses and workshops, where people swarmed like bees. She called it the stone hive, and she'd never been allowed out.

She couldn't see anything from her room, which gave on to a shadowy passage, but sometimes she managed to escape her slaves, and then she would race across the Great Court and up the stairs to the topmost balcony. From there she could look down over olive groves and vineyards, across barleyfields and forests, to the great twin-horned Mountain of the Earthshaker.

When you're twelve, she would tell herself, you're getting out. You'll drive a chariot and climb the Mountain, and have a dog.

Knowing this had made it bearable. Yassassara had promised: when she was twelve, she would be free.

The night before she turned twelve, she was so excited she couldn't sleep.

The next morning she learnt the truth.

'But you *promised!*' she'd screamed at her mother. 'You promised I'd be *free!*'

'No,' Yassassara had calmly replied. 'I promised I'd let you out. And so I will. Today you leave the House of the Goddess: to sail to Lykonia to be wed.'

Pirra had raged and bitten and screamed – but deep down, she'd known it was useless. High Priestess Yassassara had a will of granite. She'd ruled Keftiu for seventeen years, and she would sacrifice anything to keep it strong, including her only daughter.

In the end, Pirra had gone quiet. In sullen silence she'd let the women dress her in purple linen spangled with gold, and when Userref had come in, she'd ignored him. Even he, who was like a big brother, had betrayed her. He'd been part of the lie.

'I'm sorry,' he'd said quietly. 'I wasn't allowed to tell you.'

'How long have you known?' she'd said without looking at him.

'The harvest before last.'

'That's *two years.*'

He didn't reply.

'So that's why you were so keen that we learn Akean,' she'd said bitterly. 'You said it'd be fun to learn it from the old man in the weavers' shed; you said it'd be "something to do".'

'I thought it'd help if you could speak their tongue.'

'You let me go on believing I'd be free.'

Frowning, he'd smoothed his kilt over his knees. 'You needed something to hope for,' he'd muttered. 'Everyone does. It's what keeps them going.'

'Even if it's a lie?'

'Yes. Even then.'

Coldly, she'd sent him away, but after he'd gone she realized that he'd been speaking of himself. He'd been ten when he was snatched from Egypt and sold as a slave to the House of the Goddess. That had been thirteen years ago, but he'd never stopped wanting to go home.

Uncomfortably, Pirra shifted position in the hold. Userref had given her a waterskin, so she'd managed to wash off the worst of the sick; but the smell was thick in her nostrils, and she kept finding bits between her teeth.

In the gloom she made out the gifts intended for the Chieftain of Lykonia as her bride-price: man-high jars of strong black wine and bales of richly dyed linen; alabaster phials of perfumed oil that stank of almonds; ingots of the all-important tin. Pirra's heart fluttered angrily against her ribs. She'd been packed in among them like part of the cargo.

Her mother had known exactly what she was doing when she'd punished her daughter for daring to protest. Pirra was cramped and humiliated, but not really in danger; and her mother had given orders that when they reached Lykonia, they would make land away from the coastal settlements, so that Pirra could be let out and cleaned up well before the Chieftain set eyes on her.

Before they'd left Keftiu, Userref had tried to reassure her. 'I'll be there too,' he'd said. 'You won't be on your own.'

She clung to that. But when she thought of the future, she couldn't breathe.

All she knew about Akea was that it was a long way north of Keftiu, and peopled by warlike savages who couldn't be trusted – and that Lykonians lived in the south, and were the roughest of the lot. Akeans didn't build Houses of the Goddess, and they weren't ruled by priestesses; instead they had Chieftains with strongholds. That was where she would live, in a stronghold. Her mother said she would stay in it for the rest of her life, and only leave it when she was carried to her tomb.

Panic rose in her throat. From one stone prison to another . . .

'Let me out!' she cried, beating the planks with her fists. *'Let me out!'*

Nobody came.

You're not here, she told herself fiercely. *You're not in the hold of a ship, you're out in the sky with that falcon.*

Squeezing her eyes shut, she tried to go back to the moment when Userref had slipped off the blindfold, and she'd stood on the deck, blinking in the glare.

That first sight of the Sea. The white doves fluttering on the golden shore, the green sails billowing in a sky of limitless blue.

That was when she'd seen it. One moment she'd been craning her neck at the clouds – and the next, she'd heard a sound like tearing silk, and a bolt of darkness had come hurtling out of the Sun.

In awe she'd watched it swoop upon the doves. They'd scattered, but it flew too fast, and in the blink of an eye it struck; then it eased out of the dive in a graceful curve and flew off with leisurely wingbeats, a dead dove dangling from one talon.

'What *was* that?' she'd breathed.

Userref had bowed to the dwindling black speck. '*Heru*,' he'd murmured, lapsing into his native tongue. 'May He live for all time and eternity.'

'It came out of the Sun,' mumbled Pirra. 'Where – where does it live?'

'Anywhere. Everywhere. It's a falcon.'

To live wherever you wanted. To go wherever you liked . . . 'I never saw anything so fast,' she said.

'You never will. Falcons are the fastest creatures in the world.'

Huddled in the hold, Pirra ran her fingers over her sealstone. It was an amethyst engraved with a tiny bird that she used to think was a sparrow; but now she knew it was a falcon.

Suddenly she caught her breath. She pictured herself perched like a falcon on the mast of the ship – then spreading her wings and flying away.

Until now, she'd never thought about escape. She had believed her mother's lie: that soon she would be free. But what if – what if she could get away?

Excitement kindled inside her. Her thoughts began to race.

Even if she did escape, she'd never survive on her own in

a strange land; so that meant she had to get back to Keftiu – which meant putting an end to this match with the son of the Lykonian Chieftain.

But how?

Then it came to her. At the Feast of Green Barley, her mother had found a crack in one of the offering vessels. 'Get rid of it,' she'd said with disdain, and a slave had taken it and flung it over the outer wall. Pirra had climbed to the upper balcony and spotted it lying in a clump of poppies. She'd envied it. It was flawed, but it had got away.

At the time, she hadn't thought any further than that. But now . . .

Damaged things had no value in the House of the Goddess. Damaged things got away.

She was jolted out of her plans by a change in the ship's motion. It was no longer rolling from side to side, but bobbing up and down. She heard men calling to each other, and loud grinding sounds; she guessed that was the oars being pulled in. Suddenly the planks above her were being levered aside, and she was taking great gulps of salty air, and Userref was reaching down to pull her out.

The Sun was blinding. She heard the splash of surf and the cawing of a crow. 'Are we – is this L-Lykonia?' she stammered.

Userref's grip tightened on her hand. 'Be brave, Pirra,' he said. 'This is your new home.'

8

The crow in the thorn tree stared at Hylas with bright, unfriendly eyes.

'Go 'way,' he panted.

The crow laughed at him. In the time he took to wipe the sweat off his face, it could fly as far as he'd come all day. The coast was a tangle of spiny yellow gorse and mastic scrub that gave off an eyewatering smell of tar, and the glare was merciless. He'd long since emptied his water-skin. The Sea was taunting him: so much water, and nothing to drink.

He was furious with himself for losing the raft. He'd only left it for a while to scout out the coast, but when he'd returned the Sea had taken it, carrying it out of reach across the waves. Since then he'd been struggling over one rocky headland after another.

We'll find a boat and follow the coast, Telamon had said, *then make land on the other side and head in from there.*

Find a boat? How? Apart from a few shepherds' huts on

the hills, there were no signs of people. And this was the third day that Issi had been alone in the mountains.

Again the crow laughed. Hylas lobbed a stone at it. The crow lifted into the sky and flew away – purposefully, as if carrying a message.

Hylas wished he hadn't thrown that stone.

The monster ship floated in the bay. It was ten times bigger than any boat Hylas had ever seen. It had a beak-like prow with a great yellow all-seeing eye. Oars jutted from its flanks like the legs of an enormous centipede, and from its back grew a tree with vast green wings. Once, Telamon had mentioned that some ships had wings so that they could fly before the wind, but Hylas hadn't believed him.

Below him, on the shore, men were pitching tents and heading into the surrounding pine forests to look for fire-wood. They weren't Crows; they were Keftians. Like the young man in the tomb, they were beardless, and wore kilts bordered with spirals and cinched at the waist. Their weapons were splendid bronze double axes with curving twin blades, like back-to-back crescent Moons; but they'd left them casu-ally propped against the rocks, as if they didn't think they'd need them. Didn't they know about the Crows? Weren't they afraid?

Then Hylas saw something that made his heart race. Tethered to the stern of the ship was a little wooden boat. Like a calf keeping close to its mother, it bobbed in the shallows. He could swim for it.

As dusk came on, he picked his way down the slope into

the scrub between the tents and the woods, and settled down to wait.

The Keftians had brought animals with them; he watched them kill and skin a ewe. While it was sizzling on a spit, they gutted a netful of fish and set them to bake in the embers, then poured wine from jars and mixed it with water, toasted barley meal and crumbled cheese. Soon Hylas caught the dizzying smells of roast mutton and sizzling fat.

The flaps of the largest tent twitched and a woman stepped out – and suddenly stealing the boat became a whole lot harder.

She wasn't a woman, she was a priestess. Her tight green bodice was cut away to reveal her breasts, and at her neck she wore a collar of blood-red stones the size of pigeons' eggs. Her ankle-length skirt was a Sea of overlapping waves of purple and blue, spangled with tiny glittering fish like little bits of Sun. Golden too were the snakes entwining her arms and her crinkly black hair. Her pointed fingernails were yellow as the claws of hawks, and her haughty face was painted stark white.

Even from twenty paces, Hylas felt her power. Now what? To steal from a priestess would be the worst thing he could do. Who knew what curses she might send after him?

A slave handed her a stone bowl so thin it seemed filled with light. Chanting in her strange clicking tongue, she flicked wine on the fire, then moved to the shallows and cast gobbets of fat upon the waves. The offering over, her men settled down to eat, but she stayed at the water's edge, staring out to Sea.

A crow swooped for a scrap of fat from the shallows, then glided past her. She watched it intently. Hylas had a horrible feeling that it was the same crow he'd seen earlier, and that it was telling her about him.

Sure enough, she turned to face his hiding place. He froze. Her dark gaze swept towards him. He felt the power of her will. He fought the urge to jump to his feet and give himself up.

At that moment a girl burst from the tent and shouted something furious in Keftian.

All heads turned. Hylas breathed out. The eye of the priestess was averted.

The girl had the same dark eyes and crinkly hair, and he guessed they were mother and daughter; but if the priestess resembled a handsome hawk, her daughter was a scrawny young fledgling. She wore a purple tunic spangled with tiny golden bees, and a thunderous scowl. As she stalked across the pebbles, she snarled incomprehensibly at her mother.

With a word and a chopping motion of her palm, the priestess cut her short. The girl stood seething with her shoulders up around her ears. The priestess turned back to the Sea. The girl was defeated.

A young man – a slave? – approached the girl and touched her arm, but she shook him off. The young man didn't look Keftian; Hylas didn't know *what* he was. His skin was reddish brown and his eyes were rimmed with black. He wore a kilt of unbleached linen, and the amulet on his chest was a single staring eye. Like the Keftians, he had no beard; but even stranger than that, his smooth brown head was bald.

Again he touched the girl's arm and gestured to the tent. The fight went out of her and she followed him.

The wine had its effect and the camp grew noisy; men stumbled into the pinewoods, then back to the fire. The Moon rose. At last things began to quieten down, and the tents went dark. A single guard remained by the fire. Soon he too was snoring.

Holding his breath, Hylas crept past the tents and ducked behind a boulder a few paces from the fire. Now for the dangerous bit: the pebbly shore. He wished the moonlight wasn't so bright.

He was about to make his move when a shadowy figure slipped from the priestess's tent and stole towards him. In consternation he recognized the girl.

Go away, he snarled at her in his head.

For one heartstopping moment she passed so close that he heard the clink of her bracelets. She didn't see him. When she reached the fire she halted and stood scowling down at it. Her fists were clenched, her body taut as a bowstring.

What does she have to scowl about? thought Hylas. Somewhere in the mountains, Issi was battling to survive – and here was this rich girl who had *everything*: slaves, warm clothes, all the meat she could eat. What more could she possibly want?

Suddenly the girl snatched a stick from the fire. She blew on its tip to make it glow red. She stared at it with alarming intensity, her bony chest rising and falling. Hylas saw that the spangles on her tunic weren't bees, as he'd thought, but tiny double axes. Still she went on staring at the stick. He wondered if she was mad.

Suddenly she sucked in her breath – and pressed the burning brand to her cheek.

With a cry, she threw it away. Hylas couldn't repress a start. She caught the movement and saw him. Her eyes widened. She cried out. The guard woke up, spotted Hylas, and shouted the alarm. Men burst from the tents.

Warriors appeared at the edge of the woods. *Crows.* To his horror, Hylas realized that there must be a camp in there: a whole dark, silent camp of Crows that he'd never suspected.

The first warrior reached the shore and spotted him. He saw the notch in Hylas' earlobe. He shouted, 'It's one of *them!*'

Hylas blundered past the girl and flung himself into the Sea.

He went under and came up spluttering. Shouts behind him, and sounds of running feet. His food sack and water-skin were dragging him down. He shrugged them off. Arrows whistled past him. He dived underwater and swam blindly for the boat.

His hand struck wood. Somehow he scrambled in and untied it, found the oars and started rowing clumsily into the bay. He was used to handling light reed crafts, but this was much heavier; it bucked in the swell like a startled donkey.

Over his shoulder he glimpsed men pushing another boat into the shallows – where had that come from? Already they

66

were leaping in and hauling on the oars, and at the front an archer was crouching to take aim. Hylas ducked. The arrow hit the side of the boat and stuck there, quivering.

He rowed till his muscles burned. *Fool*, he berated himself. The Keftians weren't afraid of the Crows – *because they were in league with them.*

As he struggled past the dark bulk of a headland, the swell strengthened and he felt it pulling at the boat. Then he was heading into a white wall of fog, and behind him the shouts of the Crows were abruptly muffled. The Sea was *helping* him.

Hope lent him strength, and he rowed deeper into the fog.

He paused to listen.

No voices. No splash of oars. Just the slap and suck of waves against the sides of the boat, and his own sawing breath.

'*Thank* you,' he murmured to whatever spirits might be listening.

He rowed till he could row no more. With the last of his strength, he drew in the oars and curled up in the bottom of the boat. Fog beaded his tunic and lay clammily on his skin, and the Sea rocked him gently on her salty, sighing breast . . .

He knows he's asleep, and he's furious with the mad Keftian girl for sneaking into his dream. She's standing on the shore, waving a burning stick and sneering at him.

'Where's my sister!' he shouts at her.

'She's gone!' she taunts him in Keftian, which somehow

he understands. 'You went the wrong way, you'll never find her now!'

Her arm becomes longer and longer and she jabs the stick at the boat, burning a hole in it. The Sea rushes in. The mad girl howls with laughter. 'The Fin People got Issi – and now they'll get you too!'

Hylas jolted awake.

The fog had cleared and the sky was beginning to grow light. The Sea was still gently rocking him.

Blearily, he sat up. To the east, the Sun was waking: dawn was bleeding across the sky. To the west . . .

To the west, the land was gone.

In panic, he turned north – south – east – west.

The land was gone.

Around him there was nothing but Sea.

9

The Sea sounded different at night. Pirra felt as if it was mocking her failure to escape her fate. She'd thought that if she spoilt her face, she would avoid being wed. She was wrong.

Her cheek was a blaze of agony. She kept reliving the moment she'd done it. The smell of burnt flesh. The wild boy staring from the dark. And all for nothing.

'Take these,' said Userref. He knelt at the entrance to her tent, holding out strips of fine linen and a small alabaster bowl of green sludge. His cloak was beaded with fog, his scalp and chin shadowed with stubble. His handsome face was stiff with disapproval. Like all Egyptians, he believed beauty was a gift from the gods. To him, what she'd done was blasphemy.

'What's in the bowl?' she said.

'A salve, Favoured One.'

Favoured One. He only called her that when he was angry.

Without a word he passed her the bowl, then sat back on his heels. She dipped her finger in the sludge. She touched it to her cheek. Pain flared. She willed herself not to cry.

'You're doing it wrong,' he muttered. Snatching the bowl, he soaked a strip of linen in the salve, tilted her head sideways, and laid the wet dressing on the burn. She clenched her jaw so hard that it ached.

Userref's scowl deepened. 'You'll have a scar.'

'That was the point,' she said.

'*Why?* Why do such a thing?'

'I thought no one would want a girl with a ruined face. I thought they'd send me back, and on the way I could escape.'

'Tcha! How many times have I told you? You can't fight your mother! You'll never win!'

She didn't reply.

Her mother had shown no emotion at what she'd done. Calmly, she'd appraised her daughter's face. Then she'd said, 'You know that this changes nothing.'

'I wouldn't be so sure,' Pirra had retorted. 'The Lykonians will take one look at me and say no.'

'No, they won't. They can't. Keftiu is too strong. You'll go to Lapithos as agreed. All you've achieved is to make yourself into a creature no one wants to look at.'

Userref fastened the dressing in place with a band of clean linen tied under her chin. 'There. That's the best I can do.'

To keep him talking, Pirra asked what was in the salve, and he told her poppy juice and henna and a little *wadju*.

That cheered her up a bit. He couldn't be that angry with

her if he'd used some of his *wadju*. It was a special kind of rock, ground very fine, and to Userref it was very precious as it was the same fierce green as the face of his god. He used it as powerful medicine, and when he was homesick he smeared a little on his eyelids, to make him dream of Egypt.

Men's voices drifted through the fog, and she asked him what was happening. 'It's the Crows coming back,' he said. 'They lost the boy in the fog.'

'Who was he anyway, and why were they after him?'

'They say he's just some goatherd. They say he tried to kill their Chieftain's son.'

'"They say"?'

His lip curled. 'You know I never believe what strangers say; only Egyptians.'

It was an old joke between them. She would have smiled if it hadn't hurt so much.

'Two fishing boats have put in as well,' he added. 'They were scared of the Crows, but they got over it when we bought their catch.' He made to withdraw, but she held him back.

'Userref? You will still be with me, won't you? I mean, at the Chieftain's stronghold?'

Something about his hesitation made her go cold. 'I was to have gone with you,' he said gently. 'But then you did this to your face, and now your mother says I must leave you and return to Keftiu.'

A black chasm opened before her. 'But – I can't be without you.'

'It isn't up to me, Pirra. You know that.'

'But – *why*?'

'I told you. She means to punish you for spoiling your face. She knows this will hit hardest.'

'No!' Pirra clutched his arm. 'No, she can't do this!'

'I'm sorry, little one. I – I said I'd look after you. And I can't.'

'Userref!'

But he was gone.

Pirra huddled in the dark, clutching her knees. She felt hollow and sick. Ever since she could remember, Userref had looked after her. Her first memory was of toddling along the top of a high wall, and him hauling her off it just before she fell. He'd caught lizards for her to play with, and told her stories of his animal-headed gods. He was more than a slave. He was the older brother she'd never had.

The walls of the tent pressed in on her. She couldn't breathe. Without stopping to put on her sandals, she ran out into the dark.

Fog stole down her throat, and stones were sharp beneath her feet. She stumbled past shadowy figures in long black cloaks. They ignored her, heading for their camp among the pines.

Pirra hated the Crows. They'd emerged from the woods as the ship dropped anchor, like real crows descending on a carcass. They *said* they'd been sent by the Lykonian Chieftain, but Pirra didn't believe that. Those hard-faced warriors with their sinister obsidian arrows weren't sent by anyone. She had been around powerful forces all her life, and she knew the smell of evil. In the Crows she sensed a darkness that made her skin crawl.

Through the murk, she glimpsed a battered rowing boat drawn up on the pebbles. She realized that she'd reached the end of the bay.

Next to the boat, an old man sat mending a net by the light of a smoky fish-oil lamp. He stank like a dunghill, and his tunic was the filthiest Pirra had ever seen. His straggly beard was crusted with snot.

She stared at him and he threw her a rheumy glance. Then his gaze dropped to the gold bracelets on her wrists.

Up in the hills, a bird called. *Kee-yow, kee-yow.*

Pirra recognized it. Userref was good at bird calls, and he'd done this one because she'd wanted to hear the cry of a falcon.

Suddenly she knew. That falcon was calling to her. It was telling her that this was her chance.

Slipping one of the bracelets off her wrist, she held it out to the fisherman – and pointed at the Sea.

10

Telamon quickened his pace, while the falcon wheeled overhead. It had flown up from the south. He hoped this meant that Hylas had reached the Sea.

He was sore from last night's beating, and the food sack was chafing the weals on his back. His head was in a whirl. After the beating, his father had talked to him late into the night. 'It's time you played your part,' he'd said grimly. That turned out to mean wedding some Keftian girl from across the Sea, and shouldering the burden of who he was. His father had spoken of the Chieftaincy, and why he'd sought to distance Lykonia from what was happening in the rest of Akea. Afterwards, Telamon had lain awake, feeling as if he was in a bad dream from which he couldn't wake up. When he couldn't bear it any longer, he'd slipped from the stronghold and run away. He tried not to think of his father's face when he found out his son was gone.

Telamon had taken the shortest trail up the Mountain,

and around noon he reached the top of the pass. He ran to the rock where he and Hylas and Issi sometimes left messages. There was a pebble in the secret hollow, with a sign scratched in charcoal: a leaping frog. Telamon chewed his lip. Had Issi left it for Hylas, to tell him she was still alive? Or had Hylas left it for her? Or had one of them left it for *him*, to tell him – what?

Hurriedly he scanned the ground for tracks, aware that he should have done this first, instead of trampling them. Hylas wouldn't have made a mistake like that. Hylas knew all about following a trail: he could track a ghost over solid rock.

From the moment he'd first seen Hylas, Telamon had wanted to be his friend. It was four winters ago, and he'd been hunting with his father. As they were passing the village, they'd come upon some boys chucking stones at a small girl in a grimy badgerskin cloak, who was laying about her with a stick, even though they were twice her size. Then another boy had emerged from the woods, a scruffy figure in a filthy hareskin cape and rawhide boots caked with mud. Grabbing the girl by the belt, he'd faced the bullies and said, 'Touch her again and I'll break your legs.' They'd jeered at him – and he'd stared. Just stared. And they'd seen that he meant it, and slunk away.

More than anything, Telamon had envied that boy. Those village boys had known at once that he would do what he said. Telamon feared that if it had been him, they would have put him to the test, and he would have failed.

Near the meeting rock, he found several of Issi's foot-prints and one of her brother's. There'd been a storm in the night, and from the prints, he guessed that Hylas had been here before it, and Issi after.

Her trail led west, down towards the marshes of Messenia. From where Telamon stood, he could just make them out in the distance, and beyond them the blue-grey blur of the Sea. Maybe he could catch up with her and together they'd find Hylas, coming to look for them. What a reunion that would be . . .

He was about to start west when he saw the old woman crouching under the pine tree.

She squatted on her haunches, her mountainous flesh juddering as she rocked on her heels. Telamon knew her. Everyone did. He was instantly on his guard.

He should have guessed that Paria wouldn't be deterred from roaming the Mountain. What did she care about warriors? She was Neleos' mate and the village wisewoman; she could read the will of the gods in the ashes of a fire or the rustling of leaves, and she was skilled in curses and spells. No one wanted to cross a wisewoman, not even warriors of the House of Koronos.

'You're far from home, young master,' she said, baring a foetid ruin of black teeth.

'And you, Old One,' he said warily. Drawing nearer, he caught her stink of stale urine, and saw lice moving in the folds of her tunic.

'Where are you off to?' she said with an obsequious bow.

He flushed. They both knew that her servility was a sham and a form of mockery. She knew he was scared of her.

With a wheezy laugh, she patted the pine trunk. 'Paria

came to hear what her oracle has to say. But you, young master, you're heading the wrong way. The Chieftain wants you at Lapithos.'

He bristled. 'You can't know what my father wants.'

'Ah, but Paria knows much without being told. Bad things afoot at Lapithos. Thestor wants his son.'

Telamon hesitated. Should he follow Issi west, or turn back for home? 'Read the leaves,' he told the wisewoman. 'Tell me which way I should go.'

From between her pendulous breasts she drew a little birdskin pouch. Shaking grit into her palm, she sprinkled it over the tree's roots. 'Bones,' she told him with a chuckle. 'Bones ground fine, to feed my tree. The rich pay to ask the seer, while the poor pay Paria to listen to a tree – but it's the same god that speaks through them both.'

'If you want payment,' Telamon said impatiently, 'you'll have to wait.'

She leered at him. 'Paria is patient. She knows the young master will pay.'

From nowhere a wind got up and soughed in the pine, and she cocked her head to listen, fixing Telamon with her black beetle eyes. He wanted to look away, but he couldn't. Sweat trickled between his shoulder blades and stung the weals on his back. He felt her probing the dark corners of his spirit.

At last she spoke. 'The ways of men are tangled as roots. So is your heart, young master. That's what my tree says.'

'Th-that's no answer,' stammered Telamon.

Another foetid grin. 'But it's the truth.'

'I didn't ask for a riddle,' he cried angrily.

Paria laughed and went back to feeding her tree.

He paced up and down, thrashing at thistles with a stick. He had to find Issi and meet Hylas on the other side of the mountains – but his father needed him at Lapithos. *Bad things afoot . . .*

He threw away the stick. His friends needed him more.

With a curt nod to the wisewoman, Telamon shouldered his food sack and started west, towards the Sea.

II

The seabird had been following the boat all morning, glancing down at Hylas as if to say, *What, still alive?* He'd given up trying to hit it with an oar. He always missed.

He'd been rowing north, but the Sea kept dragging him south. And still no sight of land. The Sun scorched his shoulders and made his head throb. Salt stung his wounded arm. He was so thirsty he couldn't swallow – and *hungry*. He thought with longing of his food sack, left behind at the coast.

He'd been scanning the horizon for ships till his eyes ached, but so far nothing, although he kept spotting sails in the distance that turned out to be waves. And yet he knew the Crows would come after him. They were relentless. They were like the Angry Ones in human form.

When the thirst became unbearable, he scooped up a handful of seawater and drank it. It made him retch. He peed in the boat and tried some of that, but it tasted so bad he spat it out.

He still had the bronze dagger strapped to his thigh, but he hadn't seen a single fish; just some weird see-through creatures without eyes, that floated like pulsing veils. He caught one, but it stung worse than nettles, so he chucked it back.

Then he had an idea. The willowbark twine had dried tight round his thigh, but he managed to unpick the knots and free the knife. Cutting a strip off the hem of his tunic, he dipped it in the Sea and wrapped it round his head. The wet cloth was blissfully cool. *Much* better. He splashed himself all over, soaking his tunic. Why hadn't he thought of this before?

The bronze knife shone fiercely in the Sun, and for the first time he noticed that there was a mark engraved on the hilt: a quartered circle. He wondered what it meant.

He caught sight of his face in the blade. He looked bony and determined. It made him feel stronger. There *were* things he could do – and the knife could help.

Hacking another strip from his tunic, he cut two slits in it and tied it round his eyes. At once the sun-dazzle became bearable.

Next, he took the willow twine and strapped the knife by the hilt to the narrow end of one oar. There. A fine, sturdy spear. It was much heavier than a proper spear, but as he hefted it in his hands the blade flashed, and his heart swelled with pride.

He was *not* alone. Not while he had the knife.

He'd thought the spear would bring him luck, but by mid-afternoon he still hadn't seen any fish; and the seabird was gone. Black spots swam before his eyes. He was so hungry it hurt.

He'd never imagined the Sea would be so vast and so strange. It had no smell, no shelter, no tracks. He stared at the red dust under his fingernails: the last trace of the mountains. His spirits sank. Scram was dead. Telamon and Issi were far away. He was lost in a wilderness of water.

Leaning over the side, he peered into the deep. Back at the coast, the Sea had been a sunlit blue, but out here it was nearly black. He couldn't see the bottom. Did it *have* a bottom?

Far down in the dark, something sped past.

Hylas gripped the side of the boat. He knew that the Sea was full of horrors. Paria told tales of monsters with many limbs that seized ships and dragged them to their doom; of giant man-eating fish with teeth like knives . . .

Suddenly he was sharply aware of how he must look from below, huddled in his fragile little shell, waiting to be eaten.

A splash behind him. He spun round.

The Sea was calm, except for a trail of foam rocking on the water.

Another splash, this time in front.

He saw it: a fish leaping clear of the waves. At least, it looked like a fish – *but it had wings*.

Open-mouthed, Hylas watched it glide through the air and drop back to the surface, where it thrashed its tail and leapt again, spreading its strange spiny wings in another soaring arc.

The fish that fly . . . The Keftian's voice echoed in his head. It reminded him of – what? He had a nagging sense that there was something he'd forgotten to do.

No time to think of that, the waves were alive with flying fish: leaping, churning the Sea white as they fell and flew and fell again.

Grabbing his spear with both hands, Hylas lunged, missed, and nearly fell in.

Then he spotted something familiar: not a fish but a turtle, swimming slowly in the shade of the boat. He jabbed at it. Yes! The dagger caught the soft underbelly. He leant out to drive it deeper –

He fell in.

Down he went into the cold green Sea. It roared in his ears, rolling him in a net of bubbles till he couldn't tell up from down. *Keep hold of the spear, don't let go!*

Kicking towards the light, he burst from the surface.

The boat was gone. Around him he saw nothing but waves.

The swell lifted him up, then sucked him under. Coughing and gulping air, he prayed to the Lady of the Wild Things and to the Earthshaker, the great god who rules the Sea.

The Sea bore him up again, and he caught a choppy glimpse of the boat, alarmingly far away.

Clutching the spear in one hand, he battled the waves. He'd only ever swum in shallow lakes and rivers; this was much harder. Then the swell sucked him under again – and slammed him against the boat.

Spitting out seawater, he scrambled over the side. He hauled the spear in after him and lay panting with relief, staring at the Sun. He gave a jittery laugh.

The turtle was still feebly twitching on the end of the knife. Hylas thanked it briefly for giving its body to him, and ended its pain with a twist to the neck. Then he untied the dagger from the oar, slit the creature's gullet, and drank its blood.

As long as he lived, he would never forget that salty sweetness coursing down his throat; the squelchy coldness of the turtle's eyeballs bursting on his tongue like grapes; that wonderful cool wet flesh.

Now he felt a lot steadier. Crows or no Crows, he was going to survive.

Cutting off the rest of the meat, he set it out to dry, then scraped the shell clean, gnawing every last shred of flesh. He'd lost his head-coverings in the Sea, but the shell would do instead; and he could use it to bail out the water that kept collecting in the bottom of the boat.

When he'd finished, he cleaned the knife and thanked it. 'We did well, you and me,' he told it. The bronze glinted in reply. He felt a surge of pride that it had come to him, and nobody else.

Bronze. He'd never thought much about it, but now he was struck by its magic: this stone that was not stone, that was born from earth and fire, and possessed the power of both; that never grew old . . .

He'd forgotten to make an offering.

Casting the turtle's head overboard so that its spirit could swim off and find a new body, he tied two of the legs in a bundle with a length of gut. Then, muttering heartfelt thanks to the Earthshaker and the Lady of the Wild Things, he held the offering over the side and dropped it in the water.

Giant jaws rose from the deep and swallowed it.

12

Hylas heard the gentle lapping of water. He saw little waves rocking where the monster had been.

Jaws bigger than the boat. Teeth sharp as boars' tusks. If he'd drawn back his hand an instant later, it would have bitten off his arm.

And it was somewhere beneath him.

Not daring to touch the sides, he leant over.

Sun-dazzle and shadow. It could be anywhere. He pictured it sliding through the green water – water in which he himself had only just been swimming.

He grabbed the spear; except it wasn't a spear but an oar: he'd untied the knife to cut up the turtle. He grabbed the knife – then dropped it with a clatter. He fumbled to tie it to the oar. Come on, come on.

At last it was done. Clutching the spear, he scanned the Sea.

Every wave, every patch of wind-darkened water became

the monster. He spotted a fast-moving shadow sliding towards him . . .

The seagull screeched, and its shadow faded from the Sea as it flew higher.

Hylas sagged with relief. Shakily, he took off his turtleshell cap and wiped the sweat from his face.

It was only a seagull, he told himself as he settled the shell more firmly on his head.

He froze.

The monster lay just beneath the surface on the other side of the boat.

In one appalling heartbeat, Hylas took in its pointed fin and its sickle-shaped jaws. Its fathomless black eye.

Once, Paria had told him that there were two tribes of giant fish in the Sea: dolphins and sharks. *If you ever meet one*, she'd said, *you'd better pray it's a dolphin. Dolphins are sacred, and they don't eat people. Sharks do.* Hylas had asked how you told them apart, and Paria had cackled. *A shark never smiles, and its hide is rough as granite. But if you've got that close, it's too late.*

Hylas didn't need to touch that flinty hide to be sure that this was a shark. No hunter he'd ever seen in the mountains – no lion or bear or wolf – had such a stare. There was no light in it. It was a pit opening on Chaos: on the yawning void where even the gods fear to tread.

With contemptuous ease, the shark flexed its massive tail and slid beneath the boat.

Hylas waited.

The shark did not reappear. It might be anywhere.

The wind dropped to a hush. The heat grew stifling. The sky was a sullen yellow, darkening to grey where it touched the Sea.

Something bumped against the boat; just hard enough to make it rock. Hylas rearranged his clammy hands on the spear.

Lazily, the shark lashed its tail and swam away. Hylas saw the ripple of its gills, and its grey fin scything the waves.

With alarming speed it turned and came at him again.

Bracing his legs, he readied his spear.

The shark swam closer. Hylas drew back the spear and jabbed at its head. The shark twitched, nearly wrenching the weapon from his hands. He yanked it free with a jerk that almost flung him overboard and sent his turtleshell cap flying. The shark swam under the boat and seized the shell in its jaws. Thrashing its great head from side to side, it savaged the shell, crushing it as easily as if it had been birchbark. Then it dived, leaving a scattering of shards drifting on the foam.

Streaming with sweat, Hylas lowered the spear. He could still feel the awesome power as the shark had wrenched itself free of the spear, but in the water he saw no tinge of red. He hadn't even drawn blood. No knife – not even the bronze dagger – could kill such a monster.

And it would be back.

The Sun sank towards the waves, and still the shark circled. Hylas dreaded the coming of the dark.

Then, far to the south, he glimpsed something that kindled hope: a jagged black shape jutting from the edge of the Sea. He shaded his eyes with his hand. It wasn't a ship. It was land.

He started to row – clumsily, as the knife was still strapped to one oar. Out of the corner of his eye, he saw the grey fin following. He couldn't outrun it, but if he could keep going until he reached land . . .

The wind picked up, pushing him onwards. The Sea was helping him, carrying him towards it.

The shark kept pace with the boat, sometimes hanging back, sometimes drawing closer, but it didn't attack – almost, Hylas thought uneasily, as if it was waiting for something.

He noticed that the swell was getting bigger, and that the waves were now rimmed with white foam. The boat was rocking harder, water sloshing over the sides. He had to keep throwing down the oars and bailing with his hands.

With a cold clutch of terror, he realized what the shark was waiting for. To the north, the sky was black. The shark didn't need to attack the boat. There was a storm on its way. His little boat would be no match for it. The storm would pitch him into the Sea.

The wind strengthened fast. Soon it was tearing at his tunic with invisible claws, whipping his hair into his face. The boat was bucking like an angry bull. Hylas struggled to stay in and still keep a grip on the oars.

It flashed across his mind that he couldn't do both. If he left the knife strapped to the oar, it was bound to go over-board; but if he untied it, he lessened his chance of fending off the shark. He *had* to keep the knife. Besides, what use was a spear in a storm?

Bracing his legs against the sides of the boat, he struggled to untie the knots, then frantically strapped one end of the twine round the knife-hilt and the other round his wrist. He'd scarcely finished when the Sea lifted the nose of the boat out of the water, then slammed it down with a bone-jolting thud that sent both oars flying. Hylas clung on desperately.

A deafening crash of thunder – and the storm broke and the rain hammered down. In a heartbeat Hylas was streaming wet. The Sky Father was battling the Earthshaker, with him caught in the middle. Waves as tall as trees were clawing at the clouds, the wind screaming its fury as it savaged the Sea, ripping off great stinging sheets of spray and hurling them at the sky.

Again the Sea tossed the boat clear out of the water and smacked it down, but this time the sky was gone. Hylas was in darkness – he was *inside* a wave as big as a mountain. With relentless force it sucked the boat upwards to its crest, it held him there, he was staring into an abyss; then it flung down the boat and he was plummeting faster and faster, racing towards a wall of black water . . .

The boat smashed into it and shattered like an eggshell.

13

No wind. No waves. Hylas floated under the stars on the quiet, black, breathing Sea.

He was cold. He'd been in the water so long that his skin was wrinkled and peeling. He couldn't quite believe that he was still alive.

The knife had saved him. In the storm its tether had got wrapped round a plank from the shattered boat, and as the other end was tied to his wrist, this had kept him afloat. The plank was just long enough to lie on, and at times he did, paddling with hands and feet and dagger; but he hated being unable to see behind him, so then he would sit astride the plank – only now his dangling legs felt horribly vulnerable, so he would lie on his belly again.

Either way, he'd been paddling forever, although the land at the edge of the Sea never seemed to get any closer.

The bronze knife gleamed in the light of the waning Moon. It kept him company, but it couldn't keep him safe.

He hadn't seen the shark since before the storm, but he knew it was out there.

He was exhausted, but he daren't stop paddling, because then he would fall asleep and the shark would get him . . .

Something brushed his foot. He jerked awake. The water around him was alive with fish: slivers of starlight flashing to the surface to feed, the bigger ones chasing the smaller.

He started to paddle, and the fish stayed with him. Then they were gone as swiftly as they'd come.

He stopped paddling. What was the point? He would never reach land. Like those fish, he was here to be eaten.

The dying Keftian had told him that the Sea would give him answers, but now he knew that wasn't true. The Sea was playing with him, as a lynx plays with a mouse.

A breeze sprang up, murmuring in his ear. Suddenly he remembered the promise he'd made to the Keftian. He'd promised to give his hair to the Sea, to set his spirit free.

Amazingly, the hair was still there, a sodden tangle tied to his belt. Wearily, he unpicked it and flung it across the waves. 'Take his spirit,' he mumbled. 'Let him be at peace.'

Silence.

Part of him had hoped that the Sea would give some sign to show that it had heard him; perhaps the Fin People – whatever they were – would come for the dead man's spirit, as the Keftian had said. But the lock of hair rocked forlornly on the water, and the night wind died with a defeated sigh.

Hylas lay down on his belly and shut his eyes. He couldn't go on. It was too hard. He was going to die out here, alone in the dark.

Let it be painless, he begged. *Let me slip away into the arms of the Sea and never wake up.*

In his head, he began to say goodbye. *Goodbye, Telamon. Sorry I couldn't meet you like we'd planned, I'd have had a lot to tell you. Goodbye, goats. To the ones the Crows killed, sorry I couldn't save you. To the ones that got away, you stay in the wild, don't let Neleos catch you.*

'Sorry, Scram,' he mumbled out loud. His throat closed. His eyes stung. 'Sorry I couldn't avenge you . . .' He drew a deep breath. 'Issi . . . Issi, I'm –'

His sister's name was like a slap of cold water in his face. It wasn't only *his* life he was giving up. It was hers. He was her big brother. He was supposed to look after her.

His one memory of their mother was of her telling him to do just that. He'd been lying under the stars wrapped in the bearskin, with Issi snuggled against him. It had been too dark to see their mother's face, but he'd felt her warm hand on his cheek and her long hair tickling his nose as she leant down and whispered, 'Look after your sister . . .'

If he gave up now, he doomed Issi and dishonoured their mother's memory. Something inside him – a hard, fierce kernel of strength – couldn't let that happen.

Wearily, he hauled himself upright. He struck the plank with his fist. He started to paddle.

The stars brightened. The bronze knife gleamed, urging him on.

Then he saw it. A fin, keeping level with him a short distance away. Just when he'd decided to live, he was going to die.

He drew in his legs. He heard the soft splash of wavelets against the plank. He watched the fin move ahead of him – then cut a wide, lazy ring around the plank.

The shark's head rose above the surface, then sank back. Its fin turned. It was moving towards him.

Nothing existed but the shark. Again it raised its head, and now Hylas saw its gaping jaws and its jagged in-curving teeth. Its black eye locked on his. He lashed out with the knife. The shark swerved. His fist grazed granite as it swam away.

Hylas watched the fin scythe the water in another lazy ring. It disappeared. He huddled on the plank, peering about him.

The shark erupted behind him. He jabbed at it – missed – and nearly fell off the plank. Again it swam away. Again it circled.

He knew now what it was doing; in the mountains he'd seen wolves do the same thing. It was testing the strength of its prey. It would come at him again and again till he was too exhausted to fight, and then it would make the kill. He didn't think it would have to wait long.

Something slithered against his thigh. He cried out.

It was only the Keftian's hair, drifting on the waves. With the tip of the knife he flicked it from him, and it lay like a snake on the black water.

Wildly, he cast about – but he could see no sign of the shark. The Moon's path was a trail of beaten silver across the Sea.

A black fin cut across it. It turned and started towards him. With a moan, he drew in his legs.

In the distance, he caught a strange blue glimmer.

Steadily, the shark came on.

The glimmer was getting bigger. Brighter. It was racing towards him. His eyes darted from it to the shark and back again.

Around him the Sea began to glow strangely, as if it had turned to cold blue fire. The unknown thing was arrowing towards him down the Moon's path, and as it drew nearer, he saw the gleaming curve of a great back – and then another and another, all swimming towards him, arching and diving in unison.

One of the creatures leapt clear of the water, and it was a giant fish made of pure blue light. Twisting round to look at him, it dived into the Sea with a luminous splash.

The shark was going to reach him first. Gripping the plank with his free hand, he brandished the knife. He stabbed at it. The blade glanced off its flank. The shark sank – then surfaced and turned to attack again.

At that moment the Sea exploded. An enormous fish burst from the waves in a rain of blue fire – but it wasn't a fish, it was a *dolphin*, Hylas saw its great shining body and mysterious smile as it plunged into the burning Sea, then leapt again, arching right over his head, so close that he saw its pale smooth belly and a raking of fine white scars on its nose.

For an instant the dolphin's eye met his and its spirit called to him – then it disappeared into the bright water. It surfaced at once, and with startling deftness snagged the lock of the Keftian's hair on its flipper. With a flick, it tossed it to another dolphin following behind. The second one caught the hair in its jaws and dived with it into the deep, while the first – the big one with the scars – powered into the shark and butted it with punishing force. The shark twisted round to bite, but the dolphin was agile. The shark snapped empty air.

Now more dolphins were joining the attack, surrounding the shark and butting it from all sides. Hylas gave a shout of triumph. The shark broke through and fled, and the dolphins raced after it, their radiant trails flickering and fading into the night.

But many more had stayed with him, and the Sea was churning with dolphins: leaping, slamming the burning blue waves with their tails; and now he heard them calling to each other in high, otherworldly squeals. He heard the soft *pfft* of their breath and saw the holes on top of their heads blink open and spurt glittering spray; he caught the gleam of their wise dark eyes.

He forgot his terror and despair. In awe he watched them arrow beneath him, trailing streams of luminous bubbles, then burst out to drench him in cold blue fire.

And they will come to fetch my spirit, the Keftian had told him. *You will see them leaping over the waves – so strong, so beautiful . . .*

The shark was gone.

The Fin People had come.

14

As night wore on, the fire faded from the Sea and the dolphins turned from shimmering blue to sleek silver; but still they wove a shining ring around Hylas. Their eyes threw back the moonlight like the eyes of wolves, and they swam so close he could have touched them if he'd dared.

They were creatures from another world. Often they moved in unison, twisting and turning as one; and though they were mostly silent, at times they pierced the night with alien shrieks. They seemed to breathe through the hole in the top of their heads, arching out of the water just long enough to exhale with a soft *pfft*, then diving under again. And although they passed within reach, they ignored him, intent on some mysterious purpose of their own.

They had saved him from the shark. But why? They belonged to the Lady of the Wild Things – and She, like all immortals, could create as well as destroy. What did She want with him?

Suddenly the ring widened and they began to play. The scar-nosed one was back – did that mean the shark was dead? Hylas saw that it often swam with a smaller, dark-grey dolphin with battered flanks and a notch bitten out of one tail fluke. She looked older; Hylas guessed she was the mother. A baby dolphin swam very close to her. Its nose was stubbier than those of the grown-ups, and it hadn't learnt to breathe properly; it spluttered through its blow-hole. When its mother broke the surface it had to jump right out to keep up, beating the air with its tail.

The scar-nosed dolphin – its big brother? – raced past and scooped a scrap of seaweed on to his snout, then tossed it to the mother. She caught it on her flipper and flicked it back to him, right over her baby's head. They kept this up for a bit, then the scar-nosed one let the baby catch it. Now Hylas was certain: definitely the big brother. When Issi was little, he'd sometimes let her win – until she'd guessed, and got annoyed.

The dolphins' play grew wilder, and his unease returned. There was a fierceness to their piercing shrieks and unchang- ing smiles. Summoning his courage, he tried to break through by paddling the plank forwards. The response was terrifying. The dolphins closed in and started slamming the waves with their tails – *bang bang bang* – so loud it was like a hammer beating on his heart. Why were they angry? What did they want?

After an endless time the tail-slamming ceased, but still they hemmed him in, and now they were clashing their jaws and diving so close that he had to draw in his legs. They'd saved him from the shark, but they wouldn't let him go.

Watching them was making him dizzy. He lay on the plank with his legs curled up. The dolphins never slowed down, never stopped moving . . .

He woke to the grey gloom before dawn. The dolphins were gone.

He missed them. They'd frightened him, but without them he felt horribly alone.

The land appeared slightly closer – he made out cliffs and a white rim of surf – but it was still hopelessly out of reach. He would never have the strength to paddle that far.

Suddenly a pale-green form arrowed beneath him, burst into the air, and smacked down on its belly with an enormous splash. The dolphin poked its scarred nose out of the water and looked at him.

Never in his life had Hylas been so glad to see a living creature. He croaked a greeting.

The dolphin uttered a shrill whistle and sank out of sight.

'Come back! Please! Don't go!'

The dolphin bobbed up on the other side of the plank, then went under again, surfacing a surprising distance away and swimming up and down. It was dark grey on top, shading to greyish white on its belly; the scars on its nose were three pale straight lines that looked as if they'd been raked by teeth. Why had it come back? Where were the others?

Suddenly the dolphin put down its head and rushed the plank, giving it a tremendous shove with its nose that sent Hylas headfirst into its blue-green world.

Down he tumbled, and the water was alive with eerie whistles and rapid high clicks. The dolphin came looming out of the blue, trailing silver bubbles from its blowhole. It swam astonishingly fast, even though it was scarcely moving its tail up and down, and as it raced towards him it clicked faster and louder. In panic, Hylas kicked for the surface, but the dolphin wouldn't let him escape; it was circling him with incredible agility, clicking so fast that the sounds blurred to a shrill buzzing whine that made him tingle all over. He lashed out with his foot and struck a solid dolphin flank. The dolphin vanished. Hylas broke the surface with a gasp.

An arm's length away, the dolphin nodded at him and made a squawking noise that sounded a lot like laughter.

Badly shaken, Hylas swam for the plank and scrambled back on. 'Why'd you do that?' he shouted. 'I didn't do anything!'

Again the dolphin laughed.

'I didn't *do* anything!'

The dolphin whistled. Weirdly, the sound didn't come from its mouth, but from its blowhole. How could you make sense of a creature that didn't even talk through its mouth?

The dolphin went under and came at him again.

Hylas bashed it on the nose with the flat of his knife.

The dolphin twisted round and thwacked him with its tail, sending him flying once more.

He came up spluttering.

The dolphin nodded and clacked its jaws.

Angry and frightened, Hylas swam back to the plank. 'It isn't funny!'

The dolphin went on smiling its infuriating, unchanging smile.

It had smiled at the shark too. All the dolphins had. In fact, they never *stopped* smiling.

It occurred to Hylas that maybe it wasn't smiling at all. Maybe it couldn't help it; that was just the way its mouth was made.

And that laughter . . . Maybe it wasn't laughter. Maybe the dolphin was angry.

To see if he was right, he imitated it. Smacking the water with the flat of his hand, he squealed and clacked his jaws.

The dolphin swam past, looking startled, then thwacked the Sea with its tail.

For the first time, Hylas looked, really *looked*, at it. Its eyes were dark brown and clever; and although he couldn't be certain, he thought it seemed puzzled.

'I'm sorry,' he said.

The dolphin went on swimming up and down.

'Sorry I hit you. But you scared me. What do you want?'

The dolphin swam closer. Hylas had an impulse to reach out and touch its nose, but he didn't dare. Its mouth was open; he saw a blunt pink tongue with oddly crinkled edges, and conical white teeth that looked sharp enough to snap off his hand.

'What do you *want*?' he said again.

The dolphin sank beneath the waves and disappeared.

15

Everything was going wrong. The pod was off hunting, but the dolphin hadn't gone with them because he needed to help the boy – only the boy wouldn't *let* himself be helped. Why?

The dolphin could see him on the Edge, drifting on his little scrap of tree, and holding that horrible stick in his flipper. The dolphin was scared of the stick; he could hear that it was sharper than coral. But he felt sorry for the boy.

Like all humans, he wasn't made for the Sea. His body was as flat as a flounder, and he had seaweed growing out of his head. Instead of a tail he had legs like a crab, but only two, and unlike a crab they were soft, and easily bitten off. His front flippers were even worse, as they were split into wiggly bits at the ends, which made them hopeless for swimming, although very tasty to sharks.

The thought of the shark made the dolphin prickle with alarm. He and his pod had chased it into the Black Beneath, where they'd butted it so thoroughly that it wouldn't be back; but there were more sharks in the Sea, and the boy was easy prey.

The trouble was, the dolphin couldn't get him to understand that he meant no harm. He'd tried, but the boy just got angry and biffed him on the nose – which made the dolphin angry too, so then they were both slamming the waves and calling bad things.

In frustration, the dolphin left the Edge and swam down through the Blue Deep, searching the tangled water for sharks. Nothing. Good.

When he returned to the Edge, the boy wasn't moving.

At first the dolphin thought he was dead. Then he saw his leg twitch, and realized that he was doing that weird thing which humans did, when they simply *stopped*. It was alarming, but the dolphin had learnt that it was their way of sleeping.

The dolphin surfaced, and the boy woke with a jerk, crying out in his odd, blunt human speech. The dolphin felt the boy's terror crackling through the water. He heard the frightened fluttering of his poor little puny human heart.

Everything was going wrong. The dolphin didn't know how to make the boy not be scared of him; and he feared what might happen with that stick.

Hylas missed the dolphin. Why had it disappeared again? What was he doing wrong?

He was weak with hunger and thirst, and so tired it was

an effort to stay on the plank, let alone paddle. His lips were cracked, his flesh spongy and pale from being in the water so long. The scab had come off the wound on his arm, which was throbbing and sore. He was finding it increasingly hard to stay awake.

Issi's voice came and went in his head. 'Come on, Hylas, hurry up and find me. I'm *hungry!*'

Telamon was here too, clicking his tongue with impatience. 'Surely you're not giving up? And after all the trouble I had to steal that chariot!'

A wave slapped him awake.

Only it wasn't a wave; it was a scrap of seaweed.

The dolphin was back.

Hylas was glad and scared at the same time. His heart began to pound as he gripped the plank in one hand, the dagger in the other. Was it going to rush him again?

This time it wasn't laughing or clacking its jaws. It swam quietly, arching above the surface just long enough to breathe before dipping under again. Maybe it wasn't angry any more?

Tentatively, Hylas took the seaweed and trailed it in the water.

The dolphin swam past – not glancing at him, but clearly aware of what he was doing. The second time it passed, Hylas saw it eyeing the knife in his fist. He swapped hands, laying the knife on the plank and trailing the seaweed temptingly with his free hand. He was tense. The dolphin was tense.

Hylas cast the seaweed over the waves and waited.

The dolphin swam past and took the seaweed lightly on the leading edge of its flipper, tossed it in the air, caught it deftly on its nose, swam on its side for a bit, then passed Hylas again, still with the seaweed.

Hylas reached for it. He missed.

For a while the dolphin played toss and catch by itself. Then it forgot the seaweed and dived. Anxiously, Hylas peered after it. Would it be back?

Suddenly he saw it far beneath him, rising with astonishing speed. He floundered to get out of the way. The dolphin surfaced right next to him, flexed its tail, and flicked something out of the Sea, right over his head.

Whatever it was fell with a splash. The dolphin swam after it and did it again. A fish. It was flipping a fish out of the water. Was it – was it trying to *help* him?

For a third time it tossed the fish high, and this time Hylas managed to catch it. With a triumphant cry, he killed it by bashing it on the plank, then sank his teeth in its belly. Blood squirted deliciously over his parched tongue. Spitting out scales, he gobbled the sweet, slithery guts.

After gouging out and eating the eyes, he cut off the head and threw it into the Sea for an offering; then on impulse he whistled and lightly patted the waves with his palm.

The dolphin appeared. Hylas did it again. 'Here,' he croaked, 'this is for you.' He tossed over the tail, and the dolphin caught it neatly and swallowed it whole.

'Thank you,' said Hylas.

The dolphin swam past him; then back again, a little closer.

Hylas put out his hand.

The dolphin brushed lightly against his fingers. Its skin was cool and incredibly smooth, the smoothest thing he'd ever felt. Again it swam past, rubbing its flank gently against his palm, and this time it met his gaze. Its eye was brown and wise and friendly, and it seemed to see inside him and sense all that he'd been through: his fear of the Crows, his grief for Scram, his shame at not having been able to protect Issi; his loneliness. And yet he could tell that it didn't belong to his world. Its gaze was as deep as the Sea, and though it was a living creature of flesh and fin and bone, it was also a spirit of the Sea, who belonged to the Lady of the Wild Things.

'Thank you, Spirit,' Hylas said quietly.

Spirit swam round him, then put his nose to the plank and gave it a gentle shove.

At last Hylas understood. The dolphin hadn't been trying to throw him off the plank. He'd been trying to push him towards land.

After that, things were much better. Hylas knew not to be frightened, and Spirit knew not to push too hard. He even seemed to know when Hylas needed a rest, and would circle, softly blowing, until Hylas was ready to go on.

But at last Hylas was too exhausted even to stay on the plank. He felt himself sliding off into the Sea, and knew he didn't have the strength to climb back on. Spirit seemed to know it too, because he swam underneath Hylas, as if offering to carry him on his back. Without even thinking about it, Hylas took hold of the dolphin's fin with both hands – taking care to ensure that the dagger didn't touch the soft grey hide – and Spirit began to pull him smoothly towards land.

It came closer with startling speed. Through a blur of exhaustion, Hylas made out a high ridge shaped like a boar's back, and dark red cliffs streaked with bird droppings. He thought he heard the guttural cries of cormorants, and something else, just beyond the edge of understanding: a faint, uncanny, gurgling singing.

A breeze shivered the Sea, smoothing the waves in great dark patches, like the footprints of some vast unseen being. Spirit swam past a headland, and Hylas glimpsed the shadowy mouth of a cave. From within he caught snatches of that weird, echoing song. What *was* this place?

The words of the dying Keftian drifted back to him. *The Fin People will take you to their island . . . the fish that fly and the caves that sing . . . The hills that walk and the trees of bronze . . .*

Then all that was forgotten as Spirit carried him into a wide, calm bay where wavelets lapped a beach of white pebbles and the water was a bright, sunlit blue.

His foot struck sand. *Sand.* With a moan of relief, he let go of Spirit and sank into a patch of slippery purple seaweed. Crawling clear of the waves, he collapsed on the shore.

The last thing he heard before he passed out was the *pfft* of Spirit softly blowing as he swam up and down in the shallows.

16

Pirra had never seen a bird swim, actually *swim*, underwater. It was black with green eyes. Was it a magic bird because it lived on this island, or did lots of birds swim underwater, and nobody had told her?

Enviously, she watched it surface with a fish in its beak and gulp it down. Her belly growled. It was a day and a night since the fisherman had abandoned her here with only a waterskin and a couple of dried mullet. Since then she'd eaten nothing but a handful of dusty sage.

On Keftiu she'd never had to think about food. When she was hungry, she simply clapped her hands and a slave would bring whatever she wanted: delicious little fried cheese balls rolled in sesame seeds; roast octopus stuffed with sorrel; fig cakes smothered in crushed walnuts and honey.

But here. There were fish in the rock pools, but whenever she leant over, they vanished. She'd never expected fish to move so fast. She'd only seen them in paintings or in a dish.

The island didn't want her. Seabirds screamed at her, and

sharp stones hurt her feet. The Sea heaved endlessly in and out of her narrow little inlet, splashing her with spray that stung her burnt cheek; but she daren't camp in the big bay on the other side of the headland. She had to stay hidden, in case her mother or the Crows came after her. She missed Userref, although he probably didn't miss her, as she must have got him into so much trouble by running away. She hated being so helpless and so scared. She had no sandals or cloak, which meant no shade by day and no warmth at night; and no idea how to wake up a fire. Sleeping in the open was frightening, with all the noises. The sky was immense and the stars glared down at her. Alarming shadows flitted across them that might be birds or bats – or worse. There was a cave where she went to refill her waterskin, but nothing could have made her sleep down there. Caves led to the underworld. You entered at your peril.

Shortly after the fisherman had abandoned her, a storm had blown up. Miserably, she'd sheltered under a juniper tree, getting soaked. Then she'd experienced what every Keftian dreads: the ground had begun to shake. Cowering under her tree, she'd begged the Earthshaker to stop. Was He angry because she was here, where she didn't belong?

The shaking hadn't lasted long, but she'd lain awake all night, waiting for the Bull Beneath the Sea to start stamping again. At dawn she'd thrown her earrings into the shallows as an offering, uneasily aware that she should have done this earlier.

She shouldn't be on this island; it was all wrong. She'd told the fisherman to take her to Keftiu, but he'd said it was too far, and despite her protests he'd set her down here. He'd been scared and in a hurry to get away. She hadn't known why until the next morning, when she'd recognized the shape of the ridge from a hundred Keftian paintings.

The fisherman had left her on the Island of the Goddess.

On Keftiu they told tales of the people who'd lived here in the old times. It was said that they'd grown proud, and angered the gods. Then they'd vanished, never to be seen again. Now the island was a deserted, sacred place, haunted by the ghosts of the Vanished Ones. Only priestesses came here from time to time, to make sacrifice, and perform secret rites to propitiate the Goddess . . .

The Sun rose higher, and Pirra got hungrier and hungrier. At last she decided to risk a venture into the bay. When the fisherman's boat had first drawn near the island, she'd spotted a shipwreck further down the coast. Maybe there she would find something to eat.

Her mind shied away from what would happen if she didn't. Cliffs barred the way inland; as far as she could tell, she was confined to the inlet, the bay, and the point on which the ship had been wrecked.

After a scratchy, midge-ridden climb, she reached the top of the headland. Panting and streaming sweat, she stared down at the sweeping arc of the bay.

There was a body on the beach.

Pirra dropped to a crouch and dodged behind a boulder.

The body lay on its front with the foam licking at its heels. Probably some drowned sailor washed up by the storm.

Pirra thought fast. Robbing the dead would be horrible.

But . . . It was wearing a tunic. She could use that to keep herself warm at night. And wasn't that a knife at its side?

At the back of her mind lurked an even more appalling idea. She needed food. *Could* she eat a person? Raw?

Summoning her courage, she took another look.

The body was gone.

For one dreadful moment she pictured a corpse creeping up behind her. Then she spotted it further down the beach.

It wasn't a corpse; it was a boy, stumbling over the pebbles. With a jolt, she recognized him. It was the Lykonian peasant who'd stared at her the night she'd burnt her cheek. His hair was oddly lighter than before, but it was definitely him: the same narrow eyes and straight nose that made an unbroken line with his forehead.

Her heart began to pound. The Crows were after this boy. They said he'd tried to kill Thestor's son. Pirra had a shrewd idea that that wasn't true, just an excuse they'd told Userref to fob him off. But still. This boy was dangerous. *And he was trudging straight for her end of the bay.*

Heart pounding, she shrank behind the boulder.

The crunch of pebbles as he came nearer. Then silence. He'd stopped at the foot of the headland.

Scarcely daring to move, she peered round the boulder and down the slope.

He was directly below her. There was seaweed in his strange, sandy hair, and his tunic was ragged and salt-stained.

His wiry limbs were covered in bruises, and there was an angry wound on his upper arm. In his fist he clutched a large bronze knife. Pirra held her breath.

The boy started to climb.

No, she told him silently, *not up here!*

He seemed to think better of it and dropped down again. He wandered back along the beach.

Shakily, Pirra breathed out.

She watched him go to the foot of the cliffs, where he found a stick and started digging a hole. Why? Then he left that and plodded to the shallows, where he found a plank drifting on the foam. Hauling it up the beach to a clump of boulders, he propped it against them. He fetched more driftwood. Oh, no. He was building a shelter – not twenty paces from where she hid.

The morning wore on, and still Pirra watched. The boy finished the shelter with thorn branches laid on the driftwood. Then he found a flattish piece of wood and cut a notch in it with his knife. Now what was he up to? Puzzled, Pirra watched him sit down and steady the wood with one foot, then take a stick and stand it upright in the notch. He rubbed it rapidly between his palms. He went on doing this, working his hands up and down the stick. Suddenly Pirra spotted a wisp of smoke. Still working the stick, the boy bent over and blew softly. *A flame.* He added bits of dried grass, then small twigs, then whole branches. Soon he had a fire briskly blazing.

Pirra was astonished – and annoyed. This grimy Lykonian

peasant had managed something she couldn't. She'd been outdone by a goatherd.

In consternation she watched him whittle three sticks to points, then deftly tie them with twisted grass to one end of a piece of driftwood, to make a three-pronged spear. After that he went down to the rocks and crouched.

He struck fast, and stood up with a small fish wriggling on the end of his spear. He ate it raw, which made Pirra feel sick. Then he speared two more fish and set them to roast over the fire.

By now it was well into the afternoon, and she was giddy with hunger. The boy ate every scrap of roast fish except for the heads, which he placed a few paces from his shelter – she guessed that was some kind of uncouth sacrifice – and added a few peelings of skin from his sunburnt shoulders, which she thought was absolutely disgusting.

Returning to the hole he'd dug earlier, he scooped out water in his cupped hand, and greedily drank. Pirra realized that it must have seeped up from the ground, which was why he'd dug the hole. That was clever, but there didn't seem to be much of it. At least when it came to this, she'd done better than him; he hadn't found the underground stream in the cave.

Having speared two more fish and put them in the embers, he dragged a mound of dried seaweed into his shelter and crawled inside.

Dusk came on. The smell of baked fish drifted on the breeze. Pirra couldn't bear it. She forgot the danger. She forgot everything except the smell of that fish.

Stealthily, she crept down the slope. As she drew nearer, she heard whiffling coming from the shelter. Good. Fast asleep.

Through the quivering heat she spotted a blackened fish tail jutting from the ashes. Silently, she picked up a stick to poke it free.

A hand shot out of the shelter and grabbed her wrist.

17

irra kicked and scratched, but the boy was horribly strong and he wouldn't let go. With her free hand she tore at his hair. He wrenched her arm behind her, forcing her down on to the stones. She clawed his face. His fist caught her an agonizing blow on her bad cheek. She screamed, startling him into slackening his grip. She wriggled loose and shot off across the pebbles.

Quick as a snake he was after her.

She spun round. 'Stay back!' she hissed in Akean. 'Or I'll put a spell on you!'

That stopped him.

'I mean it!' she gasped, pointing a shaky finger. 'I'll make you cough up your guts and – spit blood and *die*!'

'You couldn't do that,' he panted.

'Yes, I could,' she lied. 'D'you want to find out?'

He glared at her, wiping his mouth with the back of his hand. But he didn't come any nearer.

Close up, he didn't look any older than she was, although

frighteningly tough and capable of anything. Through his tangled yellow hair he watched her narrowly. It was like facing a wild animal.

She told herself that as long as she showed no fear, he'd *have* to obey. He didn't know she couldn't do spells.

Bracing her legs to stop them trembling, she said, 'Don't you know where you are, goatboy? This is the Island of the Goddess – and I'm the daughter of the High Priestess. That means you do what I say.'

He glanced at the little gold axes on her tunic. 'My name isn't goatboy. It's Hylas. And I'm a warrior.'

She snorted. 'You're a liar, like all Akeans.'

Ducking into his shelter, he brought out his knife and brandished it in her face. 'See this? It's a warrior's knife.'

It was bronze, very finely made. She pretended she wasn't alarmed. 'You stole it,' she said scornfully.

'No I didn't, it's mine.'

She hesitated. He took a step forwards. She took a step back.

'Where are the rest of them?' he demanded.

'Who?'

'Your people! The Crows!'

'I'm on my own – and the Crows are *not* my people.'

'Well you can't deny that you were camped with them. Where's their ship?'

'I told you, I'm on my own! I paid a fisherman to help me escape. He betrayed me and left me here.'

'Why would I believe that? You're mad. And you gave me away to the Crows.'

'I'm not mad!'

He tossed his head. 'Their ships are on the other side of that headland right now, aren't they?'

'If they were, d'you think they'd send me to steal a *fish*?'

He had no answer to that.

'I told you,' she said, 'this is the Island of the Goddess. There's nobody here!'

For a moment he studied her. Then he turned and went back to his fire.

Pirra was outraged. On Keftiu, no one turned their back on her. It was the height of disrespect.

When he continued to ignore her, she said, 'That fisherman will tell my people where I am and they'll come after me. They'll bring the Crows. You need to get off this island just as much as I do.'

He went on scraping ash off the baked fish. It smelt incredibly delicious.

'I found a shipwreck,' she added. 'If I show you where it is, you can make a boat from what's left, and we'll get away.'

He ate swiftly, cramming the flaky white flesh in his mouth and crunching up the skin.

'Give me some,' ordered Pirra.

'Catch your own,' he snarled with his mouth full.

'How dare you! Give me some!'

'Catch your own or go hungry, I don't care.'

She tore one of the gold spangles off her tunic. 'Here.'

He scowled. 'What's that?'

'It's gold. It's precious. You use it to buy things.'

'Then it's no good here, is it?'

116

'Don't you know what this is worth? You could buy whatever you want.'

He looked around him. 'From who?'

Pirra set her teeth. 'If you don't give me some of that fish, I won't show you where the wreck is.'

He gave a nasty laugh. 'I can find it without you.' Wiping his fingers disgustingly on his tunic, he pushed past her and sauntered down to the Sea.

Pirra stalked after him. She was so angry she was blinking back tears, and her cheek was on fire after that blow.

It flashed through her mind that if she stole his knife she could *force* him to obey; but that had occurred to him too, and he'd stuck it in his belt. There was also the fact that she'd found water and he hadn't; could she use that? But if she told him about the cave, he'd hurt her till she said where it was.

Out in the bay, something glinted. Then a great shining creature leapt from the Sea and splashed down in a shower of spray.

The boy broke into a grin and ran into the shallows. He gave a piercing whistle.

In the bay, the creature turned and swam towards him.

Pirra's jaw dropped.

The dolphin was much bigger than she'd imagined, and far more beautiful than any painting in the House of the Goddess. In awe she watched it arch out of the water, then roll under the waves: in and out, in and out, in a graceful, undulating rhythm. As it came closer she heard its soft, snorting breath. She saw its sacred smile. She put her fist to her forehead and bowed.

The boy waded waist-deep, and waited. The dolphin swam closer. *It brushed against him.*

Pirra was astounded. In disbelief she watched the dolphin circle the boy, who was splashing it gently with water, which it seemed to like. He waded deeper and began to swim. The dolphin slowed as it approached him again. The boy took hold of its fin with both hands, and it pulled him along. It swam faster and he lay at full stretch, skimming the waves as if he were flying.

Pirra stood speechless as boy and dolphin headed out into the bay. Who *was* this boy, that a creature of the Goddess should come to him?

After making a wide circle, they turned back for the shore. The boy let go of the dolphin and waded into the shallows, where he stood watching it swim away. He was smiling, his bony face briefly transformed.

He saw Pirra and his smile faded. 'So,' he said brusquely, 'this is how it will be. You will do what *I* say. Now show me that wreck.'

18

Hylas was almost certain that the girl was lying about the spells – but was she also lying about there being no Crows on the island? He made her go in front of him with the knife at her back, in case she was leading him into a trap.

'Ow, ow,' she kept saying as she picked her way over the pebbles. Hadn't she ever gone barefoot before?

He didn't believe her story about running away. Why would she run away? Even bedraggled and dirty, she was clearly the daughter of a leader. All that gold at her wrists and neck, and on that purple tunic. Unless she really was mad, and they'd left her here to get rid of her. The angry sickle-shaped burn on her cheek seemed to bear that out.

Whatever the reason, she was in his way. She clearly couldn't fend for herself, and he had enough to do keeping himself alive without having to feed her too. He decided to put up with her for long enough to build the raft, then leave her behind.

With painful slowness, she led him to the far end of the bay, then over a rocky point. He breathed out. No Crow warriors on the other side, and no ships drawn up on the beach. There was no beach. Only the wreck, just like she'd said.

It had been a sturdy ship with a full-bellied hull, but the Sea had smashed it as easily as if it had been made of bark. Hylas stared at the angry waves surging in and out of the gap that separated the wreck from the point. It was too wide to jump, and if he tried swimming, he'd be cut to bits or drowned; probably both.

And even if he reached it, what then? He'd have to manhandle every scrap of timber and rope across that gap, then build a raft, then find his way back to Lykonia over the shark-infested Sea . . .

'We could use the plank from your shelter,' said the girl, 'to make a bridge.'

'Mm,' he said doubtfully, although he'd just had the same idea.

'Once you're over there, you could throw things to me.'

He snorted. 'Too scared to risk it yourself?'

'I'm not scared. I can't swim.'

'I thought Keftians worshipped the Sea.'

'We do. But I've never been allowed out.'

He blew out his cheeks. She was even more useless than he'd thought.

They fetched the plank, but she kept dropping her end, so he shouldered it by himself. He managed to ease it over the gap and wedge it in the wreck, steadying the other end with stones; then, filled with misgiving, he crawled on to the makeshift bridge. The wood was slippery and sagged under his weight. The Sea churned beneath him, drenching him in spray. But the plank held firm, and he made it across.

Warily, he picked his way over a dismal ruin of half-submerged timbers that lurched treacherously underfoot. He found mounds of sodden sailcloth and tangled rawhide rigging, but to his relief, no bodies, just a mouldy cap and a sandal with a broken thong. He thought of the men who now lay at the bottom of the Sea, staring sightlessly at the fishes swimming through their hair.

Who had they been? Not Keftians. With irritating confidence, the girl had declared that the ship's nose was the wrong shape; she said it was Makedonian, whatever that was. He wasn't sure whether to believe her. He wished the ship had been full of Crows. He wished they were the ones who now lay at the bottom of the Sea, being eaten by sharks.

Kneeling by the sunken hold, he saw tiny fish darting in and out of huge, shattered jars. Something long and thin shot into a crevice. He drew back sharply.

'What is it?' the girl shouted from the point.

He peered in.

From the crevice, something peered back. It wasn't a snake. Hylas didn't know *what* it was. 'Some kind of – monster,' he called, trying not to sound alarmed.

'What's it look like?'

The thing emerged, spotted him, and withdrew. 'Body like a sack. Big eyes. Lots of legs, like snakes but – not.'

'Oh, you mean an octopus. They're sacred – but very

good to eat. See if you can spear it. Don't be scared, it won't hurt you.'

'I'm not scared!' he yelled. But he wasn't stupid enough to do what she said. It had to be a trick.

Poking around in the wreckage, he found a scrap of goatskin that would do to make a slingshot, and a scabbard of woven leather, only slightly rotted, and a perfect fit for his knife; then a small hide pouch tied at the neck with complicated knots like a nest of vipers. It felt empty, but when he described it to the girl, she said – with that irritating assurance – that it was a wind pouch: sailors bought them from seers and untied the different knots depending on what kind of wind they needed; hadn't he heard of them?

Setting his teeth, he went on exploring. He found a small earthenware jar that had survived intact, right down to its wax seal. 'Here!' he shouted at the girl. 'Catch!'

She missed. The pot shattered on the rocks, and olives bounced into the Sea. 'Can't you do *anything*?' he cried.

'You didn't give me any warning!'

'Oh, shut up and go and fetch some water! I suppose you can *find* my waterhole? It's near the cliffs, behind my camp. Wait – you'll need something to carry it in, won't you? Take the biggest bit of that pot you just broke. And be quick, I'm burning up!'

She stalked off with her shoulders around her ears. When she came back, he was astonished to see her fling down a full waterskin. 'There!' she snarled.

'Where'd you get that?'

'I'm not telling.'

'Why didn't you say you had water? I'm *thirsty*!'

'Oh, what a shame.'

In stony silence, Hylas crawled over the plank and drank his fill, then crawled back again. After that, they didn't speak.

Salvaging was hard work. He was still tired from his ordeal at Sea, and his muscles screamed for rest. He had a long, sweaty struggle just to untangle one oar.

Spirit came and swam up and down, trying to attract attention. Hylas splashed him for a bit, which he knew the dolphin liked, then went back to work. That seemed to annoy Spirit, who kept nodding and clacking his jaws. It was as if he wanted something. Hylas didn't know how to explain that he was busy, and eventually Spirit gave up and swam away.

At last the oar was freed, and Hylas hauled it higher up the wreck, out of reach of the waves.

It occurred to him that if Telamon had been with him, this would've been fun. Telamon would have been good at planning how to salvage the wreck, and they could have broken off to wrestle and splash each other. And Issi would have loved the Sea, and all the new creatures. And Scram would have padded up and down, swinging his tail and chasing seagulls . . .

'Why'd you stop?' called the girl.

'Why don't you go and find us some food?' he shouted. 'There's plenty of grass to make a fish trap, and you could set a couple of snares.'

She looked blank. 'What's a snare?'

He threw up his hands. She was unbelievable. It was amazing she'd survived this long.

He had a lengthy struggle to free another oar, and when he next raised his head, the Sun was getting low and the girl was gone. So was the plank.

In disbelief, he spotted it drifting out to Sea. She must have flung it away on purpose.

He was wondering how he was going to reach land when he saw her coming over the point with the waterskin, which she'd refilled.

She saw the plank and her jaw dropped. 'I didn't mean that to happen,' she said. 'I just pulled it in and left it on the rocks. I thought it'd stay there while I was gone.'

'Why did you do it at all?' roared Hylas.

'How are you going to get back?'

Ignoring her, he lashed the oars together, manhandled them to the edge of the wreck, and pushed them towards her. 'Grab hold,' he shouted. '*And don't miss!*'

By the time he'd got ashore he wanted to strangle her. 'You really are mad, aren't you? Don't you realize that if I'd been washed off and drowned, you'd have starved?'

'And if you'd followed me and seen where I found the water,' she shot back, 'you wouldn't need me any more – and then you'd *leave* me to starve!'

He was tempted to retort that he could find out where she got water any time he liked, by tracking her; but he didn't want to put her on her guard. 'If you try another trick like that,' he said, 'my dolphin will eat you.'

'Dolphins don't eat people.'

'How d'you know mine doesn't?'

That shut her up.

In the end, the only things they salvaged that day were some rope, the wind pouch and a bundle of sailcloth that they spread on the pebbles to dry.

Back at camp, Hylas made a slingshot and downed a seabird with a lucky shot. He baked it in the embers and ate the lot.

The girl was outraged. 'That's not fair!'

'Yes it is. First rule of survival: only help those who help you. And you didn't help.'

'What d'you mean? I found the wreck *and* the water!'

He shrugged. 'I'd have found them anyway.'

Fuming, she stalked off. Some time later she returned, with three of those sea-hedgehogs in her skirt. She ate them raw, scooping out the gooey insides with a stick.

This made Hylas suspicious. 'How come you don't know what a snare is, yet you know about sea-hedgehogs?'

'I've seen slaves preparing them in the cookhouse,' she said. 'And they're called sea *urchins*.'

'What's a cookhouse?'

She stared at him.

A bit later she said, 'What's a hedgehog?'

'They're the size of a boar,' lied Hylas. 'They've got huge fangs and they lurk behind bushes and leap out at night.'

In alarm she glanced behind her. Serve her right for losing the plank.

He wouldn't let her share his shelter, so she had to build her own. It was hopeless, and as she hadn't thought to fetch any dry seaweed to sleep on, she had to lie on the stones. He almost felt sorry for her. Then he reminded himself that her people were in league with the Crows.

Over his shoulder, he saw her huddled under her miserable pile of sticks on the other side of the fire. She was awake. Probably on the alert for hedgehogs.

Night deepened, and he lay listening to the foam hissing over the pebbles. He missed Issi. He missed her chatter and her never-ending questions. 'The thing about Issi,' Telamon had once said, 'is that she always has to be making some kind of *noise*. Either she's talking, or singing, or humming, or just chucking stones. I think it'd actually *hurt* her to keep quiet.'

Hylas shifted uncomfortably on his bed of seaweed. He missed them both. It felt like months since he'd last seen them. It was frightening to think that it was only a few days.

As he drifted off to sleep, he heard Spirit softly blowing in the shallows. Earlier, the dolphin had been trying to tell him something. Had he come back to try again? Hylas was too exhausted to find out.

Tomorrow, he told himself. He'll be there tomorrow.

The dolphin was getting really anxious. His pod had vanished. This had never happened before.

At first, while he'd been helping the boy, everything had been fine. He'd heard them calling each other's name-whistles as they hunted a shoal of mullet; then they'd gone off to take a belly scrub in one of the island's sandy inlets. After that he'd been too far away to hear, but he wasn't worried. He knew he could find them whenever he liked.

But not this time.

As soon as he'd got back, he'd searched the Blue Deep, but found nothing except a few scraps of mullet. He'd circled the island. He'd searched the Black Beneath, clicking anxiously as he tried to pick up their familiar, well-loved shapes.

Nothing. They'd disappeared in the flick of a flipper, leaving him alone.

Poking his snout through the Edge, he'd whistled their names at the Above. This time, he'd caught a faint reply. They sounded oddly muffled – as if their voices were coming through land. How could that be? He could hear that they weren't far away, but he couldn't *find* them. What did this mean?

The boy could help. He was clever for a human, much cleverer than the dolphin had first thought. He could swim a little and even hold his breath for a few clicks, and although he couldn't make himself understood in the swift-flowing dolphin way, his speech had a rough warmth in it and much feeling, so the dolphin could usually grasp what he meant. If the boy *knew* that the pod was lost, the dolphin was certain he would help find them.

The trouble was, he wouldn't listen. Ever since that girl had come, he'd been too busy fighting.

The dolphin wasn't sure about the girl. Once, when she was by herself in the little inlet, she'd waded into the water on her spindly crab legs, as if she wanted to make friends. The dolphin had swum closer and given her a gentle nudge, but she'd fallen over and splashed about, gulping, so he'd gone off in disgust. Another one who couldn't swim.

On the land, all was dark and quiet. Both humans lay in that deathlike, unmoving sleep which the dolphin found so disturbing. He hated it when the boy stopped moving. The dolphin never stopped moving. He couldn't imagine what it would be like. It was frightening even to think about.

Impatiently, he swam up and down. The humans wouldn't wake until it was light. Meanwhile, what to do? He was too anxious to hunt. Besides, he had to stay at the Edge, where he'd last heard the pod.

Being lonely *hurt*. He missed the soft sigh of his mother's blowhole, and the sound of her beautiful sleek shape as she sped through the Blue Deep. He even missed his little sister, and her ridiculous attempts at hunt-the-seaweed.

It was still dark in the Above when the dolphin decided. He had to find his pod, and he couldn't do it alone. He was fed up with being ignored. He had to make the boy *listen*.

And to do that, he had to go where no dolphin had ever been before.

Hylas woke with a start from an irritating dream in which the mad Keftian girl had stolen his knife.

The Sun wasn't yet up and the sky was just turning grey. The knife was still at his side, but the waterskin was gone. The girl wasn't in her shelter, and he couldn't see her on the shore. She'd probably sneaked off to refill it while he slept. Or else she'd fallen into the Sea and drowned, which would be annoying, because he needed her to help build the raft.

Thinking of this, he saw her emerge from the thornscrub at the foot of the headland.

'Glad that's cleared up,' he said drily. 'Now I know where you get your water. What is it, a spring?'

She didn't seem to hear him. She was breathless and pale, and the burn on her cheek was a livid red sickle.

'I found your dolphin,' she panted. 'It's bad.'

19

The dolphin had only wanted to make them listen. He'd thought that if he could get on to land, they'd *have* to take notice, and then they would help him find his pod. But the Sea had been angry with him for trying to leave. She'd pushed him further and further up the inlet, and now he was stuck.

For a while the surf had kept his tail cool, but then it had ebbed away, leaving him stranded. He'd wriggled and thrashed, but he couldn't get back. He was frightened. He could hear the surf, but he couldn't reach it.

He'd only ever been in the Above for a few clicks during a leap, and he'd always splashed down again into the cool blue waves. But now. He was trapped in this terrible place, where everything was scratchy and brown and dry and *hot*.

The dolphin had never been hot in his life. His skin felt tight and his flippers hurt. Sand kept drifting into his blowhole, and he felt so dreadfully heavy that he hardly had the strength to cough it out. Worse even than that, his beautiful green Sun, who lights the Sea to help dolphins hunt fish – this same Sun was now an angry white glare.

It was so angry that he couldn't open his eyes, so instead he tried clicking, to listen to the shapes around him. *Nothing came back.* It seemed that in the Above, clicking didn't work.

Even ordinary sounds were blunted, and yet painfully loud. Instead of the Sea's soothing murmur, the surf was a crashing jangle, and the squawks of the gulls made his teeth ache.

But the heaviness was worst. In the Sea he was light and swift as a dolphin should be, but here it was as if some dreadful weight were squashing him to the sand. It was a huge effort just to breathe, let alone move, and when a gull perched on his head and pecked his snout, it was all he could do to twitch it off.

A distant rumble of voices. The dolphin felt a flicker of hope. Had the humans come at last? He tried to squeak for help, but he was too weak. Every breath was becoming a struggle.

He couldn't see them because his eyes had dried shut, but he heard the clunk of pebbles as they raced towards him. He sensed the girl's anxiety, and the boy's terror that they'd come too late.

A sudden blissful shock of cold water splashing over his back, soothing his hot, sore fin. Dimly, he heard them running into the surf. Now more water was washing over him, and small gentle flippers were patting his flanks, and carefully keeping the water out of his blowhole. The dolphin tried to tell them how glad he was that they'd come, but he hadn't the strength to stir a fluke.

For a while, the water made him feel a bit better; but he was still hot, and the Above was still crushing him to the sand.

All at once, it came to him that the water they were pouring over him wasn't enough. It wasn't the Sea – and without the Sea, he would die. The noises of the humans began to blur. The dolphin sensed that they were still with him, but their voices seemed to be drifting further and further away.

Hope fled. He was going to die out here in this terrible, burning sand.

He would never see his pod again.

20

The dolphin had seemed to revive a little when Pirra emptied the waterskin over him, but now he'd stopped moving. His eyes were closed and his hide had gone from bright silver to lifeless grey.

'Is he dead?' she whispered.

The boy turned on her. 'Shut *up*!' But she saw the terror in his eyes, and she knew that he thought it too.

Falling to his knees, he put his ear to the dolphin's blow-hole.

'Anything?' she breathed.

He motioned her to silence.

She raced to the shallows to refill the waterskin. When she returned, he was still listening. He met her eyes without seeing. Then his face worked. 'He's alive. But only just.'

Shakily, Pirra sloshed seawater over the dolphin's back. Some trickled near his blowhole and she shielded it with her palm – but warily, for she was touching a creature of the Goddess. She noted with awe that when its blowhole was open it was the shape of the full Moon, and when shut, a perfect crescent; and beneath her hand the flesh wasn't soft, as a person's is soft, but smooth and hard, like polished marble.

'Careful,' warned the boy. 'Don't let any in his blowhole or he'll choke.'

'I know, I'm not.'

'I'll do it.' He elbowed her away. 'You fetch more water.'

'I was going to,' she muttered.

He wasn't listening. He was stroking the dolphin's flank and murmuring, 'You can't give up, I won't let you. We'll get you back to the Sea. Just don't give up!'

It was hard going, stumbling back and forth to the Sea. The dolphin was stranded only a couple of paces from the surf, but the sand was hot, and Pirra floundered ankle-deep. When she started to tire, the boy snatched the waterskin and took his turn, while urging the dolphin constantly to *hold on*.

The Sun rose higher. Pirra felt it beating down on her head, and imagined how much worse it must be for the dolphin. She looked at his constant smile and thought in horror, He's not smiling. He's dying.

'The Sun's getting stronger,' she said.

The boy glared at her. 'So?'

'I mean, we've got to keep it off him, or he'll die.'

He made to retort – then shut his mouth with a snap. 'You're right. How?'

Silence while they thought about that.

'The *sail*,' they said together.

'I'll fetch it,' he said, 'you stay and keep him wet.'

He was back astonishingly quickly, scrambling over the headland with the rope coiled over one shoulder, the sailcloth in his arms, and a pile of driftwood from his shelter on top. He threw the lot down the slope, and Pirra scrambled to collect it. While he worked at building the shelter, she went back to keeping the dolphin wet.

She asked if it had a name, and the boy said he called him Spirit; he shot her a glance as if he expected a sneer, and she said it was a good name for a dolphin.

In no time he'd planted the driftwood crosswise in the sand on either side of Spirit, and lashed it together to make a support. Pirra helped spread the sailcloth over the top – and they had a rickety tent. It wasn't big enough to cover Spirit completely – about a cubit of his tail stuck out – but the close-woven wool kept the Sun off his head and most of his body, and he rewarded them with a feeble twitch of his flukes.

Now they had to haul him back to the Sea.

Without a word they took up position on either side, grabbed a flipper each, and pulled. It was like pulling a mountain. Spirit didn't budge.

The boy seized what was left of the rope and tied it round the dolphin's tail. 'One, two, three – pull!'

No effect.

'We're hurting him,' panted Pirra. She pointed to where the rope was chafing the thin skin raw. 'It's not going to work.'

The boy didn't answer. He'd untied the rope from Spirit's tail, and now he was scowling down at his footprints in the sand. Those nearest Spirit were dry hollows, but the ones closer to the surf were full of seawater . . .

In a flash, Pirra grasped what he was thinking. 'We dig under him,' she said, 'and –'

'– and the Sea comes in and floats him free.'

Grabbing sticks, they started scooping the sand from beneath Spirit's tail, taking turns to race down and fill the waterskin to keep him wet, then hurrying back to continue the trench to the Sea. At last they broke through, and water rushed foaming and splashing under the dolphin's flukes. Pirra saw a shudder run through him. She thought how good it must feel for even part of him to be cool.

She glanced at the boy and smiled, but he didn't smile back. This mattered too much to him to smile. It mattered so much that it hurt.

The tail turned out to be the easy part: digging under Spirit's belly was much harder. He was far too heavy to lift, so the boy tried rolling him to one side to let Pirra dig underneath, but it didn't work, and he worried about squashing the dolphin and making it even more difficult for him to breathe.

'Careful with that stick,' he gasped. 'You'll give him splinters.'

'What's a splinter?' panted Pirra.

'Ow,' she said a bit later, when she got one in her thumb.

By now they were both on their knees, clawing at the sand with their bare hands. But although they'd dug about a third of the way under the dolphin's belly, they couldn't reach any further up. Water was seeping beneath him, but not nearly enough to float him free.

Sitting back on his heels, the boy wiped the sweat from his forehead. 'It's not working, he's too heavy.'

Pirra nodded. They stared at each other across the dolphin's back.

Pirra glanced at the sailcloth shading the dolphin from the Sun. 'If – if we could pull that sail far enough underneath him,' she said, 'we might be able to drag him a bit further into the trench.'

Slowly the boy nodded. 'Although he'll be in the Sun again and it's nearly noon. We'll need another shelter.' He snapped his fingers. 'Juniper.' He yanked the knife from its sheath, then hesitated. Pirra guessed that he didn't want to leave Spirit and cut the juniper himself, but if he stayed, he'd have to trust the knife to her.

'Hylas,' she said urgently, 'Spirit needs you to stay close. Give me the knife.'

He threw her a narrow look, then tossed the knife to her. She caught it one-handed – she was quite pleased about that – but he didn't notice. He was already splashing water over Spirit and scooping out the trench to stop it filling with sand, while talking constantly in a low, encouraging voice.

The juniper was tough and Pirra got liberally scratched, but she managed to hack off some branches and toss them over to him. He didn't seem to feel the prickles as he wove them deftly into a roof that kept off the worst of the Sun. Then she helped him manhandle the sail about halfway under Spirit's belly, tilting him first one way, then the other, as they eased the sail higher, bit by bit. When they'd pulled it as far as they could, they stood on either side, planted their heels in the sand, and each grabbed a corner of the sail.

As long as it doesn't tear, thought Pirra.

'*Pull*,' said Hylas.

The close-woven wool went taut – and held. Spirit tried to help by feebly flexing his backbone.

A tiny judder.

'Did you feel that?' gasped Pirra.

Hylas was straining too hard to reply.

Again and again they hauled at the sail. Again and again Spirit flexed his spine.

With each pull, Pirra felt the burden lessen just a little as the dolphin's back end juddered into the surf and the Sea began to help.

'It's working,' grunted Hylas.

Suddenly Spirit gave a tremendous thrash, his tail catching Pirra on the flank and sending her flying.

She sat up, clutching her side. Hylas was half pulling, half pushing the struggling dolphin into the shallows. 'He's in!' he shouted. In amazement, she watched Spirit roll off the sailcloth and disappear beneath the waves.

There was an abrupt, unnerving silence, broken only by the suck and sigh of the surf. Foam netted the sand, smoothing away the traces of the desperate struggle that had just taken place.

With his eyes on the Sea, Hylas backed towards Pirra. 'You all right?' he said without turning round.

'Mm,' she mumbled. Wincing, she struggled to her feet. 'Do you think Spirit's all right?'

He didn't reply.

Together they scanned the waves. Sun-dazzle and turquoise water. No dolphin.

What if we were too late? thought Pirra with a clutch of terror. What if he was in the Sun too long, and the next thing we see is a dead dolphin, floating belly up?

Hylas was scowling and shaking his head. Clearly he was thinking the same thing.

He put two fingers to his mouth and whistled.

Nothing happened.

'Spirit!' he cried. Wading thigh-deep, he patted the water with his palm. Again he shouted.

Pirra held her breath.

The breeze swirled sadly around the inlet. A gull flew past, its wingtips skimming the waves.

Suddenly the Sea exploded – and there was Spirit, leaping into the air with an ear-splitting squeal.

Pirra sank to her knees. Hylas didn't move. He had his back to her, but she saw him put his face in his hands.

Meanwhile, Spirit was swimming up and down at the mouth of the inlet, rolling on to his side and sticking one flipper in the air, then sliding under again and waggling his tail flukes, revelling at being back where he belonged.

Hylas recovered fast. With a whoop, he dived in and swam underwater, then burst out in a shower of spray. 'Come in and cool off!' he shouted to Pirra.

Rubbing her arms, she stared at the Sea – this Sea which she'd worshipped all her life, but had never been in, apart from that one near-disaster when she'd tried to make friends with Spirit, and ended up swallowing a bellyful of seawater.

'I can't,' she called back. 'I can't swim.'

'Doesn't matter! I won't let you drown.' He broke into a grin. 'I need you to help build that raft, remember?'

Still she hesitated, while boy and dolphin stared back at her: two creatures at home where she was not.

'What's your name, anyway?' shouted Hylas.

'Um – Pirra.'

'Well then, Pirra, come *on*! Come and meet Spirit properly, now that he's better!'

Pirra hesitated. She took a few steps, and the water licked deliciously round her calves. She wobbled in up to her knees. Then the ground dropped away and with a wonderful shock of cold she was in, and the Sea was lifting her off her feet, washing away the heat and scratches and tiredness; it was combing out her hair with long cool fingers and singing in her ears as she went under.

Hylas grabbed her wrist and pulled her to the surface. 'It's shallower over here,' he said. 'You can stand.'

Panting with elation and spitting out seawater, she stood swaying to the rhythm of the Sea. She felt the slippery caress of seaweed round her ankles. Her gold bracelets shone, washed clean of dust.

Spirit glided past her underwater, his sleek green body rippling with sunlight. She put out her hand, and his flank was as cool and smooth as wet silk. Her heart swelled with pride that she'd helped save his life.

'When he comes round again,' said Hylas behind her, 'take hold of his fin with both hands, and he'll give you a ride.'

She threw him a doubtful look.

'I mean it. Here he comes.'

Spirit swam just beneath the surface, with only his fin jutting out.

Pirra tensed.

'Go on, don't be scared.'

'I'm not scared,' she muttered. But she was – although not of Spirit. She was scared of the Sea.

Again Spirit swam past, and this time she didn't give herself time to think, she put first one hand and then the other on the leading edge of his fin. She felt a powerful surge as he carried her forwards, pulling her with him towards the open Sea.

'Hold on and just float!' Hylas called after her. 'Lie flat, you don't need to kick – and keep your arms straight, or it gets bumpy!'

Pirra clung to the dolphin's sturdy fin and felt coolness flowing over her. Just in front, she saw smooth water sliding over Spirit's sleek head as it rose and fell, his blowhole blinking open and shut with gentle *pffts*. She felt his powerful tail brushing her toes as it moved steadily up and down. Faster and faster they went and she laughed aloud, for she was *flying*, flying through the Sea.

After sweeping in a great glittering ring that left her breathless and exhilarated, Spirit bore her back to the inlet, where Hylas stood watching. The dolphin spread his flippers to slow down, and Pirra let go of his fin. Her feet sank into seaweed, and the Sea held her up as she found her footing.

Hylas stood waist-deep, watching Spirit arch beneath the waves and vanish into the blue. 'We did it,' he said quietly.

Still breathless, Pirra glanced down through the glassy water. Her feet were pale green and half buried by swaying purple fronds. Among them, something glinted.

'We should make an offering,' said Hylas, 'to thank the Sea for letting him live.'

'We already have,' said Pirra. 'Look down there.'

One of the little golden axes had come off her tunic and drifted down to rest.

'Ah, that's good,' said Hylas with a nod. 'Yes. That's good.'

21

Hylas hadn't thought about food all day, but suddenly he was ravenous.

He and Pirra went foraging, and the island made it easy. Hylas caught a crab in a rock pool, then downed a seagull with his slingshot, while Pirra found a weird plant that she called samphire on the rocks; he thought it looked like the fingers of a fat green baby.

Even Spirit helped, tossing a slimy grey lump on to the pebbles, where it lay feebly heaving: an octopus. Hylas was going to chuck it back, but Pirra got him to kill it. She wanted him to clean it too, but he told her to do it herself, so she scraped it out with a stick, grimacing as if she'd never seen guts before. Then they roasted it over the fire.

He let her have some of his catch, and she gave him some of hers. She said octopuses are sacred as they've got blue blood, which nearly put him off, but it turned out to be delicious, very chewy and sweet. The samphire wasn't bad either. She'd stewed it in that jar she'd smashed, and it was as crunchy as milk thistle, and tasted of Sea.

By the time they'd finished, the Sun was getting low, and shadows were creeping out from the cliffs. Hylas sat picking his teeth with a thorn, and Pirra scowled as she teased knots out of her hair with her fingers. A few more of the little gold axes had fallen off her tunic, but she still had her necklaces and bracelets. The mark on her cheek was an angry red. Hylas thought it was odd that she could wince at a tangle in her hair, and yet never complained about the burn.

He considered fetching some mallow root for a poultice, then decided against it. She'd helped save Spirit, but that didn't make her a friend. He hadn't forgotten that her people were in league with the Crows.

Besides, how could they be friends, when he had to leave her behind? He felt increasingly bad about that, but there didn't seem to be any other way. He couldn't take her back to Lykonia. He had to find Issi. He told himself that she'd be all right. He would leave her plenty of food; and some boat would be sure to come by and pick her up. If it happened to be the Crows, there wasn't anything he could do about it.

As dusk came on she grew edgy, and he guessed she was worrying about hedgehogs. At least he could do something about that. He began to tell her what hedgehogs are really like, but she looked so startled that he burst out laughing. Soon he was rolling around on the pebbles, and she was grinning and putting her hand to her cheek to protect her scab.

'I can't believe you made that up,' she said ruefully.

He wiped his eyes. 'You should've seen your face.'

144

She fiddled with her bracelets. 'You're not really a warrior, are you?'

'And you can't do spells.'

They exchanged tentative grins.

'But I am the daughter of the High Priestess. I wasn't lying about that.'

'So why'd you run away?'

Her face clouded. 'I had to.'

'No you didn't. You're rich. You've got everything.'

'Oh yes, I'm rich,' she said with surprising bitterness. 'See this tunic? This colour's Keftian purple; it's made from sea snails, thousands of them. Costs more than gold.'

He snorted. 'You made that up.'

She gave him a curious look. 'You don't know much, do you?'

'I know more than you.'

'Not about Keftiu, you don't. I bet you don't even know where it is.'

He didn't reply.

'It's a long way to the south, and it's as big as Akea, but we don't have warriors, just farmers and craftsmen and sailors. Everyone has to bring a twelfth of what they've got – crops, animals, wares – to the House of the Goddess. That's where I live. It's ten times bigger than your Chieftain's stronghold –'

'It can't be. Nothing's that big.'

'Yes it is.'

He threw her an uncertain glance. 'Why does everybody have to give it things?'

She hesitated. 'Once there was an island north of Keftiu. It was richer and more beautiful than any that's ever been, but its people angered the Earthshaker and He stamped so hard it blew up. Then a great wave came rushing over the Sea. It struck Keftiu. The Sun went dark and an earthshake brought down the House of the Goddess.' She broke off, watching the flames. 'That was long before I was born, and it's all been rebuilt, but we've never forgotten. The Sea gives life, but it also brings death.'

Hylas picked a shred of meat from between his teeth. 'We get earthshakes in the mountains sometimes, but nothing like that. Funny. You call Her the Goddess; we call Her the Lady of the Wild Things; but we both call Him the Earthshaker.'

Her lip curled. 'Even Akeans get some things right.'

'I'm Lykonian.'

She shrugged. 'Same thing; it's part of Akea.'

He put more driftwood on the fire. 'So this House of the Goddess. What's it like?'

'It's – it's full of people. Like a swarm of bees. I call it the stone hive. There's always someone watching.' As she went on talking, Hylas pictured a great village of shining white stone. He saw huge double axes of burnished bronze, and sacrificial vessels of rock crystal and hammered gold; sweet black wine in jars ten cubits tall, and bare-chested men somersaulting over the backs of charging bulls. All to placate the gods, and prevent catastrophe.

'So that's why I'm rich,' said Pirra. 'I've spent my whole life in a stone prison.'

'Sounds awful,' he said sarcastically. 'Warm clothes. Soft sheepskins to sleep on. Meat every day. How do you bear it?'

She frowned. 'I didn't expect you to understand.'

'Why'd you burn your cheek?'

She glanced at him. 'Do you know what your knife is made of?'

'What?' He was startled. 'Course I do. It's bronze.'

'But what's bronze? It's copper and tin. You dig them up from deep in the earth, and mate them in fire.'

'What's that got to do with burning your cheek?'

'Everything,' she said with sudden ferocity. 'Akeans need bronze to make weapons. They have plenty of copper, but no tin. Keftiu also needs bronze, and although we haven't got copper *or* tin, we can *get* tin, from the deserts far in the east. So. My mother struck a bargain with an Akean Chieftain. We'll trade him tin for copper. That way, both Keftiu and Akea will have bronze.'

'What's wrong with that?'

'I haven't finished.' In the firelight her expression was fierce as a hawk's. 'To seal the bargain, my mother agreed to give me in marriage. Well, I *won't*! So I thought if I spoilt my face, I'd be ugly and they wouldn't want me. I was wrong. There. That's why I ran away.'

Hylas reached for a stick and stirred the fire. 'You didn't take any food with you. That was stupid.'

'*Food?*' she cried with scorn. 'Is that all you think about?'

He looked at her levelly. 'You've never been hungry.'

'Yes I have, right here on this island –'

'No you haven't. That fisherman left you a couple of mullet. That's not hungry. Real hunger hurts.'

'Well if you were a goatherd you can't have been hungry either, you'd have had milk and meat any time you like.'

He barked a laugh. 'They weren't my goats! And there's only so much milk you can steal before someone notices and gives you a beating.'

She blinked. 'They beat you?'

It was his turn to shrug. 'So what? That's just how it is.'

'But – why didn't you run away?'

He was nettled. 'Course we ran away! But every time we did they sent the dogs after us. And the last time they caught us, they – they didn't beat me. They beat Issi.'

'Who's Issi?'

He threw away the stick. 'Dark soon,' he said shortly. 'We've got to get these shelters repaired, or we'll have nowhere to sleep.'

After they'd finished the shelters, Hylas took the crab shell down to the shallows for Spirit.

He was angry with himself. He'd let Pirra distract him with all that talk of the House of the Goddess. She'd never once mentioned the Crows.

In fact, he'd been so taken up with rescuing Spirit that he'd almost forgotten why he was here. Well, not any more. He was sick of running away; sick of merely surviving. The Crows were after Outsiders for a reason. He intended to find out why.

Spirit didn't want the crab shell; he tossed it up and down

once or twice, then ignored it. He'd recovered from his ordeal, but he seemed listless and subdued. When Hylas waded in, the dolphin put his head on one side and gazed at him sadly.

For the first time, Hylas wondered how Spirit had come to be stranded. 'Why'd you do it?' he asked softly. 'Why'd you try to get on the land?'

The dolphin sank beneath the surface, leaving starlight rocking on the water.

Why *is* he on his own? wondered Hylas. Where's his family? Is he trying to find them? Is that why he got stranded?

Was it possible that Spirit was seeking his little sister, just as he was seeking Issi?

'He must be lonely,' said Pirra behind him. She stood in the shallows, a slight figure in the gloom. 'Doesn't he have a pod? A family?'

'They've gone off. I don't know where.'

'That's why he's unhappy. Dolphins aren't meant to be alone.'

'What do you know about dolphins?' he said curtly.

She smiled. 'Every Keftian knows about dolphins; they're the guardians of the Sea. That's why it's death to harm one.'

'I knew that,' he lied.

Wading deeper, she put out her hand, and Spirit swam past and let her stroke him. 'They say that a dolphin never stops moving,' she said. 'They can hear everything in the Sea. And see in the dark. They can see *through* things, too. A dolphin can see a flounder hiding under the sand, and a baby dolphin in its mother's belly. It can see the heart beating in the chest of a man.' She paused. 'But I never met anyone who could talk to them.'

'I can't, not really,' Hylas admitted. 'Not the way they talk to each other. But sometimes I can guess what he's feeling. And when he looks at me, it's – it's like he can see into my spirit . . .' He broke off, embarrassed.

Spirit swam in a circle and flicked water in Pirra's face with his flipper. She laughed.

Hylas found himself telling her about being adrift, and the shark, and the dolphins saving him. It was a relief to tell her; but when he mentioned the blue fire, she gasped.

'You *saw* the blue fire?'

'Why? What's it mean?'

She hesitated. 'Sometimes the Goddess summons dolphins to do Her bidding. They swim so close that they're splashed with Her burning blue shadow. *Her shadow*, Hylas. That's the blue fire. That's what you saw.'

He waded ashore, and the night breeze chilled his skin. He thought of the first time he'd seen Spirit, rising out of the Sea in a fountain of luminous blue. He felt breathless and scared. He didn't want Spirit to be sacred. He wanted him to be his friend.

Pirra waded after him, wringing out the hem of her tunic. 'Not many people have seen the blue fire,' she said quietly. 'I wonder why you did?'

He thought of the dying Keftian in the tomb, and the lock of hair floating on the waves. He had an alarming feeling that he was caught up in something far greater than he knew. Why had he ended up here, on the Island of the

Goddess? What lay on the other side of those cliffs that barred the way inland?

'Hylas – who *are* you?' said Pirra. 'Why are the Crows after you?'

Odd that she'd mentioned them first. 'They're after Outsiders,' he said warily.

'Is that what you are, an Outsider? What does that mean?'

He told her. 'I think you Keftians call them the People of the Wild.'

She considered that. 'I've heard of them. Though there aren't many left on Keftiu. They're said to keep to the high mountains. But I didn't know there were any in Akea too. So why are the Crows after Outsiders?'

'You tell me, you camped with them.'

She bristled. 'My mother might have dealings with them – but *I'm* not in league with them, if that's what you think.'

'But you must know something! Why did they come after me that night on the coast?'

'I don't know! Userref said –'

'Who's Userref?'

'My slave. He said they told him you'd tried to kill Thestor's son, but we both thought that was just –'

'*What?*' He was horrified. 'That's a lie!'

'Like I said, we didn't believe them –'

'I'd never do anything to hurt Telamon, he's my best friend!'

Her jaw dropped. 'You're *friends* with Thestor's son? But – that doesn't make sense.'

'Why, because he's rich and I'm poor?'

'No, because he's the boy I'm supposed to wed, and because he –'

'*Telamon?* He and you are supposed to wed? And you didn't think to tell me that?'

'Why would I? It never occurred to me that you could be friends!'

'Why not?'

She opened her mouth to reply – then shut it again. Her face closed. Hylas could see her deciding not to say another word. She didn't trust him any more than he trusted her.

'You're hiding things,' he said accusingly.

'So are you,' she flung back. 'Where did you get that dagger? How come you know our name for Outsiders, if you'd never met a Keftian before you met me?'

He did not reply. The fragile ease that had sprung up between them was shattered. 'We'd better get some sleep,' he said brusquely.

'Right,' snapped Pirra.

That night, Hylas lay in his shelter, listening to the black water lapping at the stones.

Telamon had never mentioned the deal with Keftiu. But then, he never did talk about what was going on at Lapithos; he said it was showing off. And he would have been embarrassed about having to wed.

Unless Pirra was lying about that. Unless she'd made it up, to distract attention from the Crows.

The Sea grew quiet and the crescent Moon rose, but still Hylas couldn't sleep. Talking about the Crows had brought them much closer. He pictured sinister ships with black sails racing towards him. Would the Sea carry them here? Would Pirra betray him?

There was silence from her shelter, but he could tell from her breathing that she wasn't asleep.

She was hiding things. She must be.

Well, one thing was certain. He couldn't trust her. Once they'd built the raft, he was leaving her behind.

22

Pirra had thought that things were beginning to improve between her and Hylas, but last night had changed all that. If it was true that he was friends with the Chieftain's son – which seemed impossible – then the less she said about anything, the better.

She decided to keep her head down and help Hylas build the raft; then, once they'd reached Akea, she would slip away.

She was vague about what would happen after that. Besides, she had more pressing concerns. She was beginning to worry that Hylas might be planning to leave her behind.

She told herself that she must be mistaken. He couldn't be that ruthless, even though he was a Lykonian. But what if she was right?

Building the raft turned out to be exhausting. Hylas would crawl over the makeshift bridge while she waited on the rocks; then he'd hack a piece of timber free with an axe he'd found in the hold, tie a rope round it, and throw her the other end. This was the worst bit, as she scrabbled about, failing to catch the rope, and being shouted at. When she finally did catch it, Hylas would again make the perilous crossing and help her haul in the timber.

They also salvaged three beeswax tablets which they could melt down and use for plugging gaps, and four unbroken jars, which Pirra guessed from their seals contained olives.

By nightfall they were too tired to fight, and sat numbly by the fire, picking out splinters.

The next day they lugged everything back to camp, as Hylas insisted on building the raft behind the boulders, where it couldn't be seen from the Sea. The threat of the Crows was ever-present. They were constantly checking the horizon for ships.

Hylas worked with grim determination, pausing only to set a few fish traps or bird snares. He didn't even ask her to show him where she fetched the water, and when she mentioned the cave, he just nodded and left her to it.

She wished he wouldn't. She hated the cave. It was guarded by clumps of white asphodel with spikes taller than she was, and to get inside, she had to wriggle in backwards with her arms against her chest, then drop into the chill, wet, gurgling darkness. It was too low to stand up in, and she felt the rocks pressing down on her. But she couldn't ask Hylas to do it instead, because it was the one thing she knew more about than him.

On the whole, though, they got on all right, and she began to think that her suspicions might be unfounded.

One time, he tossed her a pair of sandals that he'd found on the wreck and trimmed to fit her. And he taught her to swim, by making her jump into a rock pool and shouting at her to use her arms and legs. She swallowed so much seawater she was sick, but she managed it in the end.

Then last night he had a nightmare, kicking his shelter and shouting 'Issi! Scram! Scram, where *are* you?' When she shook him awake he looked dazed, and not quite so tough. She asked about Issi, and he blinked and said she was his little sister who'd gone missing when the Crows attacked; and Scram was his dog who they'd killed. Pirra felt sorry for him, and envious because he'd had a dog. But she was pleased that he'd told her about Issi. She was also intrigued; she'd always wondered what it would be like to have a sister.

On the third day they built the raft. They'd salvaged nine longish timbers, two logs – which Hylas said would do for rollers, whatever they were – and four shorter planks. He laid two of the planks about three paces apart, then he and Pirra put the timbers side by side on top. The plan was to place the other two planks across the row of timbers, then lash each pair of planks together at the ends, thus clamping the timbers in between.

It proved extremely hard to do. To force the ends of each pair of planks together around the timbers, they had to pile rocks on them, and Hylas had to carve notches so that the ropes wouldn't slip off. Steering the raft posed a problem, too, until Pirra remembered a painting of an Egyptian barge in her mother's chambers, and suggested mounting an oar on a tripod of crossed sticks.

At last, it was finished.

'It looks fine,' Pirra said proudly.

'It'll do,' said Hylas. He was busy gathering the dried mullets he'd prepared for the journey, and tying the other supplies to the raft. Pirra noticed that although he'd secured two of the jars they'd salvaged, he'd left off the other two, along with a second waterskin that he'd rescued from the hold.

With a sensation of falling, she realized that those provisions were meant for her. She'd been right all along. He really did intend to leave her behind.

Desolation, rage and hurt battled within her. Rage won. Her palms prickled. Her blood roared in her ears. She wanted to batter him with her fists and scream, You rotten stinking *liar*!

'Pass me that bit of rope, will you?' he muttered.

'Fetch it yourself,' she snarled.

He glanced round. 'What's wrong?'

'Oh, I don't know,' she said sweetly. 'Maybe I'm just a bit *annoyed* that I've been working like a slave for days, and you said you'd take me with you, and you *lied*.'

He flushed.

'It's true, isn't it?'

'Yes,' he said.

'*Yes?* Is that all you can say?'

'Yes.'

She blinked. 'Have you no – no *honour*?'

He snorted. 'Honour's for people who get enough to eat.'

'What about gratitude? I helped save Spirit! I helped *build* this wretched raft!'

He rose to his feet and met her eyes, and his gaze was level and unashamed. 'I'm sorry,' he said flatly, 'but I've got to find my sister. You'd be in the way.'

'*In the way?*' she exploded. 'If I hadn't helped you –'

'Look. Pirra. It could take days to reach Lykonia. If there were two of us on the raft, what would we do for food? I couldn't catch enough for both of us and you can't fish. So either we'd both starve, or I'd have to chuck you overboard to be eaten by sharks. I'd rather leave you here to take your chances. You'll be safer.'

'Oh, so I'm supposed to *thank* you?'

'No. You're supposed to accept that this is how it's got to be.'

'You're *horrible!*' she shouted. 'You don't care about anyone but yourself!'

'Even if you did come,' he said with infuriating calm, 'what would you do when we got there? Lykonia's what you were running away *from*. And you couldn't go back to Keftiu. Where would you go?'

'I *hate* you!' she screamed. Snatching up the waterskins, she ran off towards the headland.

She was so furious that she almost forgot to be frightened of the cave.

Grinding her teeth, she wriggled through the entrance and dropped into the gloom, where she plunged the waterskins into the stream and held them under by their necks, as if she were strangling kittens.

But once she was climbing back up the headland, laden

with two heavy waterskins, her rage burned off and her spirits plummeted. Of course Hylas didn't want her. Why would he? She was useless. And shouting at him had achieved nothing – except to prove that she couldn't keep her temper, and thus wasn't worth taking along.

He was right, too, about her having nowhere to go. Desolation swept over her. No one in the whole world cared about her.

A trickle of pebbles above her, and she glanced up to see Hylas skittering down towards her.

'What is it now?' she said dully.

Grabbing her wrist, he yanked her after him down the slope. 'Quick!' he panted. 'Where's this cave?'

'What?'

'The cave, the cave, we've got to hide! *Ships!*'

23

'Spirit warned me,' panted Hylas as they scrambled down the slope. 'He kept slamming his tail.'

'How many ships?' said Pirra.

'Two. But they're too far off to see if they're Crows. Is this the cave?' They'd reached the asphodels.

'I'll go first,' said Pirra. Squirming through the cave mouth, she dropped on to the stones. Fear squeezed her heart. She pictured ships beached in the bay and men splashing ashore. Her mother was relentless; she would search the whole island . . .

'Catch!' Hylas tossed in the waterskins, then jumped down beside her.

He'd brought two sticks of giant fennel, which he'd lit at the camp fire. Pirra was astonished at his forethought, and even more that he didn't seem scared of the cave. To her, the uncertain light only deepened the darkness around her. For all she knew, ghosts were all around them, thronging this shadowy pathway between the worlds of the living and the dead. Didn't Hylas feel it too?

He was prowling about, peering into cracks, and kneeling to taste the black water sliding past their feet. 'This is good,' he muttered. 'We could hide in here for days.'

'No we couldn't,' she said quickly. 'It's too small, there's not enough air.'

'Yes there is, there's a draught.' He sniffed. 'Smells salty. Must be a way to the Sea.' He snapped his fingers. 'I just remembered, when I first got to the island I saw a cave, it opened straight on to the Sea. That's where the air's coming from.'

'Hylas –'

He was poking his head through a gap between two tall pillars of dank rock. 'Think I've found it.' Before Pirra could stop him, he'd squeezed sideways and disappeared.

'*Hylas!*' she hissed.

'Come on, it widens out!'

Setting her teeth, she squeezed after him.

She burst through into a narrow cave that was too low to stand up in, and clammy with breath. 'We'll get lost!' she panted.

'No, we won't. Just remember those tall rocks near the entrance, and that red rock like a hand we passed at the turn –'

'But why go deeper at all?'

'Because we need to see those ships. If we can't, we won't know if they've gone, or if they're heading straight for us . . .' His voice grew fainter as he rounded a bend.

Gasping for breath, Pirra followed him at a crouching run. In the wavering light of her fennel stalk, rock faces sprang at her, and shadows slithered away. She heard the echoing *plink* of water – and behind it the impenetrable silence of stone.

Something brushed her ankle. She stifled a cry.

It was a garland, so ancient and shrivelled that when she nudged it with her sandal it crumbled to dust. Her hand crept to her sealstone. The walls threw back the sound of her fear. In the gloom, she made out brittle twists of barley from summers long gone, and olive leaves as grey as death. Others had been here before her. She thought of the Vanished Ones: the people who had lived on the island in the old times, and mysteriously disappeared.

Here and there, she glimpsed lesser offerings pushed into cracks and crevices: a tiny earthenware bird, a bull, a snake. On Keftiu, people did the same thing, journeying to sanctuaries on peaks and in caves to leave the first fruits of the harvest, and little wild creatures of clay or bronze.

She glimpsed a small clay dolphin on a ledge. It lay on its side, its painted eye faded with age, yet curiously alert.

Ahead, Hylas' light had dwindled to a glimmer.

Pirra righted the dolphin on its ledge, and hurried after him.

Being stuck on the island had been very terrible, and the dolphin would never have gone near it again if it hadn't been for his pod. They were lost somewhere inside it, and he could tell by their squeals that they were getting weaker.

And now the island had swallowed the boy and the girl, too.

The dolphin couldn't abandon them. It wasn't only that they'd rescued him. More than any humans he'd ever met, he cared about them. He didn't want anything bad to happen to them.

Especially to the boy. Even when the boy was busy, he would always pat the waves with his flipper when the dolphin was near; and when the dolphin swam closer, the boy would stroke him and talk to him in his odd, pebbly speech.

Sometimes too, when the Above had gone dark and the girl was asleep, the boy would wander down and stand quietly in the shallows, and the dolphin would swim around him. Then there would be no need for speech, and boy and dolphin could be lonely together, both missing their kin.

But how dreadful to be human! To be forced to live in that terrible, glaring heat! No waving forests of cool green kelp where the succulent bream swim. No deep, dark hunting grounds where you must click hard and fast to find the stingrays hiding under the sand. It made the dolphin long to grab the boy by the flipper and dive with him, down through the shimmering Blue to the Black Beneath, to show him what it is to *be* a dolphin, at one with the Sea.

This was why the dolphin had to stay near the island: he was tied to it by a tangle of worry, pity and love. He had to find his pod, and he had to look after the humans.

But *why* had they disappeared into that hole?

The dolphin had known for a while that both the boy and the girl were hiding from something, because often they stared at the Sea, and he felt their fear crackling through the water. He'd guessed that they were hiding from other humans, and now he knew he was right, because when he'd warned the boy about the floating trees, he'd fled.

But why hide in a hole, like a pair of eels? And why in *that*, of all possible holes?

That was the hole that led to the Place of Singing Echoes. Every dolphin knew of it, but none had ever been there. It was not a place for dolphins; or for humans either. It was a place for the singing echoes and the poor, thin ghosts – and at times, for the Shining One Herself.

As the dolphin rode the tricky currents outside the cave, he wondered what to do. From deep within the island he caught the humans' muffled voices. What were they doing so far in? Didn't they know how dangerous it was?

The sky was turning a deeper blue. Soon it would be dark. And still the dolphin swam, straining to catch their voices.

Suddenly he became aware of a new threat. He felt it in his fins and in an ache along his lower jaw. He began to be afraid.

Someone was angry. And when He was angry, He slammed the Sea with His enormous tail, and brought whole mountains crashing down.

Above all else, the dolphin feared Him.

The One Beneath.

'There!' whispered Hylas at Pirra's shoulder. 'Two ships. D'you see?'

She nodded.

After the darkness of the cave, it had been wonderful to emerge into this big rocky chamber that opened on to the Sea. It hadn't been easy to get to, because an underground stream flowed through it, which meant they'd had to edge sideways against the walls, in constant danger of falling in. When at last they'd reached the cave mouth, they'd seen Spirit swimming up and down, clacking his jaws. He'd seemed agitated; Hylas couldn't tell if it was because of the ships, or something else. Pirra had scarcely noticed. As her heartbeats slowed, she'd taken hungry gulps of salty air.

Beside her, Hylas blew out a long breath. 'They're smaller than when I first saw them. They're moving away.'

Shading her eyes against the Sun's red glare, Pirra squinted at the specks on the horizon. Relief washed over her. 'They're not Keftian,' she said.

'How can you tell?'

'Sails are the wrong colour, ships' noses the wrong shape.'

'You can see all that? You must have the eyes of a hawk.'

'They're not Crows, either. I think – I think they're Phoenician.'

'How come you know so much about ships if you've never been anywhere?' He sounded suspicious.

'Because,' she snapped, 'the House of the Goddess is covered in paintings, and lots are of ships from all over the world – Makedonia, Akea, the Obsidian Isles, Phoenicia, Egypt – and I've had nothing to do since I was about three summers old but stare at them and get very familiar with what they look like.'

A wave crashed against the rocks and they recoiled, shielding their fennel stalks from the spray.

'We'd better get moving,' said Hylas.

Pirra glanced anxiously behind her, where the cave mouth gaped, waiting to swallow them. 'Can't we find another way back?'

'How?' He pointed at the sheer cliffs above them and the Sea crashing against the rocks on either side. 'If we tried to swim for it we'd be smashed to pieces. Although you'd probably drown first.'

There was nothing for it but to plunge once more into the cold and the dark. And it was darker this time, because their fennel stalks were nearly spent.

Pirra told herself grimly that she'd done it before, so she could do it again; but as the voice of the Sea fell away, she was shocked to see that the outside world had already dwindled to a pallid disc of light. Then she rounded a bend and it was gone.

There was no Hylas up ahead.

'Hylas?' she called.

Nothing but the drip, drip of water and her own urgent breath.

'Hylas!'

A sound of running – then light flared and there he was, looking strangely excited. 'I found another cave,' he panted. 'It's a perfect hiding place, we can camp there for the night!'

'*What? Camp* down here?'

'It's got everything! Water, space, air.'

'But the ships have gone!'

'They might come back.'

He saw that she was afraid, and his face hardened. 'They may not have gone far, Pirra. It'd be madness to camp on the beach where they could see us. Much better down here.'

'Well then, go ahead,' she said stonily. 'I'm turning back.'

'Don't be stupid, we can't split up now, that'd increase the chance of being seen.'

'Why can't we? You're planning to *abandon* me tomorrow.'

He ignored that. 'Listen –'

'No, *you* listen! Your nightmare is not finding your sister; mine's being buried alive. So do what you like, but I'm getting out of here!'

She ran, clutching her torch in one hand and groping at the rocks with the other. Hylas didn't come after her, which made her even angrier.

The way back felt shorter than the way in, and she soon passed the red rock like a hand that marked the turn. Just as her fennel stalk was flickering out, she glimpsed the black pillars and the blessed light pouring in through the mouth of the cave.

Chucking away the fennel, she grabbed a rock and hauled herself up. The rock came away in her hand. She grabbed another. It moved.

She just had time to wonder what was happening. Then the earth growled – and she knew. In the blink of an eye the growl grew to a roar and the rocks were shaking, the daylight above her juddering from side to side. Rocks were crashing down and the earth roaring louder and louder, roaring *through* her. The Bull Beneath the Sea was stirring in His sleep, and she was in the worst place possible: she was inside a cave.

'Hylas!' she screamed, but her voice was engulfed by the Earthshaker's furious roars.

Somehow she found a hollow and crawled in. Then she pictured it collapsing on her, and crawled out again.

Something hit the back of her head, and sparks exploded in her eyes. She struggled to get up, but the earth was shuddering so hard she couldn't stand.

The last thing she saw was the daylight turn black as the mouth of the cave snapped shut upon her.

24

Hylas opened his eyes. Closed them. Opened them. No difference. Everything black.

He lay with his arms over his head, feeling the last of the Earthshaker's anger growling through him. He was covered in dust and he coughed till his eyes ran, but amazingly, he wasn't hurt. And he still had the knife in the scabbard at his hip.

When at last the growls had died to silence, he got to his feet. Wherever he was, it was high enough to stand up, if he stooped. Behind him he caught a whiff of air and a glimmer of light. Ahead – nothing.

With pounding heart, he felt the rocks before him. Solid. The earthshake must have brought down the roof of the cave.

He called to Pirra. No answer. Only a distant gurgle of water, and the watchful hush of stone.

Again and again he called. He sounded frightened. He stopped. The silence was worse.

He couldn't take it in. One moment she'd been right there, shouting at him. Now there was only a pile of rocks and a plunging sense of loss. She'd deserved better than to be crushed by an earthshake. He hoped it had been quick, and that she'd felt no pain.

Blinking and spitting out dust, he turned and stumbled towards the light.

He hadn't gone far when he heard a faint, echoing squeal. *Spirit.*

He tried to whistle back – managed a dusty wheeze – tried again.

An agonizing wait.

Then a distant, answering call.

Hylas gulped. He was *not* alone, not while he had Spirit. He pictured the dolphin swimming up and down before the mouth of the cave, perhaps even venturing up the stream that poured from the cave into the Sea, while sending his clear call ringing through the dark, like a silver thread leading Hylas towards the light.

If he could just get back to the Sea, then with Spirit's help he could swim round into the bay. And then he could –

What about Pirra? said a voice in his mind.

What about her? countered Hylas. *Nothing I can do for her now. She's dead.*

But if she isn't. She might be alive, somewhere behind those rocks. Trapped. Injured. Terrified.

Spirit's whistles rang through the dark, drawing him to safety.

Hylas ground his fist against stone. He had to look after himself. If he didn't, he was finished, and so was Issi.

'Your nightmare is not finding your sister,' Pirra had told him. 'Mine's being buried alive.'

She might last for days, even without food or water. Dying slowly. Alone in the dark.

Pirra lay huddled on her side. She knew from the rasp of her breath and its heat on her face that she was in a horribly cramped space. She didn't dare find out how cramped.

The back of her head hurt, and the scab on her cheek was throbbing, but she didn't think she'd been injured anywhere else. It was so dark that she couldn't see her fist in front of her face. The whole world was gone. She was the only one left.

'Hylas?' she called. '*Hylas!*'

No answer. He was either dead, or trying to find his way back to the Sea. She was on her own: trapped like an ant under a mountain of rock.

Panic gripped her. She clutched her sealstone, tracing the familiar bird with her finger. She tried to see a real falcon in her head, like the one she'd watched with Userref on the ship. She tried to make it dive fast and free through the limitless sky . . .

She couldn't do it. The falcon in her head was trapped, just like her. She could almost hear its panicky fluttering as it dashed itself against the rocks.

Awkwardly, she turned on to her belly, and her hair snagged

on stone a finger's breadth above her head. She tried to stretch one arm in front. Her fingers hit stone. She flexed one leg, and stubbed her toes. Her heart hammered against her ribs. The falcon in her head went wild.

Squeezing her eyes shut, she fought the urge to scream, to lash out with feet and fists. *Breathe. Breathe. Slowly. In, out.*

Her heart steadied a little. The falcon in her head grew calmer.

This tiny victory made her feel a little stronger. She decided to pass her hands over every patch of stone around her, in case she could find a way out.

Blindly, she moved her hands over the crusted stone in front of her face. She found a hollow about the size of her fist. Inside, something rattled. A – a *drinking cup*? It was broken; she caught the earthy smell of pottery. She sniffed deeply. People had made this cup. The world above still existed.

Groping beneath her, she was startled to come upon what felt like a needle of polished bone; then an oval lump of clay with a hole in it that she recognized at once. It was a loom-weight. In the House of the Goddess, women tied groups of threads to weights like this one, to keep the wool in their looms hanging taut. On windy days, the lines of weights made a dull clacking noise. Pirra had grown up with that sound.

But what was it doing down here? People didn't offer loom-weights to the gods.

A suspicion flickered at the edge of her mind, but she pushed it away.

Her hands travelled above her and around. Not even a

crack. Ahead of her – dead end. Again her heart began to race. Biting back panic, she felt behind her with her toes.

A gap. Was it big enough to squeeze through?

Twisting like a snake, she pushed herself backwards. The spangles on her tunic scraped stone, and for one heart-stopping moment she was stuck. Then she was shooting through and half-falling, half-sliding down a clattering slope of loose rock.

She landed in a heap, streaming sweat and gulping air.

Wherever she was, it felt bigger, and less impenetrably dark. And she could see.

In the gloom she made out a long, narrow cave with a floor covered in strange, glistening mounds of yellowish stone, and a roof so low she could touch it. The roof was dark red and ridged, like an enormous mouth. At the far end, about thirty paces away, a spear of dusty light slanted down.

Pirra licked her lips. If that light could get in, maybe she could get out?

Panting with eagerness, she started towards it. The cave was too low even for crawling, so she hauled herself on her elbows, boosting herself with her toes. Grabbing one of the yellow mounds, she pulled herself forwards. The stone was slimy, and her fingers slipped. She got a better grip on an outcrop shaped like a hand . . .

She froze.

It *was* a hand. A hand turned to stone.

With a cry, she recoiled – and came face to face with the head.

Stone had flowed like thick mud over the skull, sealing in flesh and bone forever. The stone mouth gaped at her in a silent scream. Stone eyes glared with terrible hunger.

In one horrified heartbeat, the truth about those yellow mounds crashed upon her. She'd been crawling over dead people turned to stone.

Everywhere she looked, they thronged the cave: men, women and children, lying where they'd fallen as they'd crawled over each other to reach the light; frozen forever in their final agony.

This was the long-kept secret of what had become of the Vanished Ones. They must have taken refuge in these caves, just as she and Hylas had taken refuge; but the Earthshaker had brought the roof crashing down, shutting them in.

Perhaps when the earthshake had first started, they'd had time to bring a few random possessions; that would explain the cup and the needle and the loom-weight. And down here they would have had air, and they could have licked water off the rocks. They might have survived for days. But they would have known that they would never get out.

Pirra's belly tightened. To reach that crack, she had to crawl over them, trying not to wake them from their long sleep.

Baring her teeth, she started feeling her way over the bodies. Here and there the light showed her a nightmare glimpse of an arm flung out, or a knee drawn tight to a chest. She saw splayed fingers webbed with stone. Stone pooling in a mouth that would never shut.

As she passed, her shadow seemed to give them life. Was that a stone hand reaching for her ankle? She shot forwards, squeezing between two corpses that lay face to face, their crusted arms outstretched. Again her tunic snagged. She couldn't get loose. She reached out to pull herself forwards. With a brittle crack a stone finger snapped off in her hand.

A whisper echoed through the cave.

Her mouth went dry. In horror, she stared at the finger on her palm. With a cry she flung it from her.

Had that stone arm just twitched? Had that head ripped free from the rock and turned to follow her with blind, angry eyes?

Around her she saw dim hollows in the walls, where shadowy figures crouched just beyond the reach of the light. The whispering grew louder. The shadows began to move.

Whimpering, she crawled faster. Behind her she felt the dreadful eagerness of the hungry dead.

At last she reached the light. Her last hope snuffed out. The crack in the roof was too narrow; she couldn't even thrust in her fist. And before her the cave was blocked by another fall of rocks.

A sigh from the hungry ghosts. *We know . . . Ah . . . we know.*

Pirra collapsed, gasping and pressing her face into the stone.

Was this how it was for them? she wondered. Had they been dead when they'd turned to stone – or still alive?

She thought how it would be to feel cold stone hardening

over your feet. Stiffening around your legs, clogging your nose and mouth and throat . . .

Panic rose inside her. She clenched her fists.

'You are the daughter of the High Priestess,' she told herself sternly. 'You do *not* give in.'

Behind her the hungry ghosts uttered a rattling sigh, and drew back into the shadows.

'You do not give in,' she repeated.

Pirra hated her mother, but now the thought of her was oddly steadying. High Priestess Yassassara was not like other women. She lived only to serve the Goddess, and she'd never loved any living creature – but she was strong. Maybe some of that strength flowed in her daughter's veins, too.

Gritting her teeth, Pirra heaved herself to her knees and peered about her.

The Vanished Ones had gone still. Around her she made out nothing but rocks.

The one by her knee resembled a triton shell.

Shakily, she reached for it. It *was* a triton shell. She cupped her hand around the curved base in which the big sea snail would have lived, and traced the whorls that narrowed from there to the tip. But it wasn't a real shell; it was made of marble.

There was one just like it in the House of the Goddess, carved from white alabaster. It was very sacred: only her mother could touch it. She used it for the rite of First Barley – and sometimes, in times of trouble when she sought help from the gods, she would put the tip to her mouth and blow.

The triton shell that Pirra held now was flawless, except for a tiny nick in its lip. It must have been made on Keftiu; only there did they have the skill. This link with home made her feel a little better; but she didn't dare blow it. She might bring the whole cave crashing down.

Clutching the shell, she began to explore the rockfall that blocked her escape. She couldn't find any cracks. 'Well then, I'll *make* one,' she muttered.

She dislodged one small rock and placed it behind her. Then another and another. She worked faster, rolling away those too big to lift. The cave echoed with the clatter of stone, drowning out the sighs of the hungry ghosts. To Pirra, it seemed as if she was building a wall of sound to keep them at bay.

At last she paused for breath. With the tip of the triton shell, she tapped the rocks before her, listening for any hollowness that would tell her she was about to break through.

Nothing.

She tapped again.

On the other side of the rocks, something tapped back.

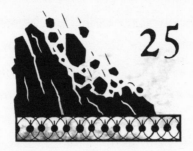

25

'Pirra!' Hylas paused to listen.

From the other side of the rocks came that tapping again; then a clicking cascade of sound, like the speech of hawks. He sagged with relief. 'Pirra, it's me! Talk Akean, I can't speak Keftian!'

An astonished silence. *'Hylas?'*

'Are you hurt?'

'Just a bump on the head. You?'

He shook his head, then remembered she couldn't see. 'No.'

He started clawing at the stones. From the sound of it, she was doing the same.

She asked how he'd found her, and he told her how he'd cleared a way through the first rockfall, then got lost in a maze of caves. He'd whistled to Spirit, and caught the dolphin's answering squeal; then he'd heard her voice. 'It sounded like you were talking to someone.'

'I was.'

'Who?'

'Myself.'

He dislodged another boulder, and felt her hand thrust through the gap. He gripped it. Her fingers were as cold as claws. 'We'll get you out,' he told her. But the gap was too small, and as they made it bigger, pebbles rattled and rocks creaked overhead.

'It's going to come down,' Pirra said tersely. 'I've got to try now.'

She was right. The rocks wouldn't hold much longer.

Hylas took hold of her wrist with both hands. 'Keep the other arm behind you,' he said, 'twist your shoulders sideways and tuck your chin to your chest. I'll pull you out.'

'What if I get stuck?'

'You won't.'

'You don't know that.'

'Breathe out,' he muttered – and pulled with all his might.

She didn't budge. Bracing his heels, he pulled again. Rocks groaned. Dust sifted down. Pirra yelped. Then she was through and they were scrambling back as the rocks came crashing down.

Coughing and covered in dust, they listened to the echoes die. It was so dark that Hylas couldn't see her face, but he heard her breathing. 'You all right?' he panted.

'Mm.' But he knew she must have been badly scratched, and he'd nearly wrenched her arm from its socket.

'Hylas?' she said in a low voice.

'Yes?'

'Thanks.'

He scowled. 'Come on. A while back I saw a glimmer of light. It might be a way out.'

He went first, groping with hands and feet. The walls were slimy, and the air smelt dank. He sensed that they were heading further from the Sea, into the unknowable heart of the island. Behind him he heard the shuffle of Pirra's sandals and the whisper of her breath. He thought what a difference it made that he was no longer alone.

He asked her how she'd survived the earthshake, and she told him a horrifying story about a lost people called the Vanished Ones, and having to crawl over corpses turned to stone. He wondered how she'd kept her wits. Perhaps if you were the daughter of the High Priestess of Keftiu, you weren't afraid of ghosts. Or perhaps she was simply brave.

They reached a place where the cave split in two. One way was black and silent, but from the other came an echoing gurgle of water and a glimmer of light.

'I don't like the feel of that one,' said Pirra.

'I don't either, but it's lighter and there'll be more chance of getting out.'

'I know, but it feels – strange.'

Hylas knew what she meant, but he didn't think they had much choice. After a brief argument, they took it.

The glimmer grew to a watery blue-green glow. The rocks around them were rippled and folded – as if they'd once been waves, and some immortal had turned them to stone. They were running wet; the cave was full of dripping, trickling, gurgling. The echoes wove in and out in a mysterious song, just beyond the edge of understanding.

Hylas' spine prickled. He'd heard that song before. It had called to him across the waves on the day when Spirit had first brought him to the island. *The hills that walk and the caves that sing . . .*

Then suddenly there were no more rocks on either side, and the echoing song was louder, and beside him Pirra gasped.

Before them yawned a vast cavern filled with a lake of astonishing blue. From the roof hung folds of pale, glistening rock. Spears of white rock rose from the still surface of the lake, and at its heart lay an islet thronged with twisted pillars standing guard, like people turned to stone. Above the islet, a shaft of brilliant blue light poured down from a rent in the roof.

Hylas swallowed. 'That crack,' he said quietly. 'It might be big enough for us to climb out.'

Pirra didn't reply, but he guessed what she was thinking. To reach it they would have to swim the lake and get on to that island, then scale one of those brooding pillars.

'We can't do it,' she said.

'I think we have to.'

The lake was cold. Rocks tilted underfoot. Something slithered past his ankle. That weird bubbling singing rang in his ears, interwoven with sounds of running water – and yet he couldn't see any: the lake was eerily still.

As they waded deeper, the blue became more intense, until they were wading in light: the same otherworldly light that the dolphins had brought with them when they'd rescued him from the shark. It washed over him, staining his flesh blue. The shadow of the Goddess.

'We can't get on to the island from here,' whispered Pirra. 'It's too steep.'

'We'll go round the other side,' he whispered back.

When she didn't reply, he turned to look at her. She wasn't a girl, but a water spirit: blue face and black lips, long crinkly black hair.

The ground shelved and he stumbled up to his chest. 'I'll swim,' he said through chattering teeth. 'If you can't remember how, hold on to my shoulders.'

Close up, the columns guarding the island were enormous: some hunched and squat, others tall and thin. All stood with bowed heads and arms clamped rigid to their sides.

Hylas felt Pirra's hands tense on his shoulders. 'If they move . . .' she breathed.

Above them, the crack was wider than it had looked from the shore. If they could reach it, they might be able to climb out.

Hardly daring to make a ripple, Hylas swam slowly round, till he found a place where it shelved more gently, as if inviting them ashore. His feet touched stone.

Suddenly Pirra's fingernails dug into him. 'Hylas!' she hissed. 'Look! *She's here!*'

He raised his head.

The way was blocked.

Not by the guardians of stone.

By the Goddess Herself.

26

She had stood for thousands of summers, and She would stand for thousands more. The Great Goddess. The Lady of the Wild Things. She Who Has Power.

Her arms were folded beneath Her sharp stone breasts, and Her smooth oval face glowed white as the Moon. Human hands had painted Her inhuman stare in ancient blood. They had set Her image here, so that when She visited this singing cave, She would breathe life into the marble flesh.

Pirra stood with tears pricking her eyes. Never in the House of the Goddess had she felt the Presence so strongly. She bowed her head, unable to bear such terrible perfection.

Beside her, Hylas stood transfixed.

'Don't look too long,' she whispered. 'You'll go blind, it's like staring at the Sun.'

He licked his lips. Then he indicated the crack in the roof. 'How do we reach it?'

She stared at him. 'We can't! It's too close!'

'We've got to! How else do we get out? That pillar, the one furthest from – from Her. If we can reach it, we can climb out.'

Pirra swallowed. Stone snakes coiled about the feet of the Goddess, who stood upon a great mound of bleached bones. Perhaps they were the remains of offerings by long-dead supplicants; or perhaps they were the supplicants themselves. To reach the crack in the roof, she and Hylas would have to climb those bones beneath the watchful gaze of the stone guardians and of the Goddess Herself . . .

But Hylas was right. They had no choice.

'First we have to make an offering,' she muttered, 'or She'll never let us out.' Already she was tearing off her jewellery. She couldn't get one of her bracelets over her fist, so instead she tore off as many spangles from her tunic as she could reach. 'Here.' She gave half to Hylas. 'We'll leave it there by that stone snake. Ask Her to let us out, but only in your head – and *don't* meet Her eyes.'

Bones crunched underfoot as they started to climb. Pirra felt the painted gaze of the Shining One beating down on her. She resisted the urge to raise her head and look.

She noticed that in among the bones were the seedheads of poppies, and seashells and the brittle wings of birds. Earth, water and air, she thought. Whoever had left these offerings had known what they were about.

The gold clinked coldly as she and Hylas set it down. The watery singing grew louder. Blue light rippled over the stone snakes coiled about the glistening feet of the Goddess. For a moment, Pirra thought one of the snakes stirred.

Hylas touched her wrist, and together they approached the guardian they had to climb. Pirra's belly tightened. The guardian was lumpy and beaded with moisture, like clammy flesh. Pirra pictured a stone arm wrenching free and gripping her in an embrace from which she would never escape.

Hylas had already linked his hands to make a step. 'You first. Quick! Climb!'

He boosted her so high that she scarcely touched the guardian. She found a ledge inside the crack and perched there, dazzled by the distant glare of the world above. Wasn't that another ledge, just within reach? And there, a peg hammered into the rock? Astonished, she made out more pegs and ledges, spiralling all the way to the top: perhaps cut to allow some priestess from an earlier time to enter the cave.

'There are *steps*!' she whispered down to Hylas.

He didn't respond. He was standing motionless before the Goddess.

'Hylas, *hurry*!'

He glanced up at her, and she was startled by the determination in his face. 'You go on,' he said quietly. 'I have to find out.'

'*What*? What are you doing?'

'I have to – I have to ask Her.'

In horror, she watched him move closer to the Goddess. Appallingly close. He knelt at Her Moon-white feet. Shakily, he reached out his hand. He touched his forefinger to one marble knee. Then put his finger to his mouth and licked.

Raising his head, he spoke to the Goddess. 'Is Issi still alive?'

'Is Issi still alive?' said Hylas, and his voice echoed through the cave. *Alive? . . . Alive? . . .*

His fingertip tingled where it had touched the Goddess, and his tongue burned. The water song rang in his head – as always, just beyond the edge of understanding.

All at once, the sounds of dripping and gurgling sank to nothing. His chest seemed to open, and he felt a sharp tug, as if a thread of light had hooked his heart and were drawing it out of his body.

Something shifted inside him, and he was suddenly intensely *aware* of everything around him. The lake blazed with cold blue fire, and in its depths he heard the currents sliding over each other. He heard fish nibbling on the bottom, and the soft suck of mollusc feet. He glimpsed the flash and flicker of water spirits with sea-green hair and fluid silver limbs. From the world above he smelt the musky scent of the wild beasts guarding the island. On his skin he felt the cool, salty breath of the Lady of the Wild Things . . .

The watery singing was *inside* him, and its tangled sounds were smoothing out, like seaweed flowing in a powerful current. The voice of the Goddess breathed through his mind. *Your sister lives . . .*

He swayed.

Slowly, he raised his head. He shielded his eyes with his arm. The marble Goddess was ablaze with light.

'Is sh-she all right?' he stammered. 'Will I find her? Why are the Crows after me?'

Immortal laughter filled the cave. *You seek the truth . . . But beware . . . the truth bites . . .*

The thread hooking his heart snapped.

He shuddered. He was back on the mound of bones, with the song of water gurgling in his ears.

'*Hylas!*' cried Pirra from above. 'Look *out!*'

On the mound of offerings, something moved. Shells clinked and bones rolled as a long, thin shadow slid towards him. One of the stone snakes was coming alive.

He struggled to his feet. The snake's forked tongue flicked out to taste his scent. He scrambled back. In the blink of an eye the snake struck. Hylas threw himself sideways. Fangs grazed his calf. With a cry he drew his knife – but the hilt snagged on the sheath, he couldn't get it out. The snake came at him again. He seized a bone and hit the flat serpent head. It recoiled with a hiss.

Floundering through the bones, he reached the foot of the guardian and clawed his way up. Below him the snake twined around it and hissed and dropped back.

'Climb! Climb!' he gasped to Pirra, a black shape against the glare.

Terror spurred him on; he found pegs and ledges and climbed till his muscles burned. Below him the echoing hisses fell away. Dust rained down on him, gritty and bitter as ash. Now all he could hear was the scrape of Pirra's sandals and his own sawing breath.

Pirra vanished into the world above – then reappeared,

reaching down to help him. He heaved himself over the edge and lay panting, unable to believe that he'd got away. He heard a falcon crying high on the wind. Above him he made out a black ridge and an angry red Sun.

A *red* Sun? But the Sun had been low when they'd entered the caves; how could it *still* be low now? Either they'd spent a whole night and a day in the caves, or else . . . or else in the caves, time didn't exist.

His mind reeled. He couldn't take it in. But Issi was still alive. He clung to that.

Pirra was looking at him strangely. 'Down in the cave, you spoke to a voice I couldn't hear.'

He hesitated. 'It said my sister is alive. It said – "The truth bites". I suppose it meant the snake.'

'Maybe,' said Pirra. 'Although the words of the Goddess can have many meanings.'

Getting to their feet, they stared about them.

Hylas sniffed an acrid smell that was horribly familiar.

Pirra raked her fingers over the ground and raised her hand, letting fall a scattering of fine grey ash. 'What *is* this place?' she said.

27

What *is* this place? wondered the dolphin as he swam through the twisting channel. The breath from his blowhole sounded scarily loud, and when he poked out his head he heard the singing echoes and the twitter of ghosts, many clicks away. But still he swam, determined to find the boy.

At first, when the One Beneath had been slamming His tail, the dolphin had swum frantically up and down outside the cave. The Sea had raged and he'd had to dodge boulders crashing down from the cliffs. How could the humans survive this?

At last the gigantic tail-slams had lessened to a rumble, then a shudder, and finally a ripple. Anxiously, the dolphin had strained to catch the sounds the boy made when he ran, or when he slapped the waves with his poor little flippers. Nothing. Just the voice of the Sea and the growls of angry stone.

The dolphin had sent out long, ringing squeals – and

finally, from deep within the earth, he'd heard the boy's answering call. Again and again the dolphin had squealed, guiding him out of the cave. But after a while, no more answers had come back.

The dolphin hadn't hesitated. When he'd been stranded in the Above, the boy had saved him. Now he had to save the boy.

Fearlessly, he'd plunged into the jaws of the cave: the cave that no dolphin had ever braved before.

With terrifying suddenness it had narrowed to a channel. The dolphin had heard how twisty it was, how spiky with limpets and coral, but still he'd swum on.

That had been a while ago. Now as he swam deeper, the channel became many: a branching tangle, like a forest of kelp. His clicks echoed confusingly. Which way to go?

He headed for where it felt coldest and sounded deepest – but it was frighteningly narrow. Weeds snagged his snout, and coral scratched his flippers. At times he could barely squeeze through, and twice it grew so shallow that he nearly got stranded. An eel poked its nose from a hole and snapped at his tail. An octopus mistook him for a rock and fastened on his blowhole; he was panicky and breathless by the time he'd managed to scrape it off.

Worse even than that, the water was turning strange. It was the Sea – and yet it wasn't the Sea. It felt weirdly thin, and it didn't carry him as well as it should. It didn't even *taste* of the Sea.

The singing echoes grew abruptly louder, and beneath them he caught a bubbling sound of laughter.

Poking his nose above the surface, he saw that before him the channel went on for a few more tail-flicks, then opened into a wide bay beneath a glittering blue stone sky. All around he saw the frail ghosts of humans, and in the still water, tall standing stones warning him back. In the middle of the bay stood an island – it sounded as if it was made of the bones of seabirds and fishes – and from this reared a terrible white stone ablaze with cold blue fire.

The dolphin's courage faltered. He would never find the boy. He had to go back.

The channel was too narrow. He couldn't turn round.

He sank deeper and tried again, twisting his snout awkwardly on to his tail, but the rocks clamped his flanks like the claws of a crab.

Frantically he struggled. The rocks held him fast.

He felt tiny tremors in the water as the ghosts drew nearer, leaning over him and fluttering their long, thin flippers over his back. He heard the bubbling laughter of the Shining One.

Desperately, he whistled for the boy.

The boy didn't come.

Something else did.

28

'What *happened* here?' said Pirra, blinking in the red glare of the setting Sun.

They'd emerged into a steep-sided valley where no green thing grew. The ground beneath her feet was covered in cinders, and she breathed the throat-catching stench of ash. She stared at strange black trees with leaves the colour of dried blood.

'It must've been a forest fire,' said Hylas. 'Only not like one I've ever seen.' He snapped off a branch of black laurel. Every leaf was intact, but scorched to an eerie dark-red sheen.

'Like bronze,' she said.

That seemed to disconcert him. 'The trees of bronze,' he murmured.

'What?'

'I don't like the feel of this. In the mountains we avoid places where there's been a forest fire, because they draw the . . .' he lowered his voice, 'we call them the Angry Ones.'

Pirra's skin prickled. 'So do we.'

They exchanged glances.

Hylas threw away the branch. 'It'll be dark soon. We've got to get out of here. I think our camp's somewhere to the west, over that ridge.'

'That's not a ridge, it's a cliff. We'll never get up there.'

He scanned their surroundings. 'Looks like the only way we can go is south.'

'Which will take us even further from camp.'

'I know. But we haven't got much choice.'

Pirra had the uneasy feeling that this was what the island wanted all along. First it had drawn them into the caves; and now it had spewed them out into this devastated valley for some shadowy purpose of its own.

There were no signs of life, but as they walked, they passed the blackened carcasses of creatures that hadn't managed to escape. Pirra found the tiny charred remains of a bird. She sensed its small spirit – and the spirits of the poor burnt trees and the other dead creatures – begging her to find out why this had happened. The island had been wounded. A great burn had seared its very heart.

The Sun vanished behind the ridge, and the light began to fail. Their feet sank with a *whump* into deep, soft ash. The sound only emphasized the stillness.

Hylas walked with his head down, limping slightly; there was a bluish mark on his calf where the sea-snake's fang had grazed him. After a while he halted. 'It's getting dark. We'll have to find somewhere to camp.'

Pirra was horrified. 'Not here! Surely once the Moon rises –'

'Pirra, it isn't going to rise. It's the dark of the Moon.'

They both knew what that meant. The dark of the Moon is when people keep a lamp burning all night, for fear of ghosts and evil spirits.

'What will we do for water?' said Pirra.

He spread his hands. She thought with longing of the waterskins they'd left behind in the caves.

A few early stars were out when they reached a shadowy gully leading off to the west. It was flanked by dark cypresses, and further in, Pirra glimpsed a lone poplar standing guard.

'That might be a way to the Sea,' she said uncertainly. 'Then we could get round by the coast.'

'I don't like the feel of it,' said Hylas. 'I think we should keep to the main trail.'

'But it's going the wrong way.'

'If we follow the animals, they might lead us to a spring.'

'What animals? They're all dead!'

'No, some managed to get away. Look at the tracks.'

'What's a track?' she snapped. Thirst was making her irritable.

'Oh, surely you know about tracks? They're footprints, they tell you things.' Impatiently, he pointed out what he said was a hare's trail, then a row of sinuous lines made by a snake; he said the gaps in between were where it had gathered its coils.

'So it's like writing,' she said. 'Well if you'd told me that to start with, I'd have understood.'

'What's writing?'

'Oh, surely you know about writing?' she mimicked. 'It's

marks that mean things.' With a stick of charcoal she scratched lines on a pebble. 'There. That's for you, it says goat.'

'What d'you mean it "says"? It can't talk, it's a pebble.'

'Oh, never mind! I'm going to take a look down that gully, I bet it does lead to the Sea.'

'Fine. Do what you like.'

'Fine.'

She stalked off, scuffing the ash with her feet. Hylas stayed behind, examining his precious tracks.

It was darker in the gully. A wind sprang up, raising columns of ash that seemed to follow her. The dead trees rattled their brittle bronze hands, and she shivered. She would go as far as that poplar tree, then turn back.

Suddenly a shadow crossed her heart. She heard a rushing high overhead, like great wings moving fast. Something dark cut across the stars.

She raced back to the mouth of the gully, where she found Hylas staring at the sky. In the gloom she saw how pale he'd gone.

'What was that?' she whispered.

He shook his head. 'I thought I saw something crouching on the ground. It flew up. At first I thought it was a vulture –'

'What's a vulture?'

'A big bird that eats carcasses. But it felt wrong. And I've never known a vulture fly that fast.'

Neither wanted to mention what was in their minds; but this time, when they headed off, they stayed close together.

They hadn't gone far when Hylas motioned her to silence. Then she heard it: a faint, echoing babble of water. 'Oh, thank the Goddess,' she muttered as they stumbled through the gloom.

Rounding a spur, they came upon a jostling throng of wild creatures: deer, lynx, wolf, all scrabbling at the ground, united by their desperate need for water. Ravens exploded into the sky. A stag raced towards Pirra – swerved – and thundered off into the dark. Then she saw the cause of the animals' desperation: the Earthshaker had buried the spring beneath a rockfall. They couldn't reach it.

'Don't move,' said Hylas, drawing his knife and stepping in front of her.

The lion was four paces away, a huge male with a matted mane and a battle-scarred nose. Its eyes threw back the starlight as it staggered towards them, uttering harsh, sawing grunts.

It halted, panting and trailing ropes of spit. Then, with an exhausted sigh, it slumped on to its side and laid its great head in the dust.

Hylas sheathed his knife. 'It's in pain,' he said. 'Look at its paws.'

Pirra felt sick. The lion's pads had been scorched to rawness by the fire. Every step must have been agony.

Forgetting her thirst, she ran to where the spring was buried and started pulling away rocks. 'If we could give it some water . . .'

It didn't take them long to clear a gap big enough to draw out a few gritty handfuls. The lion lay struggling for breath, gazing at them with weary patience; but when they trickled water into its muzzle, it was too weak to swallow.

'It's no good,' said Hylas.

'Surely we can do something?'

'No, Pirra. It's too late.'

She watched him lay his palm on the lion's heaving flank. 'Be at peace,' he told it gently. 'May you find a strong new body – and no more pain.'

The golden eyes dulled. Pirra felt a fleeting warmth on her face as the lion's spirit swept out into the night.

Pirra sat with her back against a boulder and forced down the last scrap of tough, bitter lion meat.

Hylas hadn't wanted to do it; he'd said eating the flesh of another hunter went against the old ways, but that you were allowed to if you were starving. Pirra had asked what he meant by the old ways, but he hadn't replied.

They'd camped far enough from the spring to avoid being trampled by thirsty animals. It was a hot night, so they didn't bother with a shelter. Hylas had coaxed a fire from a pile of charcoal – at least there was plenty of that – then he'd started grimly hauling away more rocks. Pirra had suggested that he wait till morning, but he'd retorted that he hadn't been able to save Scram or the lion, and he wasn't going to let another creature die if he could help it.

Together they'd cleared the spring until Hylas said a blind hedgehog could reach it; then he'd part-skinned the lion and cut a slab from its ribs, which they'd roasted and tried to eat. After that they'd dragged the carcass into the scrub for others to feed on, leaving the heart and tail on a rock for the Goddess.

It hadn't taken long for the animals to discover that the spring was clear, and from where she sat, Pirra heard a constant scuffle of feet and hooves and paws. Growls flared into short-lived squabbles, then subsided to slow slurpings and the sound of water dripping from satisfied muzzles.

She was exhausted, but she couldn't settle. She dreaded hearing the sound of wings.

She knew why Hylas had insisted on skinning the lion and unblocking the spring. He needed to keep his mind off what haunted this place.

He sat on the other side of the fire, scouring the lion's bladder with cinders to make a new waterskin. Feeling her eyes on him, he raised his head. 'Back at that gully – I don't think it was a vulture.'

She swallowed. 'Neither do I.'

A rustle of wings made them start. A raven flew past with a sonorous *cark!*

Hylas blew out a long breath. Pirra peered into the dark.

She couldn't remember a time when she hadn't feared the Angry Ones. Everyone did: priestess, peasant, slave. The Angry Ones have always existed, and they always will. They are the shadow that follows you at midnight, and the dread that turns your dreams to nightmare. When you wake in terror of the dark, or your skin prickles with fear but you don't know why – then the Angry Ones are near. They come from the Chaos before the gods, and they hunt those who've murdered their kin. You might ward them off for a while by muttering an ancient charm; you might even evade them for a time by disguising yourself, or fleeing your homeland;

but sooner or later, they'll find you, and scorch your spirit to madness.

'Why are they here?' whispered Pirra. 'They hunt people who've done terrible things; but there isn't anyone here except us.'

'I don't know,' said Hylas. 'But I wish we had some buck-thorn. Where I come from, they say it helps ward them off.'

There was silence while they thought about that. Both knew that even if you haven't done anything wrong, the Angry Ones can still destroy you if you get too close.

Hylas threw more charcoal on the fire, making her jump. 'I'll keep this burning all night. Let's hope dawn comes soon.'

Surprisingly, they both slept until sunrise, and after filling the new waterskin, they set off, feeling braver as grey light began seeping into the valley.

Around mid-morning, they stumbled on a trail that looked as if it might lead down to the Sea, but they hadn't gone far when it opened into a clearing: a clearing blocked by a great pile of charred trees.

The slopes on either side were covered in fallen pines, as if toppled by a giant's hand. Something about the way they lay aslant each other didn't look right to Hylas. He went to take a closer look.

He found axe marks on their trunks. Returning to the pile of charred trees, he unearthed the burnt bones of several oxen and some blackened fragments of earthenware. He sniffed one. He smelt oil. He blinked in disbelief.

'Someone did this on purpose,' he said. 'Someone cut down these trees and doused them with oil and set them alight. Then the wind caught the fire and blew it up the valley.'

'But – they couldn't have meant to burn the whole valley,' faltered Pirra. 'It must've got out of hand.'

Hylas stooped to examine a slab of granite that had been placed before the woodpile. On it lay a glistening pile of obsidian arrowheads. He turned one in his fingers. It was shaped like a poplar leaf. He'd dug one just like it out of his arm.

'Crows,' Pirra said in a hard voice.

'But *why*?' he murmured.

'It's said that they burn their sacrifices.'

'You think that's what this was? A *sacrifice*? But what could they hope to gain?'

'I don't know.'

'No sacrifice should be this big. They must have destroyed timber enough to build ten villages.'

'And all the poor tree spirits.'

He felt himself growing angry. All those dead creatures and defenceless trees. And the Crows had done it. Always the Crows. 'What's wrong with this island?' he murmured. 'It feels as if – as if everything's joined up.'

'What do you mean?'

'Why did that ship run aground? What happened to Spirit's pod? Why did the Earthshaker wake?' He frowned. 'Ever since the Crows attacked, I've felt there's some kind of pattern, only I can't see what it is. I feel like a fly caught in a spider's web.'

Pirra didn't reply. She was craning her neck at the fallen

trees littering the westward slope. 'D'you think we could climb out that way?'

He followed her gaze. 'Maybe. I'll try it first, you wait here.'

The trees were alarmingly unstable, and spiky with broken branches. He called down to Pirra to stand back, in case the whole lot came crashing down. Halfway up, he saw what he couldn't have seen from below: an overhang that made further climbing impossible. It seemed that the island still wouldn't let them out.

Coming down was harder, as his hands and feet were slippery with charcoal. His knife-sheath snagged on a branch and tipped upside down; the knife fell out and clattered to the bottom. Pirra ran to retrieve it. 'I've got it!' she called.

Glancing over his shoulder, Hylas spotted what he'd missed on the way up: a ravine, hidden behind a spur on the other side of the clearing. He saw a slash of brilliant green, and his spirits rose. The ravine was untouched by the fire. It had to lead down to the Sea.

He was about to call down the good news when the bushes in the ravine stirred.

He froze.

There it was again.

Someone was coming.

29

The man who emerged from the ravine walked with a limp, and he kept to the shade as if he didn't want to be seen.

He was barefoot, in a ragged tunic of salt-stained rawhide, with a half-empty waterskin slung over one shoulder, and a knife stuck in a twist of rope that did for a belt. His dark hair was long, so he couldn't be a slave; and although he looked like a homeless wanderer, he had the build of a warrior. He was too far off for Hylas to see his face, but he gave an impression of intense awareness that made Hylas' skin tighten.

From his hiding place among the fallen trees, Hylas peered down at the clearing. He could see no sign of Pirra. He only hoped she'd heard the man coming, and taken cover.

Still keeping to the shade, the man halted at the pile of Crow arrowheads. He stood looking down at them. His hand went to his knife. Slowly, he scanned the clearing.

Hylas felt the power of that gaze coming at him like heat from embers.

The man limped to the charred remains of the sacrifice, directly below Hylas. He stooped for a shard of earthenware. Sniffed it. Set it down. He found a boulder and leant against it, kneading his right thigh as if it pained him. From a pouch he shook a few leaves and crushed them in his palm. He rubbed some on his forehead and chewed the rest, washing them down with a pull from his waterskin, then wiped his mouth on the back of his hand.

'You up there,' he said calmly. 'I think you'd better come down.'

'I know you're up there,' said the Stranger. 'And we both know that the only way out of that woodpile is down.'

A beetle crawled on to Hylas' foot. He didn't dare brush it off.

The Stranger folded his arms on his chest and yawned. 'I can wait all day. How about you?'

The beetle wandered off and was replaced by ants.

'All right,' said the Stranger. 'I'll wait.'

The Sun rose higher. Hylas felt sweat trickling down his sides. A wind sprang up, blowing ash in his eyes. His mouth was dry. Pirra had their new waterskin.

'Can't be much fun up there,' the Stranger remarked. His voice was as smooth as honey, but with an undercurrent of strength that made you want to listen and obey. 'You'll be thirsty. Hungry, too. Boys like you always are.'

Hylas caught his breath. How could the Stranger know he was a boy, if he couldn't see him?

'Oh, I know quite a lot about you,' said the Stranger, as if he'd spoken aloud. 'You're skinny. Tired. Bit of a limp in the left leg. What'd you do, step on a thorn?'

Hylas began to feel dizzy. Was it possible that this wasn't a man, but an immortal in disguise?

And yet – if he was an immortal, surely he could simply *make* him come down?

And if he wasn't an immortal, why didn't he just climb up and *drag* him down? Unless – unless he *couldn't* climb up because –

'You're right,' conceded the Stranger. 'I'd rather not do any climbing with this scratch on my thigh. By the way, what's your name?'

This was so unexpected that Hylas nearly blurted it out.

The Stranger shrugged. 'Well then, I'll give you one. I'll call you Flea, because only a flea could jump up there. So now, Flea. If you don't come down, I'll have to hurt the girl –'

'No, don't!' cried Hylas.

'Ah – it can talk,' the Stranger said drily. 'And by its accent, I'd say Lykonian –'

'Don't hurt her!'

'Well, that's up to you, isn't it?'

Hylas chewed his lip. It occurred to him that if the Stranger really did have Pirra, then where was she? Was this a bluff?

Then it came to him. *Tracks.* The Stranger had read his tracks, and Pirra's, too.

The Stranger scooped up a handful of ash and watched it trickle through his fingers. 'A good sailor,' he said, 'always knows what the wind's doing. Although that wouldn't mean much to you, since you're from the plains.'

'I'm not, I –' Hylas shut his eyes.

'A mountain boy? Yes, of course, I should've guessed from your hiding place. Though you're a long way from Mount Lykas, aren't you, Flea?'

Hylas didn't answer. He felt like a mouse trapped by an alarmingly clever fox.

Pushing himself off the boulder, the Stranger started collecting branches and piling them upwind of Hylas. Now what was he up to?

Unnerved, Hylas watched him limp to the mouth of the ravine, returning almost at once with a fistful of downy grassheads. Kneeling a little awkwardly because of his bad leg, he drew his knife and deftly struck sparks into the tinder.

'You're wondering what I'm doing,' he said easily. 'Well, I'll tell you. You know how it is after the winter, when your hut's crawling with lice? So what do you do? You throw wormwood on the fire and smoke them out.' He blew on the kindling, then stood back to let the wind get at it. 'It works on fleas, too.'

In no time the wind was sending black smoke billowing up the slope. Soon Hylas couldn't breathe. Coughing and swallowing smoke, he crawled out blindly, lost his footing, and fell.

In the blink of an eye the Stranger hauled him the rest of the way, slammed him face down on the ground and jabbed the point of his knife under his jaw. 'Where are they?' he said in a voice like granite.

'Who?' gasped Hylas.

'The sons of Koronos! Quick! No lies!'

'I don't know who you mean!'

Strong hands pinioned his arms with his own belt, wrenched him upright and held him in an agonizing grip that nearly broke his collarbone. 'Where are the Crows?' demanded the Stranger. 'You must know, you're one of their spies!'

'No I'm not!'

'Not good enough. If you want to live longer than that branch I've just put on the fire, start talking!'

'I'm not a spy, I swear!'

The Stranger flipped him round and held him at arm's length. Hylas found himself staring up into a strong, wind-burnt face. He saw a sharp dark beard crusted with salt, and deep-set eyes that were strangely light, as if bleached by years of staring into vast distances. They were studying him with all the compassion of a lynx for its prey.

'If you're not a spy,' barked the Stranger, 'what are you doing here?'

'Trying to get away from them!'

The Stranger gave him a look that searched to the roots of his spirit. 'You're clever,' he said at last. 'But what you need to bear in mind is that I'm cleverer.'

Hylas swallowed. 'I – I'm clever enough to have realized that.'

The lines at the sides of the Stranger's mouth deepened, as if he would have smiled if he hadn't forgotten how. 'How old are you, Flea?'

'Um. Twelve.'

'Twelve.' A shadow of pity crossed the hard features. 'Is it possible?' he murmured. 'I've been on the run longer than you've been alive.'

'From the Crows?'

'And other things.' For a moment the deep eyes were haunted. 'So now, Flea. What do you know about the Crows?'

Hylas took a breath. 'We were on the peak with the goats and they attacked our camp, me and Issi, that's my sister. We got separated. They killed Skiros, he's an Outsider too. Thestor – that's the Chieftain – he let them on his land, I don't know why. I got away and ended up here. I'm trying to get back to find my sister. That's all I know.' That was a lie; he hadn't mentioned the Keftians, but that would have led to Pirra, and he hoped the Stranger had forgotten her.

'How many attacked your camp? What did they look like?'

Hylas described them as best he could. 'Their l-leader,' he stammered. 'Who is he?'

The Stranger spat. 'His name is Kratos. Kratos, son of Koronos.'

'What *is* Koronos?'

'Not what, who. Koronos is head of the clan that rules Mycenae. Once they were honoured and respected, but they grew drunk with power and seized what wasn't theirs. "Crows" is the name people gave them out of fear; it's come to mean the whole clan, and the warriors who fight for it.'

He paused. 'For a captive, you ask a lot of questions. Here's one for you. Why is Kratos after you?'

'I don't know. He's after all Outsiders. Maybe I'm the only one left. And Issi.'

The Stranger took that in silence, and Hylas sensed a subtle mind sifting outcomes with dizzying speed. He mustered his courage. 'Are you – are you a god?' he asked.

Again the lines around the Stranger's mouth deepened. 'I might be. How would you tell?'

'You'd have a burning shadow.'

'True. Although if I were a god, I could make you think it wasn't.' His voice had turned smooth again, but still with that undercurrent of strength. This man could make you believe that fire was water.

'Are you a shapeshifter?' said Hylas. 'Like the Man of the Sea? Or some other spirit in disguise?'

'Oh, I'm good at disguises. I've had plenty of practice.'

The fire spat. Hylas gave a start. The branch was nearly burnt up.

The Stranger had seen it too. 'What am I going to do with you, Flea? I want to believe you – but can I risk it? The Crows have set traps for me before; and I haven't survived this long by being kind.'

Hylas took a leap in the dark. 'I know where your ship is.'

The Stranger went still. 'That's convenient. A little too convenient.'

'Ow. Please. It's true. It's got – um – undyed sails and jars of olives – and – and a wind pouch, with all different knots!'

The grip on his collarbone eased. 'Any survivors?'

'I didn't find any.'

'What, none?'

Hylas shook his head.

Something showed in the Stranger's face, and Hylas saw that although he was ruthless, he had cared about his fellow sailors.

'I can take you to the wreck,' said Hylas.

'You can tell me where it is now and save me trouble.'

'If I told you now, you – you might kill me.'

'I might kill you anyway. It'd be the sensible thing to do.'

The fire hissed and the branch collapsed in a flurry of sparks.

'How far to the ship?' said the Stranger.

'Not far,' lied Hylas. 'We could be there by nightfall.'

'Where is it?'

'On some rocks just off a point, but you can reach it if the wind's not too strong.'

The Stranger hauled him to his feet and grabbed a burning brand from the fire. 'Which way?'

Hylas' mind raced. It was vital to look as if he knew where he was going, which ruled out the ravine from which the Stranger had come. 'North,' he said confidently.

As they headed back into the burnt valley, he racked his brains for a plan and came up with nothing. He only hoped that Pirra was long gone, and would have the sense to stay that way.

Huddled behind her boulder, Pirra listened to them heading off. What was Hylas up to? Why was he leading that man back the way they'd come? Did he have some sort of plan?

The thought of following them made her belly turn over. If she got too close, the Stranger would catch her and gut her like a fish. If she lagged behind, she'd get lost. She saw herself wandering alone through the burnt valley; stumbling into that haunted gully as night was falling, and feeling the dreadful presence of the Angry Ones . . .

But Hylas needed her. She couldn't let him down. If it hadn't been for him, she'd still be trapped underground.

Taking a swig from the waterskin, she mustered her courage. One thing was certain: if she ended up anywhere near that gully, she'd need buckthorn to protect herself. She didn't know if Hylas had realized it yet, but the Stranger was a haunted man.

Diving into the ravine, she frantically searched the scrub. Laurels and holly, but where was buckthorn? She had just a hazy idea of what it looked like, as she'd only seen it in a picture and some leaves in a bowl; and all the time, Hylas and that man were getting away.

With a cry of triumph, she found some. Hacking off a few branches with the knife and jamming them in her belt, she scrambled back to the clearing.

It was empty. Hylas and the Stranger were gone.

She raced after them – or rather, after where she guessed they'd headed; there were more trails than she remembered, and tracking turned out to be a lot harder than it looked.

Wild plans of rescue swirled in her head, all of them hopeless. The Stranger looked like a beggar, but moved like a warrior; and if she was right about him, he was even more dangerous than that. If she was right, he'd committed the worst of crimes.

Hylas must have guessed by now, even if he hadn't heard the spell the Stranger had muttered as he'd crushed those leaves in his hand.

Pirra couldn't remember when she'd first heard that spell whispered in the House of the Goddess, but she knew that it had been said on Keftiu for thousands of years – and in Egypt, too; Userref had told her that. Terrified people had whispered it long before the very first House of the Goddess was ever built, or the mountains of stone that the Egyptians had raised in the desert. It was older even than the wild tribes who'd dwelt in caves before the gods taught men how to farm.

It was the oldest spell in the world.

The spell against the Angry Ones.

30

Shadows were creeping out from under the trees, and fear was thickening in Hylas' throat. Beside him the Stranger kept glancing about uneasily, and snuffing the air like a stag scenting danger. 'Why this way, Flea?' he growled.

'It's the way to your ship,' lied Hylas.

'It'd better be.'

The Stranger held the burning brand high, as if to ward off the night. At times he chewed another leaf from his pouch, or muttered a charm under his breath. The leaves were buckthorn, and even if Hylas hadn't already guessed, the charm would have told him why the Stranger wore no amulet or sealstone. He didn't want to give himself away to what hunted him: the Angry Ones.

The sky was overcast and tinged with red. The valley was hushed, holding its breath. The haunted gully wasn't far off. Hylas thought of darkness moving under the black cypresses. He strained his ears for the sound of wings. Just by being with this man, he was in mortal danger.

The light was failing when they reached the spring. Thirsty beasts had trampled it to a muddy wallow, but now it was deserted, clouds of midges the only signs of life.

No bats, thought Hylas. With so many midges, there should be bats.

'We won't stop long,' muttered the Stranger. 'We have to get out of here before dark.'

Tying Hylas to a tree stump and setting the brand against a boulder, he drank swiftly, refilled his waterskin, and splashed the wound on his thigh. Then, to Hylas' surprise, he brought over the waterskin and gave him a drink, too.

'Thanks,' said Hylas.

The Stranger didn't seem to hear. The brand was almost spent; he was prowling about seeking another branch.

Hylas couldn't make him out. He was ruthless and frightening, and he must have done something terrible to be pursued by the Angry Ones, but at times he showed flashes of kindness; and despite himself, Hylas wanted to like him. It was as if there were two men inside that powerful frame: one who didn't want to hurt him, and another who would do whatever it took to survive.

A gust of wind whirled the dust into twisting spirals. Quick as a lizard, the Stranger snatched the brand and spun round, sweeping the shadows. His face was wild, and his teeth glinted in his beard.

The wind dropped. The Stranger lowered the brand. His

forehead glistened with sweat. He caught Hylas staring. 'Funny thing about fear,' he said. 'Live with it long enough, it becomes a companion. But you know that, don't you, Flea? You know what's wrong with this valley.'

Hylas nodded. 'What did you do, that they're after you?'

The Stranger looked down at him. 'You're too young to understand. Too young for any of this. You should be at home, tending your goats.'

'The Crows killed them. They killed my dog.'

The Stranger frowned. Then he startled Hylas by asking what had happened to his knife. When Hylas didn't reply, he said, 'You have an empty sheath at your belt, so where's the knife?'

'I – I lost it.'

The Stranger considered that. 'Do you know why the Crows burnt this valley?' he said quietly.

Hylas shook his head, wondering where he was leading.

'Think about it, Flea. People sacrifice because they want something. The Crows must have wanted something badly to burn a whole valley.' Carefully, he lit the new brand with the old, then moved to Hylas' tree stump and sat beside him. 'I've been asking myself why Kratos would go to the trouble of hunting Outsiders,' he said. 'A snake strikes when it's threatened. So ask yourself, Flea, why do they feel threatened? How could a skinny little Outsider threaten the Crows, the all-powerful rulers of Mycenae?'

'I don't know,' said Hylas.

'I'll tell you. To threaten the Crows, you take the thing that keeps them in power. Do you know what that is?'

Again Hylas shook his head.

'The power of the Crows is rooted in a dagger.' He paused to see how Hylas took that. 'Odd, isn't it? Not an alabaster cup, or a collar of purest gold. Just a plain bronze dagger. Three rivets, and a simple mark on the hilt: a chariot wheel to crush their enemies. With that dagger they're invincible. Without it, they're not.'

Hylas fought to keep his face from betraying him, but inside he was reeling. His mind flew to the tomb where the dying Keftian had urged him to take the dagger. *It's precious. I stole it. Keep it hidden.*

'B-but – how could they do that?' he stammered. 'How could their power be in a dagger?'

'I'll tell you,' said the Stranger, still watching him intently. 'The first Chieftain of the House of Koronos fought a great battle with his enemies. He killed the leader with a blow that split helmet and head in two. Later, from the cloven helmet, he forged a dagger. He quenched the heated bronze with blood from his own battle-wounds. Then he sacrificed seven bulls, and called on the Sky Father to steep the dagger with the power of his clan – and to give them the strength and endurance of bronze. The Sky Father sent an eagle as a sign that the prayer was heard. As long as the House of Koronos keeps the dagger, it is invincible.'

He paused, his deep eyes never leaving Hylas' face. 'When I saw that great burnt sacrifice at the head of the valley, it told me something. It told me the Crows have lost their dagger. That's why they came to this island. That's why they made that sacrifice. To beg the gods to give it back.'

The wind had died. The only sound was the babble of the spring.

Suddenly the Stranger leant close to him. 'Is that why they're after Outsiders, Flea? Did an Outsider steal their dagger? Did *you?*'

Hylas met his eyes. 'I didn't steal it. On my sister's life, I swear it.'

'But you know of it.'

'– Yes.'

'Where is it now?'

'I don't know.'

'How did you come to know of it at all?'

'Just now, when you told me.'

'When did you last see it?'

He hesitated. 'A few days ago. It's lost, it fell in the Sea . . .' He tried to look away, but the Stranger's gaze held his. He saw that Hylas lied.

'Has your girl got it? The girl whose tracks I found in the clearing?'

'N-no,' faltered Hylas. 'I don't *know* where it is! That's the truth!'

Another penetrating look. 'Oddly enough, I believe you. So it seems that we're both in the dark.'

He took a few paces, as if pondering something: something he didn't like. Then he squared his shoulders and threw Hylas a fleeting look of pity. 'I'm sorry, Flea,' he said. 'Why did you have to lead me here, to this terrible place?'

Hylas' mouth went dry. 'What are you going to do?'

Shouldering the waterskin, the Stranger untied Hylas and

pulled him to his feet. 'Come on,' he muttered. 'Let's get this over with.'

The spring was left behind, and in no time the black cypresses loomed out of the darkness.

'No,' said Hylas. 'That's the wrong way.'

The Stranger ignored him.

The lone poplar stood like a sentinel in the middle of the gully. Sticking the brand in the crook of a branch, the Stranger made Hylas sit on the roots; then he tied him to the trunk. He worked quickly, glancing often at the darkening sky.

Hylas' teeth were chattering. 'What are you going to do?'

The Stranger drew his knife and hacked off a lock of his own hair, then tied it round Hylas' neck. Grabbing a piece of charcoal, he held Hylas steady, and scratched marks on his forehead and chest.

'I hate this, Flea,' he said fiercely. 'To do such a thing to a child . . . But I have to. I can't let them get me. It's not just my life at stake – and there is no other way.'

Rising to his feet, he seized the brand and called to the shadows thronging the gully. 'Spirits of air and darkness! See this mark on his head and heart! This is the mark of Akastos! Come for him. Take him. Feed on *him*!'

'Akastos,' panted Hylas. 'That's your name. You've put your sign on me. You've marked me with your hair. I'm – I'm *bait*. You're going to leave me here for the Angry Ones.'

The man called Akastos limped towards the mouth of the gully.

'If you leave me,' called Hylas, 'you'll never find your ship!'

'Yes, I will,' Akastos replied. 'You said it's easy to reach if the wind isn't too strong. The wind's been in the north-west since my ship foundered, which means the wreck is on the north-west coast.'

'But – even if you find it, you'll be trapped when the Crows get here! And they will come! I know a place to hide, I can help –'

'I don't need your help.'

'*Please!*'

Something in his voice made Akastos stop.

'Don't leave me,' pleaded Hylas. 'I haven't *done* anything!'

'I know,' said Akastos in an altered voice. 'But I can't let that get in the way.' He rubbed a hand over his face. 'We're alike, you and I. Both survivors. Maybe you'll think up something to cheat them of their due.'

'*Akastos!*'

But he was gone.

The silence after he left was dreadful. Through the black branches, Hylas watched the last glimmer of daylight drain from the sky. A few pale stars glinted. Then clouds snuffed them out. The darkness deepened. It would be a night without a Moon.

Hylas felt the tree's rough bark digging into his shoulder blades, and Akastos' marks stiffening on his skin. He smelt charred wood and the stink of ash.

He heard the rushing of wings.

31

Hylas struggled wildly. The bindings held fast. He tried to rub off Akastos' marks, but his arms were pinioned against his sides; he couldn't reach.

A deeper darkness sped across the sky.

He searched his memory. He began haltingly to mutter the charm.

The darkness swept past, and the sound of wings faded into the night. He strained to listen. He knew they would be back.

The Angry Ones hunt those who have murdered their kin, and he hadn't murdered anyone, but he knew that wasn't going to save him. The Angry Ones don't care who gets in their way. If you're too close to their quarry – or if you bear his mark – they'll hunt you too.

Akastos had known what he was doing. He'd bound Hylas to the tree with knots that couldn't be undone, and put his mark on him twice, so that there would be no mistake. Hylas was as helpless as a goat staked out as bait for a lion.

A huge shadowy form blotted out the sky. It dropped on to the rim of the gully. It folded its wings with a leathery *thwap*.

Hylas' spirit shrank.

More wingbeats. Another shadow lit on to the rim. Hylas heard the clink of claws on cinders. He smelt the stink of charred flesh. He saw the darkness move.

A terrible, listening silence.

From the rim of the gully he seemed to see darkness congeal and snake down, swaying from side to side. Seeking *him*.

In his mind he felt them. Their flesh was burnt black by the fires of Chaos. Their raw red mouths were gaping wounds.

Could they see in the dark? Could they hear his laboured breath and the sweat trickling down his sides? Could they smell his terror?

He had no buckthorn to ward them off. All he could do was mutter the charm – but under his breath, in the desperate hope that he wouldn't give himself away.

At the corner of his eye, something stirred on the ground.

There. At the mouth of the gully. He strained to pierce the blackness, but it was too dense.

Above him, on the rim, the dark was churning, long necks snaking down to find him.

Again that movement on the ground – but closer now, a shadow stealing towards him. The charm stuck in his throat. Dread squeezed his heart . . .

'Hylas!' whispered the shadow on the ground. 'It's me! Pirra!'

It was so dark that she had to grope her way towards him. If it hadn't been for his fair hair, she would never have found him.

'Are you all right?' she whispered, tugging at the knots behind his back. They were like granite; she couldn't undo them.

'Have you got the dagger?' he panted. 'Quick! Cut me free!'

She hacked at the rawhide, but it was too tough.

'*Hurry!* They're right above us!'

She raised her head. Terror washed over her.

A dark shape wheeled down and settled in the cypresses at the mouth of the gully. Pirra heard the scrape of claws and the leathery crackle of wings.

Again she attacked the rope. Her hands were shaking. The blade bounced off.

'He put his mark on me,' hissed Hylas. 'That's what they sense. I can't reach it – can you?'

'Where?'

'Brow and breastbone. And he tied his hair round my neck.'

Frantically, she felt for his face and rubbed off the charcoal with her fingers, then did the same for his chest. The hair round his neck was too slippery to untie. She tried to cut it. She'd never imagined that hair could be so strong. At last she managed it and cast the hair aside. As she started on the rope, she remembered the buckthorn leaves in her belt.

'Why'd you stop?' whispered Hylas.

'I've got buckthorn –'

'It won't work, they're too close!'

Thirty paces away, a shadowy form dropped from the cypresses and hit the ground with an appalling thud.

They froze.

Pirra renewed her attack on the rope. 'I can't,' she muttered. 'It's taking too long.'

'Find a stone,' gasped Hylas, 'and a scrap of charcoal. Scratch his mark on it and – and tie the hair round.'

She grasped what he meant. 'A decoy?'

'Do it now, untie me after!'

'But –'

'Pirra if we don't make that decoy right now, it won't matter how fast we run!'

She grabbed a stone and snapped off a branch from the poplar. 'The marks,' she breathed. 'What did they look like?'

'I – I never saw them.'

Her mind raced. 'Did he tell you his name?'

'Akastos.'

'What did the marks *feel* like?'

The shadow at the mouth of the gully swayed. Pirra heard a dreadful snuffing sound. Dread darkened her mind.

'It felt like – like a dagger pointing down . . . and I think – bars at either end of the hilt –'

'I know it, it's the first sound of his name.' Blindly, she scratched what she hoped was the right mark on the stone.

But where was the hair? She scrabbled in the dust. Couldn't find it. Panic closed in.

Got it. With trembling hands, she tied it round the stone.

'*Hurry*,' urged Hylas.

The snuffing ceased. The shadow went still. It had caught the scent.

As if at some signal, another dropped from the ridge, whirling down in a gust of foul wind to settle in the cypresses. Then another.

At last the hair was tied. Pirra drew back her arm and flung the stone as far as she could towards the mouth of the gully.

'Cut me loose!' panted Hylas.

The shadow on the ground halted – swayed – and lurched after the stone.

Feverishly, Pirra hacked at the rope.

'Don't hack,' said Hylas, '*saw*, like you're sawing wood!'

She'd never sawed wood in her life, but she grasped what he meant. He twisted and strained. The rope burst.

Leaping to his feet, Hylas grabbed the dagger in one hand and Pirra's wrist in the other. Together they fled the only way they could: up the gully, into the unknown.

As they ran, Pirra glanced back – and glimpsed winged shapes that would live in her nightmares forever, dropping from the trees and converging on the place where she'd cast the stone.

'Are you all right?' Pirra said quietly.

Hylas nodded.

'You don't look it.'

'Thanks.'

'I only meant –'

'No, I mean – thanks. For coming to find me.'

'Oh.' With her heel she hacked at the dust. 'Well. I wouldn't have survived very long if I hadn't.'

Hylas hugged his knees and wondered when he would stop shaking. It had been horrible, stumbling through the gully in the dark, dreading at any moment to hear the Angry Ones coming after them. They'd reached a dead end; then the sky had cleared and in the starlight he'd found a ravine winding west. After an endless scramble it had opened out and they'd glimpsed the Sea, a sheet of dull silver in the stillness before dawn.

As the Sun woke, they'd sheltered under a thorn bush and shared what was left in the waterskin – which, amazingly, Pirra had managed to keep with her.

'Let's go,' she said, wrenching him back to the present.

'You start, I'll catch up,' he muttered.

She seemed to realize that he needed to be on his own, and headed down the slope.

Numbly, he stared at bees bumping about among clumps of purple thyme, and hoverflies buzzing around yellow thistles. It didn't seem real. How could all this exist when They did too? Where did the darkness go when the Sun came up? Where were the Angry Ones now?

He could still feel them, like a stain on his spirit. He thought of Akastos, and that haunted look in his eyes. *I've been on the run longer than you've been alive . . .*

He longed for Spirit. He wanted to dive with the dolphin through the shimmering Sea, and feel it washing away the darkness inside him. Spirit would understand without having to be told.

Pirra was coming back. He watched her scrambling up the slope. Something was wrong. He rose to his feet.

'Get down!' she whispered.

'What is it?'

'A ship! They're just coming ashore. I didn't stop to look, but I think they're Crows!'

Hylas thought fast. 'Where is it?'

'Like I said, on the beach!'

'Yes but where?'

She pointed south.

'That's something. I think our camp's to the north, so at least we don't have to get past them.'

Together they crept downhill.

Suddenly Pirra pulled him behind a boulder. 'There,' she breathed.

The ship was drawn up on the shingle about a hundred paces to the south. Hylas took in its furled sail the colour of dried blood, and the men leaping over the sides in long black cloaks and boar's-tusk helmets. He saw the glint of their leader's bronze armour. He saw their faces.

He saw their faces.

He swayed. There was a roaring in his ears. He felt as if he were falling from a great height.

One of them was Telamon.

32

The Crows were passing directly beneath them: Pirra counted five men and a boy, each with a bronze dagger at the hip.

They walked purposefully, with their heads down. Pirra breathed out. They weren't tracking. They were gathering driftwood.

Beside her, Hylas had gone still. 'That's Telamon,' he said in a hoarse whisper.

'What?'

'Telamon. He's a Crow.'

She squinted after the men moving off down the beach. So that was the boy she was supposed to wed.

'A Crow,' Hylas repeated. 'Telamon's a Crow.'

She was puzzled. 'Of course he is. He's part of the House of Koronos. Come on, we've got to get out of here! D'you think we can make it over that headland?'

'Why didn't you tell me?' he said in a low voice.

'Tell you what?'

'That he's a Crow.'

'Hylas – we have to get *out* of here!'

'Why didn't you *tell* me?'

Something in his voice made her look at him. Beneath the ash and the grime, his lips had turned grey. His tawny eyes were almost black.

Once, in the Great Court of the House of the Goddess, she'd seen a bull-leaper tossed by a bull. He'd been carried off alive, but his face had been as drained and shocked as Hylas' was now.

'Why?' he demanded.

'I thought you knew, of course! Now come *on!*'

The coast was densely wooded, and they found their way over the headland without being seen. No sign of pursuit, but every moment Pirra dreaded seeing warriors coming after them.

They plunged into a thicket of chestnut and sycamore that was noisy with sparrows. It gave good cover, and she breathed more easily. Still no pursuit.

Some time later, they stumbled on a spring. As she knelt in the moss, Pirra realized she couldn't go another step. 'I'm spent,' she panted. 'I can't remember when I last slept. How far till we reach camp?'

'I think it's still quite a long way. Maybe half a day.'

'Would it be safe to stop here for a bit?'

'Nowhere's safe,' muttered Hylas.

She hesitated. 'About Telamon – I really did think you knew. After all, you told me he's your best friend.'

'Was,' he said between his teeth. 'He *was* my best friend.'

They found a place to sleep under some saplings, and Hylas masked it with branches so that they couldn't be seen. Pirra went to look for food and returned soon after, saying that the trees grew right down to the shore, and she'd risked a dash to the shallows. She'd brought back a skirtful of sea urchins, which they ate raw, scooping up the rich sloppiness with their fingers. She kept casting him curious glances, which made him angry. He didn't want her to see him like this.

At last she said, 'I always thought it was weird that he was your friend. I mean, him being a Crow.'

He glared at her.

'When you told me he was your friend, I didn't know if I could trust you. I didn't know *what* to think. That's why I didn't say anything. Of course I did trust you later, in the caves; but then everything was happening so fast, there was never any time to talk about it.'

Hylas jammed the dagger in the earth and watched it quiver and go still. He felt sick, churning with rage and misery and disbelief. Had they *ever* been friends, or had it all been a lie? But *why*?

He thought back to the day after the attack, when Telamon had come looking for him in his father's chariot. He'd said he didn't know why the Crows were after Outsiders. *Soon as I heard, I went to warn you . . . I found Scram . . . I buried him . . .*

Was any of that true? But what would Telamon gain by such lies?

Pirra took the last sea urchin back to the shore as an offering. 'No sign of them,' she said when she came back, 'but I think I spotted our wreck in the distance. You were right, it's at least half a day off. Can we rest here till dark?'

He didn't answer. With his finger he traced the crossed circle on the hilt. *A chariot wheel*, Akastos had said, *to crush their enemies*.

It didn't seem possible that this dagger before him – this plain bronze knife – held the power of the House of Koronos. But deep inside, he knew it was true.

He thought back to what Akastos had said: that the Crows had lost their dagger and wanted it back, and that maybe this was why they were after Outsiders. Did they for some reason think an Outsider had stolen it – and that the Outsider might be him?

'Why do you keep staring at your knife?' Pirra said quietly. Her face was drawn with fatigue, but her dark eyes watched him keenly.

He told her. About finding the dying man in the tomb, and being given the knife, and how it had helped him stay alive when he was adrift, and what Akastos had said.

When he'd finished, there was silence between them. The trees stood stunned in the noonday heat. Even the sparrows had fallen quiet. Only the rasp of the crickets throbbed on and on.

Pirra was the first to speak. 'Are you sure this is the one?'

'It's got the chariot wheel, just like Akastos said.' He looked at her. 'The man in the tomb, the Keftian. Do you know who he was?'

She shook her head. 'No idea – or why he would've stolen it. And presumably they kept the dagger at Mycenae; so how did he get from there to Lykonia? And why?' She chewed her lip. 'Until now, I'd never even heard of this dagger, and I don't think anyone else on Keftiu has either. Which – I suppose – makes sense. The Crows wouldn't want anyone to know if . . .' She gasped. 'I just remembered. This must be why they asked the Oracle.'

'What Oracle?'

'When we got to Lykonia, we heard that Thestor and Kratos had gone to consult their Oracle. Maybe whatever answer they were given – maybe it had something to do with Outsiders stealing the knife.'

'But I told you, I didn't steal it!'

'I know, but you've got it. It came to you; that's what counts. And maybe – if the Oracle did say something about Outsiders, and by then Kratos knew you were the only one left in Lykonia – then maybe he assumed that you'd taken it.'

'But I've never been anywhere near Mycenae!'

'I know. But whoever stole it – that man in the tomb – he must have brought it from there to Lykonia; and then it fell into your hands, so it comes to the same thing.'

Pulling out the dagger, Hylas held it up. Not a speck of dirt clung to the blade. It was perfect. Beautiful.

He'd come to believe that it was his friend. It had kept him company when he was adrift, and in the storm it had wrapped its tether round the spar and kept him afloat. He'd thought it had been helping him, but now he saw that it had only been saving itself. So this was another friend he'd never really had.

He laid it on the ground and wiped his fingers on his thigh. 'I'll get rid of it,' he said. 'I'll chuck it in the Sea. Then they'll never get it back.'

Pirra frowned. 'I don't think that'd work. I think it knows how to look after itself.'

'What do you mean?'

'That time in the caves, when the snake was after you, and it got stuck in its sheath? Maybe it *wanted* you to be bitten, so that it could escape. And when you were climbing those fallen trees and it fell out just before that man, Akastos – before he caught you. If he'd found it on you, then he'd have it now. I don't think it wanted that either. No, Hylas. If you threw it in the Sea, it'd find some way to be discovered. To get back to the Crows.'

Despite the heat, Hylas shivered. He watched the shifting sunlight playing on the blade. He had the unnerving sense that it was listening.

'I just thought of something else,' said Pirra. 'I bet Kratos hasn't told his men that it's missing.'

'Why not?'

'It'd be a sign of weakness. Never show weakness if you want to hold on to power. My mother taught me that. Yes. Kratos has probably only told his closest kin. Maybe Thestor and Telamon, nobody else.'

Hylas stared at her. '*Telamon?* Telamon is kin to that man?'

She nodded. 'Thestor and Kratos – they're brothers. Their father is Koronos, High Chieftain of Mycenae. Telamon's his grandson. He's Kratos' nephew. That's what makes him

a Crow. He's been one since the day he was born. Hylas –
are you all right?'

He was back in the mountains, clinging for his life beneath
the overhang, while a monster of black and bronze leant
over the edge of the gorge. He saw a powerful hand smeared
with ash. He felt a slitted gaze raking the slopes to find
him . . .

Because of Kratos, Scram had been slaughtered. Because
of Kratos, Issi was lost in the wild. Kratos, son of Koronos.
Telamon's uncle.

'Hylas?'

'Leave me alone!' he burst out. 'Just – leave me *alone!*'

Blindly, he went crashing through the trees.

They're not called Crows, Telamon had told him. *They're a*
great clan: the House of Koronos . . . My father – he has no quarrel
with them . . . He's a Chieftain, that means he can't always choose
who he has dealings with.

All that was true – and yet so many lies lay buried in what
he'd left unsaid.

And still the questions churned round and round. If
Telamon really was a member of the House of Koronos,
then why had he helped Hylas escape? Why steal his father's
chariot and bring those supplies? The dried sheep's liver,
the walnut juice. *Why?*

Without knowing it, Hylas found his way to the edge of
the trees. The Sea lay flat beneath a sullen yellow sky. The
glare off the stones hurt his eyes.

Until now, whatever he'd been going through, he'd always
hoped that a time would come when he could tell Telamon

about it. *Wait till I tell Telamon*, he'd said to himself. But now there was no one to tell.

He remembered the words of the Goddess in the cave. He'd asked why the Crows were after him, and She'd said, *The truth bites*. At the time, he'd thought that She meant the sea-snake. Now he realized that She'd been warning of what he would find out.

And the truth did indeed bite deep. He felt as if someone had stuck a knife in his chest and twisted it.

He couldn't go back to Pirra. He had to be alone.

No, not alone. He needed Spirit. Spirit would understand.

There was no sign of the Crows on the shore. He darted to the rocks in the shallows and hid. He beat the waves with his palms. When that didn't work, he stuck his head underwater and shouted for Spirit in a frenzy of bubbles.

But no matter what he did, Spirit didn't come.

33

It was a huge relief to be back in the open Sea, but the dolphin was terribly worried about his pod – and about the boy and girl. It felt as if he'd been stuck in the caves forever, although what had happened there was already melting into a blue blur.

He remembered being stuck in the channel and twisting frantically to get free. He remembered the pain in his scratched flanks. He remembered ghostly flippers fluttering over his back, and bubbling laughter coming closer. Then the laughter had ceased, and he'd stopped struggling. Awe had washed over him. The Shining One was come.

Nearer and nearer She'd swum, until he was bathed in Her cold blue fire. She was vast and perfect as the Sea. On Her flippers was neither notch nor blemish, on Her flanks neither tooth-mark nor scar. Her tail was stronger than the storm, and Her eye was deeper than the Black Beneath.

With one flick of Her fin She had freed him from the rocks. She had healed his scratches, and miraculously washed away all pain. She had spoken to him in the dolphin way that needs no voice – and he had understood.

Obedient to Her will, he'd swum to the Place of Singing Echoes, and She had shown him the shell that was not shell, but stone. Carefully, he'd taken it on his snout, and the Shining One had sent him back through the twisting channels; and when he was out again, he'd left the not-shell where it was meant to be.

Now all that seemed a long time ago, and very far away. He had done the will of the Shining One, and She had set him free.

But where was everyone else?

Ripples of anxiety shivered down his flanks as he squealed and clicked and squealed again.

Nothing.

He sped to the place where he'd caught the strange, muffled sounds of his pod, coming to him through the earth. He slammed his tail and squealed their name-whistles. He couldn't hear them. What had happened to them?

He raced up the coast to find the boy. He was nowhere to be found. The dolphin swam right into the shallows, heedless of the pebbles scraping his belly. He called and tail-slammed, but the boy didn't come.

Racing back to deeper water, the dolphin listened anxiously to the voice of the Sea. It was moaning restlessly, but he couldn't understand what it was saying, and as he rode the swell, the currents were so strong that he had to swim hard to keep from being swept away.

He poked his snout above the waves, and the Above was

hot; he felt his hide beginning to tighten. And the sky wasn't blue, but yellow.

He dived, hoping to hear the familiar shape of a sardine, or even a shark. But the fish were gone. They'd left the shallows and taken shelter in the deep. What had frightened them?

The dolphin's courage faltered. For the first time in his life, the Sea felt too vast, too powerful. He longed for the touch of a friendly flipper, or a dolphin flank rubbing against his.

He swam further down the coast, clicking fast and hard to pick up any living shape. He heard the familiar hills and valleys beneath him, and the great forests of seaweed, but no fish and no dolphins.

Then he heard something else: one of those great lumbering piles of floating trees that humans use for crossing the Sea. It had floated into a bay, and now lay rocking in the shallows like a sleepy whale.

The dolphin swam closer. He saw humans scuttling like crabs on the shore around their little red fires. They were all men. He didn't like them. He sensed the violence in them.

Then he spotted a small, dark shape crouching on some rocks jutting into the bay. If it hadn't been for the men on the shore, he would have flipped nose-over-tail for joy. He'd found the boy!

Dipping beneath the waves, the dolphin sped towards the figure on the rocks.

34

Something shining rose from the Sea – and Telamon gave a start.

For a moment the dolphin met his eye. Then it rolled on its side and vanished beneath the waves.

Telamon's heart quickened. Could this be a good omen? Did it mean that Hylas was still alive?

Further out, he spotted the arch of a gleaming back. The dolphin was heading north, up the coast. For a moment Telamon even wondered if the sacred creature might be giving him some sort of sign: perhaps showing the way to his friend.

Two warriors came running over the rocks with their spears at the ready. 'We saw a fin! Was it a shark?'

'Dolphin,' said Telamon.

They lowered their spears, and one of them rubbed his hand over his face. 'Lucky I didn't try the shot,' he muttered.

'Lucky indeed,' Telamon said coolly.

He waited for them to return to camp, then went back

to scanning the waves. The dolphin was gone. The Sea was a sheet of hammered bronze.

A wave of hopelessness washed over him, and he put his head in his hands. Nothing had turned out the way he wanted, and he couldn't see how to put things right. He'd promised Hylas that he would find Issi, but he'd failed. He hated to think of her wandering alone in the mountains, and he hated himself for not having done more to find her. He'd failed Issi, and he'd failed Hylas. All he'd achieved was to anger and disappoint his own father – and deceive his uncle.

But how could he have done otherwise? Kratos had it all wrong. Hylas couldn't have had anything to do with stealing the dagger. He couldn't possibly be the Outsider whom the Oracle had mentioned.

Although maybe, Telamon reflected miserably, maybe none of that matters now. Maybe the worst has already happened, and Hylas is dead.

Telamon kept seeing the moment when the helmsman had found the wreckage of the rowing boat, during the crossing from Lykonia. The fisherman they'd brought with them had peered down at it and recognized a spar from his boat; then he'd spotted the shark, keeping level with the ship, and laughed. 'Looks like it got him! Ha! Serves him right!'

As if it was happening in front of him, Telamon had pictured the shark attacking his friend: the Sea turning red as Hylas thrashed in the monster's jaws . . .

He'd leant over the side and retched till his belly hurt.

The men had put it down to seasickness, but his uncle had cast him a thoughtful glance, as if wondering whether there was more to it than that.

'He's still alive,' said a voice behind him. It was a quiet voice, but so cold it made Telamon shiver.

Kratos had left off his bronze armour, but unlike other men, being unarmed didn't make him more approachable. His chest and his black leather kilt were streaked with ash, his eyes bloodshot from peering into the embers for signs. He was watching Telamon with an unreadable expression.

'Wh-what did you say?' stammered Telamon.

'The Outsider lives,' said Kratos. 'I saw it in the ashes. He's here, on the island.'

Telamon swallowed. 'But – even if that's true, he can't be the one you're after. He can't have the dagger, I'm sure of it.'

'So you say.'

'He's just a goatherd, he wouldn't know anything about it –' He broke off. He mustn't seem to be defending Hylas.

His uncle let the pause lengthen to an uneasy silence.

To fill it, Telamon told him about the dolphin. 'Maybe it's a good omen,' he ventured.

'Maybe,' Kratos replied. 'Or maybe our sacrifice worked, and soon we shall have our reward.'

'I – I hope so,' lied Telamon.

His uncle bared his teeth in a smile. He looked disturbingly like Telamon's father: the same high-boned features and bristly black beard. But in Kratos, all kindness had been burnt away.

But he's *kin*, Telamon reminded himself. You owe him the same loyalty you owe to Father.

He knew this, but he couldn't feel it. How could you be loyal to a man who wanted to kill your best friend?

'We'll find the girl, too,' said Kratos, still watching him.

'What?'

'The Keftian. The daughter of the High Priestess.' His lip curled. 'The girl you're meant to wed.'

'Oh. Yes. The fisherman said he left her here, didn't he. So I suppose he must have done.'

'Oh, I don't think he would have lied to me,' said Kratos with unpleasant emphasis.

Again Telamon swallowed. No one would dare lie to Kratos. Except, as it turned out, his own nephew.

So far, Telamon had been lucky. Even though his father and Kratos were brothers, there was no love lost between them, and Thestor hadn't told Kratos that the Outsider was Telamon's friend, or that Telamon had helped him escape.

But now, as Telamon stared up at his uncle, he wondered whether kinship would save him if Kratos ever found out. One glance at the cruel cut of that mouth told him the answer was no.

'I'm taking some men south,' said Kratos. 'I want to scout the coast before it gets dark. Will you come?'

Telamon licked his lips. 'No. I'll stay here. In case that dolphin comes back.' He made himself meet his uncle's gaze, and prayed that he wouldn't detect the lie.

'It's your choice,' said Kratos. He was still smiling, but

something in his tone told Telamon that he'd made the wrong one.

As soon as his uncle was out of sight, Telamon started north. He didn't have much time – it wasn't long till dusk, and he had to be back at camp before Kratos – but he couldn't shake off his hunch that the dolphin had shown him the way. Even if he was wrong, he couldn't sit on the rocks, doing nothing, while they hunted his friend.

The heat was stifling, and by the time he'd got over the headland, he was pouring sweat. The slope below him was thick with sycamores – just the sort of place where Hylas liked to hide.

Feeling more hopeful, he began his descent. It was even hotter under the trees. The rasp of the crickets made his temples throb. 'Hylas?' he whispered. 'Are you there?'

Only the crickets replied.

Further in, he tried again. 'Hylas, it's me! I'm alone. I've come to help!'

Still nothing.

Forcing his way through a prickly clump of juniper, he emerged into a little glade where pale moths flitted among man-high thistles.

He found a heel-print in the dust and knelt to examine it. *Was* it a print, or just a hollow left by a displaced rock? Hylas would have known at a glance.

Sadness welled up in Telamon. He missed his friend. He remembered all the times when he'd slipped away from Lapithos and sought Hylas on the Mountain, scrambling up to the pass to check for signs at the meeting rock, then hearing Hylas' bark of laughter as he erupted from the bushes and knocked him over, and they rolled and wrestled in the scrub . . .

Standing among the thistles, it came to Telamon that he could never go back to that time. Even if he did find Hylas, things would never be the same. The best he could hope for would be to help Hylas escape to some faraway land, and make him swear never to set foot in Lykonia again. And that would mean saying goodbye to him forever.

The mark in the dust didn't look right. It wasn't a heel-print, after all. Angrily, he scuffed it out. What was he doing, stumbling around in a thicket?

An arm hooked him by the neck and wrenched him backwards off his feet.

35

'Why?' demanded Hylas, pressing the scrap of flint to Telamon's throat. 'Just tell me why!'

'Why what?' gasped Telamon.

'Why did you lie to me?'

'I didn't – I saved you!'

'You're a Crow and you never told me!'

'I *saved* you! I stole my father's chariot; he took the skin off my back! If you don't believe me, take a look!'

Without relaxing his grip, Hylas yanked Telamon on to his belly. His shoulders were criss-crossed with weals.

In a flash Telamon twisted round and jabbed an elbow in Hylas' ribs, then clamped his legs round Hylas' head and flipped him over. Hylas landed with a winding thud and rolled sideways to dodge the attack.

It didn't come.

'I'm not here to fight,' panted Telamon as he got to his feet.

'So you say,' snarled Hylas. 'How do I know this isn't a trick?'

'Because it's *me*!' roared Telamon.

Hylas wiped the sweat from his face.

Telamon looked just the same. Same tunic, same warrior braids with the little lumps of clay at the ends to stop them coming loose. How could they be enemies?

'I'm glad you're alive,' said Telamon ruefully, rubbing his neck. 'We found the remains of that boat you stole, and we saw a shark. It was horrible.'

'Who's "we"?' said Hylas between his teeth. 'Your uncle and his men?'

Telamon blinked. 'How do you know he's my uncle?'

Hylas brushed that aside. 'What about Scram? Did you bury him, or was that another lie?'

'Of course I buried him!'

'And Issi? Did you even bother to look for her?'

'Yes, but –'

'And that plan to go round the coast to the other side of the mountains? It was a trick so I'd be washed out to Sea and never come back!'

'No, Hylas, it wasn't. The day after you went off in the chariot, I started over the pass.' Telamon flushed. 'My father sent some men. They fetched me back to Lapithos.'

'Why should I believe you? You're a Crow and you never told me!'

'Don't keep calling them Crows!' shouted Telamon. 'All I knew was that I had kin in Mycenae, I'd never even *met* them till a few days ago! But there wasn't time to explain it to you, I had to get you out of there before they caught you!'

'There was plenty of time, we've known each other four years!'

'And when did you ever show the slightest interest in my life at Lapithos?' Telamon shot back. 'You're just like the villagers, you don't want to know about the outside world!'

'So it's my fault,' sneered Hylas. 'And everything you did was to help me.'

'Why's that so hard to believe?' Suddenly Telamon slumped on a fallen tree. 'This feels like being torn in two,' he muttered. 'Just by being here, I dishonour myself and betray my kin.'

'So I should feel sorry for you?' Hylas said coldly.

Telamon gave him a strange look. 'You don't know what it's like. Until a few days ago, all I knew was that I had kin in Mycenae. Father had kept us separate from them; he said it was best.' He clenched his fists. 'Not all members of the House of Koronos are bad, Hylas. My father isn't bad, and neither am I.'

'Your father stood by while they hunted Outsiders.'

'He hated that. But there was nothing he could do. You don't know Kratos.'

'So why did Kratos hunt Outsiders?'

Telamon kneaded his forehead. 'There'd been omens in Mycenae. They said the House of Koronos was under threat from some danger in Lykonia; they didn't say what. Then a precious heirloom of our clan was stolen. Koronos – my grandfather – he sent two of his sons here, to this island, to make a great sacrifice and seek the gods' help in getting it back. He sent Kratos to Lykonia. Kratos and Father consulted the Oracle. She spoke so strangely; she said, *If an Outsider wields the blade, the House of Koronos burns.*' His face worked. 'Kratos was convinced it meant an Outsider had stolen the – the heirloom.'

'So he started hunting us down and killing us.'

'When I last saw you, I knew *nothing* of this!' Telamon said fiercely. 'But after you'd gone off in the chariot, Father gave me a beating for helping you – yes, Hylas, he'd found out about us – and afterwards, he told me. About why he'd kept us separate all these years, and about the Oracle, and what had been stolen. By then Kratos was after you alone, because – because there were no other Outsiders left in Lykonia.'

'Except Issi,' said Hylas.

'To Kratos she didn't count because she's a girl.' Again he kneaded his forehead. 'When Father's men caught up with me and took me back to Lapithos, Kratos was there. He'd had word from the coast. An Outsider boy had stolen a boat and escaped into a Sea mist. I knew it was you. I begged Father to let me go in Kratos' ship to look for you. I said I needed to – to prove my loyalty, and make up for having helped you.'

Hylas waited for him to go on.

'Father let me. He hadn't told Kratos that you and I were friends; and he believed me when I said I was trying to make amends. Do you realize what that means? It means I lied to him yet again. And it means that if Kratos finds out I'm trying to help you, he'll kill me!'

Hylas had no answer to that. He wanted to believe Telamon, but he couldn't risk it. 'How can I trust you,' he said, 'when you kept so much from me? You never told me about your kin, or the dagger, or –' He cut himself short.

Silence between them. Damselflies darted among the thistles. From high overhead came the shrill cries of swifts.

Telamon had gone very still. 'I never said it was a dagger. How come you know it's a dagger?'

Hylas did not reply. He watched the realization dawn in his friend's face.

'And I *swore* it wasn't you,' said Telamon. 'I told Father you couldn't have taken it. You didn't even know it existed.'

'I didn't steal it,' said Hylas.

'But you do know about it. And you – have got it?'

'Yes.'

Telamon backed away from him, shaking his head. 'All this time – I was *defending* you . . .'

'I told you, I didn't steal it.'

Telamon wasn't listening. 'Where is it?' he demanded.

Hylas snorted. 'Do you think I'd risk bringing it with me?'

Telamon opened his mouth to speak, then shut it again. 'How do I know you're not lying? How do I know it's really the one?'

Hylas hesitated. But he'd said too much already; there was no point denying it. 'It's got a crossed circle on the hilt,' he said. 'A chariot wheel to crush your enemies.'

'Someone could have told you that. I need more proof.'

Hylas thought for a moment. 'At dawn when the Sun hits it, the edge turns red, like it's just drawn blood. And when you hold it, you feel stronger than you've ever felt before.'

Telamon's jaw dropped. 'All this time – it *was* you.'

'I didn't steal it, Telamon. That's the truth. I didn't even know what it was until yesterday.'

Telamon snatched up a stick and paced the clearing, slashing at thistles. When he turned to Hylas he looked older, and very much the son of a Chieftain. 'Bring it to me,' he said curtly.

'*What?*'

'Give it to me. I'll say I found it. Then they won't be after you any more.'

'But once the Crows get it, they can't be beaten. Why would I let that happen?'

'Not all Crows – as you call them – are bad. Maybe Father and I can find some way to restore the honour of our House . . .'

Again Hylas snorted.

'All right, if that doesn't convince you, how about this? Giving me the dagger is your only way out.'

'No. I won't do it.'

'Don't you know how powerful they are?' Telamon burst out. 'Oh, it's all right for you, you've never *seen* Kratos when he's angry! And he has brothers, and – there's Koronos himself!'

Hylas looked at him. 'You're scared of them,' he said. 'Scared of your own kin.'

'Well of course I am!' shouted Telamon. 'And so is my father – *my father*, Chieftain of Lykonia! So would you be if you had any idea what they can do! Hylas, this is your only chance! I'll tell them I saw your body floating near the coast, but that I couldn't reach it. I'll say I found the dagger in the shallows. I'll help you escape. You'll be safe!'

'What about Issi?'

Silence. Telamon ran his thumb over his bottom lip. 'I – I know where she is.'

Hylas went still. 'Tell me.'

'Hylas –'

'*Tell me!* Have they got her? Is she all right?'

He advanced on Telamon, who took a step back. 'They haven't got her and she's all right, but . . .' He paused. 'I'll only tell you where she is if you give me the dagger.'

Hylas stared at him as if he'd never seen him before. 'You would do that? You'd bargain with my sister's life?'

'I'm not! I'm saying that I won't tell you till I've got the dagger. Can't you see, Hylas, if they don't get it back, they'll never stop hunting you? But if I tell you where she is now, you'll never give it up!'

Hylas wanted to rage and shout. But Telamon was right. 'Dawn,' he spat. 'Head north. You'll come to a shipwreck on the rocks. Meet me there at dawn. I'll bring the knife.'

Telamon gave him a searching look. 'Do you mean this?'

'What do you think?'

He chewed his lip. 'It'll be hard to get away. Kratos –'

'I don't care. If you're not there by dawn, you'll never see me or the dagger again.'

36

'**B**ut it's a trap!' Pirra said in a hoarse whisper.

'If it was a trap, he'd have sprung it by now. Besides, he wouldn't do a thing like that.'

'Oh, no? I've met boys like him in the House of the Goddess. They talk about honour, but that's just words.'

'You don't know Telamon.'

'And you do?'

Hylas didn't reply.

It was the middle of the night, and their camp was dark as pitch. Angrily, Pirra groped her way to the spring, where she washed off the soot of the burnt valley, and finger-combed her hair. She was furious with Hylas, and annoyed with herself for being so shaken when she'd woken and found him gone.

The cold water stung her cheek, but made her feel better; so when Hylas came for a wash, she made room for him. He'd clearly never combed his hair in his life, so she showed him how to tease out the knots; but most were so bad that he simply cut them off.

With a twinge of unease, she watched him tie back what was left with a twist of grass. Warriors purify themselves before battle. He was expecting a fight.

And he was keen to get moving. He said he wanted to reach the wreck before Telamon, in case he didn't come alone.

'Ah, so you do think it might be a trap,' said Pirra.

He didn't answer.

They kept to the wooded slopes: Pirra bumping into trees, Hylas moving as silently as a shadow. At length he halted at a clump of boulders that leant together as if sharing a secret.

'Why'd you stop?' panted Pirra.

For answer, he asked if he could cut a strip from the bottom of her tunic. She asked why, and he muttered that she'd see. Once he had the scrap of linen, he found a stick the same size as the dagger, and wrapped it up. Then he handed Pirra the real dagger, keeping the bundled-up stick for himself.

'This is a good place to hide,' he told her. 'Stay out of sight till I get back.'

She blinked. 'But – I'm coming with you.'

'No. You can't help me this time. And I need you to look after the dagger.'

She made to reply, but he talked her down. 'If I don't come back, stay hidden till you're sure they've left the island. And whatever happens *don't* let them get the dagger.'

Already he was heading off into the trees. She ran after him. 'Don't be stupid, Hylas, I'm coming with you! – Hylas?'

But he'd vanished into the dark. She knew it would be hopeless to try to find him.

It was uncomfortable, huddling behind the boulders and waiting for dawn. Strange birds clattered about in the trees, and some huge creature came snuffling so close that she caught its peppery smell. Clutching the dagger, she growled at it to go *away* – and to her astonishment it did, crashing down the slope. She wondered if she'd just met her first boar . . .

She woke stiff and cramped, with ants crawling over her legs. The sky was just beginning to turn grey.

Peering down through the trees, she made out the heaving Sea and a pebbly strip of shore. A boy was walking along it. She recognized Telamon, the Chieftain's son. He'd come alone, as he'd promised.

So what? Pirra thought sourly. Hylas was clever, but he hadn't grown up among the plots and counter-plots of the powerful, as she had. Did he really think Telamon was going to tell him where to find his sister, with or without the dagger?

A breeze shivered the Sea, smoothing out the waves in great dark patches like the tracks of some vast, unseen being. Pirra's spine tingled. Those were the footprints of the Goddess as She walked over the water to wake the Sun. Pirra had the uneasy feeling that the Shining One was leaving the island: let these mortals fight it out among themselves.

Pirra thought of Hylas waiting at the wreck. Did the Goddess even know he existed? Did She care?

Below her on the slope, something moved.

She froze.

The warrior was twenty paces away. He walked slowly, with his helmeted head down. He was following tracks.

In one appalling heartbeat, Pirra took in his bronze armour and the sword at his hip; the heavy spear clenched in his hand. The hand was smeared with ash, the fingernails stained black.

Kratos.

Keeping his head down, he moved off along the trail.

Pirra's thoughts raced. If he reached the wreck, Hylas was finished. But if she followed him she'd have to leave the dagger behind, or he might get it – and without the dagger, what good was she to Hylas?

Kratos glanced back over his shoulder – and went still. Pirra couldn't see his face, but she sensed that he'd spotted something.

Not daring to breathe, she watched him turn and walk back the way he'd come. Towards her.

Now he was directly below her.

He stooped and plucked something from the trail. He straightened up. Pirra saw the change in him: the tension of the hunter sensing prey.

Raising his head, he scanned the slope.

He can't see me, she told herself. He can't know I'm here.

Then she saw what glinted in his palm, and her belly turned over.

It was a tiny, gold double axe.

The Sun was red as a warning, and as it appeared above the edge of the world, it set fire to the sky.

Hylas stood in the surf, craning his neck at the ruined ship.

It looked wrong. Until now, he'd been too far away, but as he drew nearer, he realized his mistake. The wreck he and Pirra had salvaged didn't perch on a tall hill of black rocks, and it didn't lie beneath a headland that loomed over it like a wave about to break.

It wasn't their wreck.

Wondering what this meant, he scanned the rocks for a way up. Whether or not Telamon came alone, he wanted a good position with plenty of scope for escape.

Jumping at full stretch, he grabbed a juniper halfway up, and after a tricky scramble, made it to the top. Only when he was there did he realize that if he'd kept to the slopes, he could have walked down from the headland and straight on to the wreck.

The Sea had flung the ship sideways on to the rocks. It leaned drunkenly, hammered by the waves. Hylas picked his way over the slimy timbers. One nearly tipped him into the hold, where a pool of black water lay in the shadow of the mast. The mast had snapped nearly in two. It tilted crazily overhead, creaking and groaning as the Sea crashed against the hull.

Hylas could see nothing that would do for a weapon, except a length of rope. Clutching it in one hand and the bundle in the other, he found a hiding place behind a pile of shattered jars, and settled down to wait.

He didn't have to wait long.

Telamon had kept his word and come alone. At the foot of the rocks he halted. 'Hylas – are you there?' he called above the noise of the waves.

Hylas did not reply.

'I'm alone. Unarmed. I – I've hidden some supplies outside our camp, by a big sycamore with a broken branch.'

'Why'd you do that?' said Hylas, stepping into the open.

Telamon squinted up at him. He saw the rope in Hylas' fist, but made no remark. 'Soon as I've got the dagger, we'll leave the island. You can pick up the supplies when we've gone.' He scanned the rocks for a way up.

'Stay where you are,' warned Hylas.

Telamon frowned. 'If you want. Have you got the dagger?'

Hylas held up the bundle.

Telamon gave a curt nod.

The Keftian purple had been a good touch, thought Hylas. But he felt horrible about tricking his friend.

'Show me,' called Telamon.

'Issi first. Tell me where she is.'

'Not till I have the dagger.'

Hylas shook his head. 'Not till I know where she is.'

The Sun rose: a silent explosion lighting a red fire under the dark clouds building in the sky. The Sea clawed tirelessly at the wreck.

Telamon had always been a bad liar.

'You don't know where she is,' said Hylas.

Telamon hesitated. 'I found her tracks at the meeting rock. She'd left a pebble with a frog scratched on it. Her trail led down towards Messenia. I hadn't followed it for long before Father's men caught up with me.'

'So when you said you knew where she was, you lied.'

Telamon's chin jutted defiantly. 'You know more now than you did before I told you.'

'You lied. Here. Take it.' He flung down the bundle.

Telamon caught it one-handed and tore off the linen. The stick fell at his feet. 'You lied too,' he said.

They exchanged stares – and in that moment, Hylas knew that their friendship was over. 'Did you think I'd let you have the dagger?' he said.

'I thought you'd keep your word.'

'Like you?'

Telamon opened his mouth to reply. Then suddenly his eyes widened in horror. '*Hylas, look out!*'

Hylas spun round and saw a spear hurtling towards him. He leapt sideways. The spear hissed past his temple and clattered on to the shore.

Telamon ran to retrieve it. 'I didn't know this would happen!' he shouted.

Hylas didn't answer. A warrior was walking down the headland towards him. His armour glinted dark red in the rising Sun, and his face was hidden behind a high bronze neck-guard and a boar's-tusk helmet stained lightless black.

It was Kratos. In his fist he held the dagger of the House of Koronos.

37

Kratos moved easily, despite his armour. He didn't need to hurry. Hylas wasn't going anywhere. He was trapped. Behind him the wreck and the crashing Sea; below him Telamon with the spear in his hands.

Hylas took a step back. 'Where's Pirra?' he shouted above the noise of the waves.

Kratos opened his free hand and let something fall. It bounced over the stones. A tiny, golden double axe.

The blood roared in Hylas' ears. 'What have you done to her?'

Kratos reached the foot of the headland. He took off his helmet and placed it on the ground. He did the same with his neck-guard. The curl of his lip said it all: no need for full armour against a mere boy. 'Telamon,' he called to his nephew, 'throw me my spear.'

Down on the shore, Telamon hesitated. 'But you don't *need* it!' he cried. 'You've got the dagger! He can't do us any harm!'

'He's an Outsider. While he lives he's a threat.'

'What threat can I possibly be to you?' shouted Hylas. 'What threat was my dog? What threat was my sister?'

'Telamon,' called Kratos. 'The spear.'

'I *can't*!' yelled Telamon, but there was a pleading note in his voice. 'I won't let you do this!'

Kratos ignored him. He didn't need the spear. He had the sword at his hip and the dagger of Koronos in his fist.

He stepped on to the wreck and it creaked beneath him. His carapace of bronze flashed in the Sun. He was invincible.

Hylas grabbed the sharpest potsherd he could find. It would be useless. He chucked it away. He was a boy with a rope against a seasoned warrior three times his size. If it came to hand-to-hand combat he'd be dead in a heartbeat.

As he cast about for somewhere to hide, he thought, All that running and hiding, all that struggling to survive – and it's going to end like this?

And still Kratos came on. Hylas heard the clink of his armour. He caught the bitter stink of ash. In the rising Sun, the warrior's face seemed etched in bronze. His dark eyes gleamed. He was enjoying this. He'd enjoyed killing Scram and making Issi run for her life. He'd enjoyed whatever he'd done to Pirra.

'Where is she!' Hylas burst out, not knowing if he meant Pirra or Issi, but needing to shout, to do something instead of just standing there and submitting to his fate. 'Where is she? What have you done to her?'

Pirra struggled to her feet, then sank back with a moan. Her head was swimming. She was going to be sick.

She couldn't believe that someone so big could have moved so fast. Like a nightmare he'd come crashing up the slope, and like a nightmare her sandals had slipped and branches had snagged her tunic, holding her back. Then she'd felt an agonizing grip on her shoulder. She'd screamed and bitten his hand. With a roar he'd struck her a blow that sent her flying. After that – nothing. He must have thought she was dead, because when she came to, he was gone, and so was the dagger.

She finished retching and wiped her mouth on the back of her hand. Her cheek was on fire and her shoulder hurt. The ashy stench of his sweat was still in her nostrils, the taste of his blood in her mouth, beneath the taste of sick.

Grabbing a sapling, she hauled herself to her feet and started after him.

Tracking was even harder among trees, and she swiftly lost his trail. It didn't matter. If she kept the Sea on her left, surely she'd have to find the wreck?

Hurry *up*, she berated herself as she scrambled across the slope. It occurred to her that if she made her way down to the shore, the going would be easier; but then Kratos might see her, and she shied away from what that would mean.

Suddenly there were no more trees and she was out on a windswept ridge, with a falcon's-eye view of what was happening far below.

She saw that the Sea had smashed not one ship, but two. The ship that she and Hylas had salvaged lay to the north, while another lay to the south, directly below. Between them she saw the turquoise slash of an inlet, but its mouth had been blocked where part of the cliffs had fallen into the Sea. Within the inlet she caught a flicker of big silver bodies.

In a heartbeat she realized that she was looking at Spirit's missing pod. They must have entered the inlet days ago, perhaps to scratch their bellies on the sandy bottom; then an earthshake had trapped them inside, probably the same one she'd felt on her first night on the island. They'd been there ever since: trapped, starving, unable to get out.

All this flashed through her mind in an instant.

Then she saw Hylas.

He stood on the wreck with his back to the Sea. Kratos was advancing on him. Telamon was on the shore at the foot of the rocks, brandishing a spear and cutting off Hylas' escape. Hylas was turning his head this way and that, but he had nowhere to go. He was defenceless. And Kratos was moving steadily closer.

Gritting her teeth, Pirra scrambled down the slope, fighting her way through a thicket of thorns.

She got lost. Furious with herself, she wasted precious time trying to find a way through. When at last she did, she was horrified to see that instead of staying on the headland, she'd come out below it, on the shore.

Stupid, stupid, she told herself as she stumbled across the shingle. Her breath sawed in her chest and her sandals kept slipping. She tore them off and ran on.

Telamon hadn't yet seen her. He was shouting and trying to find a way up the rocks, on to the wreck. If she could sneak up and knock him out with a rock, she could grab that spear and find her way on to the wreck and . . .

Telamon leapt for a juniper bush halfway up and started to climb.

'Hey, you!' screamed Pirra.

He glanced round and nearly fell off in amazement.

'Haven't you done enough already,' she yelled, 'you slimy little *weasel*?'

His face contorted with rage. 'Stay out of this! You don't know anything!'

With a snarl she hurled herself at the rocks, but they were slippery and she couldn't reach the juniper, couldn't find a way up.

From somewhere above, Hylas gave a wild yell. What was happening?

Telamon was still climbing – awkwardly, with the spear in one hand – but he'd nearly reached the top. Grabbing a handful of pebbles, Pirra started pelting him. 'Traitor!' she screamed.

'I'm trying to *help* him!' he bellowed.

'Liar!'

Stepping back to take aim, she trod on a rock that rolled beneath her foot, and tripped. She went down hard on the pebbles, and the Sea surged in and splashed her in the face.

On her knees, she froze. She stared at the rock that had made her lose her footing. She no longer heard Telamon shouting, or the noise of wind and Sea. It wasn't a rock at all.

This isn't possible, she thought.

And yet there it lay with the foam washing over it: rolling seawards, then back towards her.

What lay before her was a triton shell, carved out of pure white marble.

It was the same triton shell she'd found in the caves.

38

Kratos came at Hylas with his sword in one hand and the dagger in the other. Hylas edged sideways round the hold, clutching his useless length of rope.

Shouting from the shore. He made out Telamon's voice and someone else – could it be *Pirra*?

Kratos attacked from the right. Hylas jumped to the left. It was a feint. Kratos lunged to the right. Again Hylas leapt. The dagger missed him by a whisker. An oar rolled beneath him. He slipped and grabbed the mast. It tilted, and he lurched over the hold, getting an alarming view of black water before he scrambled back. A glance behind him revealed that he'd reached the edge of the wreck: below him was a sheer drop to the hungry waves.

And still Kratos came on.

Further out to Sea, a shining form leapt from the waves.

You can't help me now, Hylas told Spirit silently. *Swim away as fast as you can, before you get hurt.*

Again Spirit arched out of the Sea, this time coming down with a resounding splash. In a heartbeat, Hylas understood what the dolphin was telling him. *Jump! I'll carry you to safety!*

It was his only chance – but something held him back. 'Where's my sister?' he shouted at the Crow leader. 'What did you do to her? You're going to kill me anyway – tell me first!'

The dark eyes glittered as Kratos came at him again. Hylas lashed out with his rope. Amazingly, it caught the warrior's swordhand, and with a hiss he loosened his grip. Hylas gave a yell of triumph as the sword fell with a splash into the hold.

Kratos seized an oar and jabbed at him like a fisherman dislodging a crab from under a rock. Hylas grabbed the other end of the oar. Bad mistake. Kratos jabbed again, and the force of the thrust nearly knocked Hylas off the wreck.

Panting, he staggered out of range. He'd lost his rope. There was nothing else within reach.

Kratos flung away the oar. The dagger of Koronos glinted in his fist; that was the only weapon he'd need. Hylas saw that he'd tied it to his wrist with a thong – so no chance of knocking that into the hold.

Despite the heat, Kratos moved with the same muscular ease as before, while Hylas was soaked in sweat and panting for breath. He wouldn't last much longer.

Suddenly he realized that he'd got himself on the wrong side of the hold: below him, rocks jutted like giant teeth from the Sea. He'd missed his chance. If he jumped now, Spirit couldn't save him, he'd be dashed to pieces.

And still Kratos came on.

Clouds were massing and the wind was getting up, whipping Pirra's hair across her face. She had to act fast, or Hylas was finished – but she couldn't move, couldn't take her eyes off the white marble shell rolling before her in the foam.

It was dangerous. She feared even to touch it. Who knew what would happen if . . .

Shouts behind her. In horror, she saw a black tide of Crow warriors sweeping towards her up the shore. Their dark cloaks flew, and they carried a thicket of spears.

Another cry from the wreck. Was that Hylas?

Pirra seized the triton shell and ran, heading blindly for the trees. The marble was cold and smooth, and its power thrummed through her. There was a ringing in her ears. She no longer heard the shouts of the Crows. It *was* the same shell she'd found in the caves, she was sure of it; she recognized that tiny nick on the lip.

The warriors were almost upon her.

She halted. She took a deep breath. Then she put the tip of the shell to her mouth – and blew.

39

At first, Hylas thought it was the blowing of a ram's horn – but this was deeper, an echoing boom that surged and receded like the Sea.

He halted. Kratos halted. On the shore, the Crows went still.

Abruptly, the booming ended. The echoes died.

As if a spell had broken, the Crows hefted their spears and ran forwards. Kratos advanced. Hylas had nowhere to go. That booming call hadn't saved him; it had only delayed the inevitable.

Suddenly he was sick of being frightened. He had a wild urge to leap out into the open with his arms flung wide and shout, *Go on then, get it over with!*

At that moment there was a deafening crack on the headland. Hylas saw a boulder teeter and crash down on to the rocks. The earth began to growl. The wreck juddered. He struggled to stay upright. Even Kratos was bracing his legs.

The growls grew to a roar, and a crack opened at the foot

of the headland, as if an unseen axe were hacking through the rock. The crack widened to a bolt of black lightning that came zigzagging towards the wreck. The wreck shook, tossed this way and that by the rage of the Bull Beneath the Sea. Hylas fought to keep his footing as the wreck buckled and heaved under him, crashing down with such force that it pitched him into the hold.

He came up spluttering, waist-deep in black water. Where was Kratos?

Above him the mast was rocking, oars and rigging falling around him. The walls of the hold were tilting crazily: the wreck was sliding off the rocks into the Sea. Then the waves smashed through and swept him off his feet.

He hit his head against a beam jutting from the hold. Desperately, he clung to it as the Sea sucked him back, then surged in again and smacked him against the side of the hold.

Kratos exploded from the water beneath him. Hylas twisted sideways. Not fast enough. He cried out as the dagger nicked his arm. Kratos grabbed him by the hair. Hylas fought, but his fingers clawed bronze. Kratos yanked back his head and raised the dagger to cut his throat.

With a startled grunt, Kratos fell forwards on top of him. Wriggling out from under, Hylas glimpsed a silver form vanishing into the murk. It was Spirit: he must have slammed into Kratos from behind, and now he was swimming off to gather speed for another attack.

As Hylas broke the surface he saw the dolphin's fin racing towards Kratos – but this time the warrior was ready. Spirit swerved to evade the dagger. Hylas saw the water flush red. Whose blood? Spirit's or Kratos'? Where was Spirit?

Hylas seized his chance. With Kratos distracted, he scrambled up the side of the hold, grabbed the end of the mast with both hands, and swung with all his weight. For an instant the massive beam didn't move, but then it tilted. He heard it groan and finally snap. He leapt out of the way just before it went crashing down on Kratos.

The roars of the Earthshaker diminished to growls – then rumbles – then silence. Hylas heard the slap of the waves and his own heaving breath. He saw a few last pebbles rattling down from the headland. There was no sign of Kratos. The mast must have killed him outright.

No sign of Spirit, either. Had he swum out to Sea?

The wreck was still sinking: now the waves were up to Hylas' waist. He was exhausted. He didn't think he'd have the strength to climb out of the hold, or swim round to the shore; and if Spirit didn't come for him – if Spirit was . . .

Come *on*, Hylas, he told himself. You can't give up now.

The walls of the hold towered above him. Gasping for breath, he snatched at a tangle of rigging and tried to haul himself up.

A granite hand gripped his ankle and dragged him down.

Frantically, he kicked, but Kratos' grip was relentless, dragging him back. Like an eel, Hylas wriggled and thrashed, dreading the bite of the dagger.

It didn't come. Kratos dragged him underwater, and in the swirling darkness, Hylas saw why. The warrior was fighting one-handed: the mast had crushed his dagger-hand, pinning down both him and the dagger.

With a judder, the wreck sank deeper. Now the water was up to Hylas' chest. Kratos' black hair floated like snakes as he fought to keep his head above the surface and struggled to wrench his trapped hand free.

He couldn't do it. Hylas met his eyes and saw the warrior realize that he was going to drown. Kratos glared back at him, unafraid. *Yes, I'm going to die – but I'm taking you with me.*

Hylas stamped down hard with his free foot. The grip on his ankle slackened for an instant – and he yanked free.

As he floundered to the other side of the hold, he heard Kratos chanting in a strange, harsh tongue. There was a deafening clap of thunder. Then the clouds burst and the rain hammered down.

Kratos gave a horrible gurgling laugh. 'The gods have heard me!' he gasped. 'You'll never do it now!'

With the last of his strength, Hylas grabbed the rigging and heaved himself out of the hold. Over his shoulder he saw the warrior gulping air. He saw the wild triumph in the black eyes: Kratos was drowning, but he'd retrieved the dagger of Koronos.

Again Hylas heard that horrible gurgling laugh. Then the Sea crashed over Kratos' head and silenced him forever.

The Bull Beneath the Sea had ceased to stamp, the cloud-burst had passed on, and Pirra staggered to her feet. Part of the headland had collapsed, and a great jagged crack had split the shore in two. Telamon sat on the pebbles looking dazed, rubbing his temple. In the earthshake, he'd fallen from the rocks and hit his head.

As if in a dream, Pirra watched warriors race past her and swarm up the rocks, while others splashed into the shallows. They weren't after her, they were after Hylas. He crouched on the last scrap of wreck that remained above water, with the waves washing over him. Before she could scream a warning, he saw the Crows taking aim, and leapt off into the Sea.

It wasn't going to save him. They were too close. His fair hair blazed in the Sun, an easy target in the dark water.

Wading into the shallows, Pirra attacked the nearest Crow, but he pushed her off with insulting ease. She saw Telamon jumping up and down, ordering the warriors not to shoot. He might as well have shouted at the wind. The Crows were jabbing at the waves and casting their spears into the Sea. They were going to spear Hylas like fishermen skewering pike.

Suddenly they faltered. With startled cries they drew back. They lowered their spears.

Telamon was staring out to Sea, shading his eyes with his hand.

The dolphins came out of the Sun. Leaping, diving, arching out of the waves as they raced towards Hylas.

So many dolphins, thought Pirra as she watched the glistening bodies arrowing through the water, weaving a ring of shining silver around Hylas. The Earthshaker had freed

Spirit's family from the inlet – and now they were coming to Hylas' aid.

Yelling in triumph, Pirra watched the warriors edge back from the Sea. No one dared risk the anger of the Goddess by harming Her creatures.

Pirra saw Spirit burst from the waves and leap right over Hylas. The dolphin surfaced and swam alongside him, and Hylas grabbed his fin with both hands.

As the awestruck warriors looked on, Spirit made another great arching leap, with Hylas flying behind him.

Then boy and dolphin splashed down together and vanished into the deep.

40

The dolphin was *happy*. The One Beneath had stopped slamming His tail, and his pod was free!

At first he'd turned snout over flukes in an ecstasy of greeting, rubbing nose to nose and flank against flipper with his mother and little sister and all the others. Together they'd raced through the Blue Deep and squealed till the Sea sang with dolphin joy, and he'd felt the loneliness peeling off and floating away like an annoying scrap of seaweed.

Then, with the whole pod at his tail, he'd sped back to the Edge to protect the boy from the bad humans; and now they were once again diving into the Blue Deep, after fish.

And best of all, he was taking the boy with him. At last the dolphin could show him his beautiful Sea! Together they would chase the shimmering shoals, and the boy would know what it was to be a dolphin on the hunt: the thrill of trapping anchovies in a web of silver bubbles, the delight of scrunching up wriggling mouthfuls of flesh and fin and bone.

And after that, he and the boy would play together, and dive deeper and deeper into the Black Beneath.

In a heartbeat the threat of the Crows was left behind and Hylas was safe; he was flying with Spirit into a world of soft green light.

Holding tight to the dolphin's fin, he pressed his cheek to the smooth hard back, and felt Spirit gripping his calves with his flippers so that he wouldn't fall off. Silver-green dolphins flashed past, and kindly dark eyes met his for an instant, then faded into the blue. The Sea was alive with whistles and clicks, and the dolphins' joy became his, tingling over his skin and trilling through him.

Moments later, Spirit was hurtling down the flank of an underwater mountain. Hylas glimpsed a rippling forest of seaweed, and the red-and-gold flicker of fish. Then the mountain was gone and the blue was darker – and he was cold.

Enough, he told Spirit in his head. *I need to go back.*

But Spirit was happily clicking away to himself, and didn't hear.

Hylas struck the solid flank with his fist, but Spirit seemed to feel nothing but an affectionate tap. Hylas struggled to wrench his legs free, but the dolphin's flippers were too strong; and Spirit thought he was keeping him safe.

Darkness closed in, and the clicks of the pod quickened to a buzzing whine, trapping him in a web of sound. As they swam deeper, a sharp pain pierced his skull. He swallowed, and with his fingers squeezed his nostrils shut. The pain eased a little, but it soon came back.

Again he punched Spirit's flank. No response.

He felt a crushing weight on his chest. He was getting dizzy. He fought a desperate urge to breathe.

I need air! he shouted in his head. *Spirit! I've got to have air!*

As if he'd heard him, Spirit suddenly flipped up his nose, and with a mighty beat of his tail they were surging back the way they'd come.

With astonishing speed, Hylas heard the clicks of the pod fading below him. Far above, he glimpsed a glimmer of light. The glimmer became a glow. His dizziness and pain fell away. But still he fought that terrible urge to breathe.

As they sped higher, he heard a roaring sound, and made out white waves crashing overhead. Then they were bursting into the light and he was taking great heaving gulps of air.

Gasping and shuddering, he slumped on Spirit's back as the dolphin bore him gently towards the shore. He heard the quiet, steady *pfft!* of dolphin breath. With a pang he realized that the ordeal which had nearly cost him his life had been, for Spirit, but the briefest of dives.

At last they reached the shallows, and Hylas slid off and lay on his back in the seaweed, feeling the surf rocking him. His eyes burned with salt. His head ached.

As his wits returned, he remembered the Crows, and weakly raised himself on one elbow.

Spirit had brought him to a little inlet overhung with

junipers. Hylas didn't recognize it; but it seemed well hidden, and he could see no sign of Crows. He thought of Kratos and Telamon and the dagger. It seemed as if it had happened to someone else.

He felt Spirit gently nosing his toes, and guessed that this was the dolphin's way of saying sorry. *I didn't know you can't be underwater like me. Sorry.*

Clumsily, Hylas stretched out his foot and gave him an answering nudge.

He wanted to tell Spirit that he understood, and was sorry too. *Sorry I can't be with you under the Sea.*

But he wasn't quick enough. Spirit was gone.

Be at peace, Telamon told Hylas silently as he threw a branch of black poplar on his uncle's funeral pyre.

Did it count if you pretended you were grieving for your uncle, when really you were mourning your friend? Would the gods still hear you?

Right up to the moment when he and the girl had found the scrap of bloodstained tunic on the shore, he'd kept hoping that Hylas was alive. Even afterwards, he'd found it impossible to believe. Hylas dead? Never coming back?

The fire crackled and spat as it devoured the oil-soaked driftwood and started on the body.

After yesterday's cloudburst, the sky was clear, the Sea as smooth as milk. Telamon stood blinking in the sunlight. He felt the greasy smell of burning flesh steal down his throat. Turning his head, he watched the wavelets sucking sadly at the pebbles. He thought of Hylas' body lying somewhere out to Sea, with no rites to help his spirit on its way.

Scooping up a handful of hot ash, he smeared it on his face. It stung, but he needed that. He needed to punish himself. Everything was his fault. If he hadn't met Hylas at the wreck, Kratos would still be alive. And so would Hylas.

From a distance, the men were watching him with new respect. They'd seen him prise the dagger of Koronos from his uncle's cold, dead fingers, and now they saw him smearing ash on his face. They approved. This was how it should be: the young kinsman taking over from the dead.

Telamon knew he should be proud. After all, he'd regained the dagger, the heirloom of his House. Instead, he felt ashamed.

It didn't help that until they reached Lykonia, he was supposedly in charge. He knew he wasn't up to it, and he suspected that the men did too. A boy of thirteen summers, leading warriors twice his age?

Yesterday Ilarkos, his uncle's second in command, had asked if they should burn Kratos' body according to the rites he'd followed, or take it back to Lykonia for burial in the usual way, at the Place of Ancestors. Telamon hadn't known what to do. He hated the idea of burning a corpse, just as he hated the rites his uncle had practised; but he daren't say so, and in the end, Ilarkos had made the decision for him.

'So now you're a hero,' said a sneering voice behind him.

Telamon bristled.

The Keftian girl looked like a bedraggled little hawk. She was filthy. Although she'd been overjoyed to see the

Egyptian slave whom her mother had sent with them to look after her, she'd refused his offer of a clean tunic; and she'd scraped back her hair, as if to draw attention to the scar which scythed across her cheek like a new moon.

'Go away,' snarled Telamon.

'How does it feel?' she said sweetly. 'You've got your precious dagger back, and Hylas is dead. Are you proud of yourself?'

'*Proud?*' He glanced around to check that no one could hear. 'He was my best friend!'

The pyre collapsed in a flurry of sparks. The girl regarded him with narrowed eyes. 'I suppose you know that your kinsmen burnt a whole valley?'

'Shut *up!*'

'I sent my slave to take a look. He says it's already turning green. Soon it'll be as if they'd never made their sacrifice.'

Telamon strode off down the shore, but to his fury, she followed. 'What's going to happen to me?' she said.

'We'll take you back to Lykonia,' he muttered. 'That's where your mother is, she can deal with you.'

'No, I mean –'

'I know what you mean. I don't care if she did strike a bargain with my father, I'm not mating with you.' Pointedly, he stared at her scar. 'You're too ugly.'

She barked a laugh. 'Well, that's something, I suppose.'

He picked up a stone and hurled it at the Sea.

Near the ship, Ilarkos was sacrificing a pig to the Earth-shaker, in the hopes of gaining a safe crossing to Lykonia. It put Telamon in mind of the first sacrifice he'd ever seen.

He'd been four summers old, and astonished by the jet of blood spurting from the ram's fleecy throat. 'Will it work?' he'd asked his father, and Thestor had squeezed his hand and said, 'That's for the gods to decide.'

Now, as Telamon watched the greasy black smoke twisting skywards, that struck him with the force of a revelation. Of *course*, he thought. *Everything* is the will of the gods. Why didn't I see that before? It's because of *them* that I've been torn between Hylas and my kin. *They* decreed what I did. I had no choice.

No choice, he thought. He felt a little better. It meant that none of this was his fault.

He made a promise in his head. Soon as I get home, I'm going to the meeting rock on the Mountain. I'm going to sacrifice a calf for Hylas and Issi.

'Yes,' he said. 'That's the right thing to do.'

He'd spoken aloud, and he braced himself for another sneer from the girl; but she wasn't listening. She was shading her eyes and pointing at the shallows, where the ship lay at anchor.

'Look,' she murmured. 'The dolphin's back.'

Ilarkos came up, with some of the men. 'It's the same one that came for the Outsider,' he told Telamon. 'We don't know what it means.'

'I'll find out,' the girl said coolly.

Telamon snorted. 'No, you won't! If I let you anywhere near the Sea, you'll try to escape –'

'Then tie me up,' she snapped. 'Tie me to that tree on

the point and set sentries to watch from the ship, if you're scared I'll get away.'

He flushed. 'I'm not scared. I just don't trust you.'

She drew herself up: a scrawny girl in a filthy tunic, but with an authority that made the men stare.

'You can't stop me talking to a creature of the Goddess,' she told Telamon. 'I'm Keftian. We know the dolphin speech.'

When Telamon didn't reply, she addressed the men. 'If you don't let me talk to that dolphin – *alone* – the Goddess will be displeased. And then you'll never get home.'

41

'Hylas!' whispered Pirra. 'Are you there?'

Leaning out over the rocks as far as her tether would allow, she watched Spirit swim past. A short distance away, the guard on the ship was watching too, fingering his amulet and muttering a charm. She gave him a cold stare and turned her back.

Below her, on the side of the point that the guard couldn't see, a fair head emerged from a clump of junipers. She sagged with relief. 'You *are* alive! I found a pebble with a mark on it, and I guessed that you'd left it as a sign, but I wasn't sure. Are you all right?'

'Are you? They've tied you to a tree!'

'That's just to stop me trying to escape.'

He made to climb up, but she warded him back. 'Stay where you are, they're watching from the ship.'

'They won't see me, I can –'

'I mean it! It's not worth the risk.'

He scowled. He was barechested; what was left of his

tunic was tied round his hips. He looked exhausted. Pirra wondered what had happened with Kratos on the wreck, and whether Hylas would tell her if she asked.

They exchanged glances, and she felt the constraint between them. It was as if everything they'd been through together hadn't really happened.

I'm back where I started, she thought bitterly. An object to be pushed about by my mother, like a piece on a gaming board.

Would Hylas understand if she told him, or would he growl at her to be glad that she had enough to eat? Suddenly he seemed a stranger: a sharp-eyed Lykonian, only out for himself.

'Were you alone when you found the pebble?' he asked.

'No.' She told him about her and Telamon finding the bloodstained scrap of tunic, and her guessing that Hylas had left it on purpose; then spotting the pebble nearby, with its spiky scratched-on mark. 'You took a chance that I'd know it was a hedgehog,' she said.

'Did Telamon see it?'

'No. I made sure of that.'

'So he thinks I'm dead.'

She nodded. 'When he saw the tunic he sat down and cried. The odd thing is, I think he meant it.'

Hylas' scowl deepened. Then he said, 'It was you who woke the Earthshaker. Wasn't it?'

She hesitated. 'I couldn't think how that triton shell had got all the way from the caves. Then I realized. It must have been Spirit.'

They watched the dolphin swim past them again, then veer towards the ship, where men were leaning over the side, dangling offerings of fish. Pirra remembered the day when she'd taken hold of Spirit's fin and flown with him through the Sea. All over now, she thought. She felt sick.

'They've got their dagger back,' said Hylas between his teeth.

'But they didn't get you. While you live, you're a threat. The Oracle –'

'I don't care about the Oracle. All I care about is finding Issi.'

'It's the words of the Goddess, Hylas, it means something. It all comes back to Her. She sent you here –'

'For *what?*' he burst out with such violence that she hissed at him to be quiet; but the guards were busy watching Spirit snapping up mackerel.

'For *what?*' Hylas whispered fiercely. 'I'm back where I started – no sister, no friend, no *nothing*! Even if I can get off the island, what then? I'll be alone on a raft in the middle of the Sea, just like before!'

Pirra twisted off her last gold bracelet and tossed it down to him. 'There,' she said crossly. 'If a ship comes by, you can pay for your passage with that – and then you won't need your wretched raft.'

Doubtfully, he turned the bracelet in his fingers. 'But would it get me as far as Lykonia?'

'Hylas, it's *gold*, it'll take you all the way to *Egypt* if you want, and you'd still have enough left to buy the whole ship!

Chop it in pieces. A scrap the size of an olive will get you to Lykonia.'

'Oh. Well, thanks.'

'It's nothing,' she said shortly. What good was gold? It couldn't buy freedom. A wave of dejection swept over her.

Two warriors were starting towards her across the rocks. With them was Userref, who'd just seen that she'd been tied up, and was looking outraged.

'They're coming for me,' said Pirra. 'You'd better hide.'

'What will you do?' asked Hylas.

She swallowed. 'Try to avoid whatever my mother's planned for me. Try to escape. Again. What about you?'

'Find a way back to Lykonia. Find Issi. Find some place where we can be free of the Crows.'

'That's a lot of finding,' said Pirra.

He gave a lopsided smile. 'For you too.'

'*Hide*,' she urged.

But instead of hiding, he started climbing towards her. 'I just remembered, I found this. Quick, take it!'

Straining at her tether, she reached down and snatched it: a small slate-coloured feather, banded with bluish grey.

'It's a falcon's,' he said. 'I found it in an inlet. I thought it'd make a good amulet.'

'It's the best thing I've ever had,' she mumbled. 'And I've got nothing for you.'

He flashed her a grin. 'Pirra, you've just given me a lump of gold!'

'No, I mean an amulet.' The awful thing was, she did have

one for him, but she'd left it in the camp. Userref had brought back one of the lion's claws from the burnt valley, and she'd been planning to give it to Hylas; but now it was too late.

She glanced down to find him watching her through his tangled fair hair. 'You escaped once,' he said. 'You'll do it again.'

She tried to reply, but her throat had closed.

'You're brave and you don't give up. You'll do it, Pirra.'

She forced a smile. 'Good luck, Hylas.'

'Good luck.'

She wanted to ask if he thought they'd ever meet again, but Userref and the warriors had almost reached her; and when it was safe to look back, Hylas had gone.

Long after the ship had carried off Telamon and Pirra, Hylas remained watching on the shore.

A brisk wind had sped them on their way, but now it had sunk to nothing, and the island was hushed. Not even a gull glided over the water. There was no sign of Spirit. He was probably off hunting with his pod.

Hylas told himself that this was good, it meant that Spirit was happy; but he couldn't feel it. He knew now that he and Spirit couldn't be together. The dive had proved it. Spirit had tried to show him his beloved Sea, and it had nearly killed him.

Did Spirit know it, too? It was impossible to tell. Apart from that brief appearance by the ship, the dolphin hadn't come near him.

Hylas found Telamon's supplies exactly where he'd said, under a sycamore tree with a broken branch. There was a full waterskin, a tunic, a belt and even a plain bronze knife; also a goathide sack crammed with pressed olives, hard cheese and salted mackerel. Telamon had kept his word, after all. Hylas didn't want to think about that.

Trudging north, he came to the crack the Earthshaker had opened in the shore. There was no trace of the wreck. Where it had been, the Sea broke tirelessly.

In his mind, Hylas heard Kratos' terrible gurgling laugh. What had he shouted in that strange, harsh tongue? Why had he cried, *You'll never do it now?*

After bridging the crack with driftwood, Hylas made his way over the headland, then past the wreck that he'd salvaged with Pirra. He didn't want to think about her, or about what lay ahead: setting off alone on the raft, and saying goodbye to Spirit.

It turned out that he wouldn't be getting anywhere near the raft, as it was heading briskly out to Sea. The man who'd stolen it had fitted it with a mast and a scrap of salvaged sail, although this now hung limp in the windless calm. He stood with his legs braced and one hand on the steering-paddle, letting the current carry him past the rocks. He'd chopped off his hair to disguise himself from the Angry Ones, but Hylas knew him at once.

'Akastos!' he shouted as he splashed into the shallows.

Akastos turned, and for a moment his face went still; then he gave a shout that might have been laughter. 'Flea! You survived!'

Hylas was furious. 'No thanks to you! That's my raft! Bring it back!'

Akastos gave another almost-laugh and shook his head.

'But it's *mine*!' yelled Hylas. 'I built it!'

'True,' called Akastos, 'but you used my ship. And you didn't do a bad job, for a boy from the mountains, even if you did forget a sail.'

Desperate to keep him talking, Hylas asked how he'd managed to stay hidden from the Crows.

Akastos stiffened. 'The Crows? They were here? On the island?'

'Down the coast! There was a battle on the shore. Then Pirra – she woke the Earthshaker. But now they're gone.'

'And I never knew,' said Akastos to himself. 'Looks like the gods have tricked me again.' Then to Hylas, 'But you're wrong about the Earthshaker, Flea, He didn't wake. That was the merest twitch of His tail in His sleep. When the Earthshaker wakes, mountains crack apart and spew rivers of fire, and the Sea attacks the land . . . When the Earthshaker wakes, you'll know it.' He turned back to the steering-paddle.

'Take me with you!' shouted Hylas. Akastos was ruthless, but he wasn't a Crow; and even a man pursued by the Angry Ones was better than being left on his own. '*Please!*' he begged.

'I can't, Flea. You're bad luck, and I've got enough of that already.'

From nowhere a wind sprang up and filled the little sail. 'Well now, that's a surprise,' said Akastos, his voice carrying across the water. 'That wind pouch actually works. And I thought it was a fake.' He raised his hand to Hylas. 'Good luck, Flea. Don't let the Crows get you!'

Hylas dived in and started to swim, but already the wind was speeding the raft on its way. 'My name's not Flea!' he cried. 'It's Hylas!' But Akastos was too far off, and Hylas didn't think he heard.

As the raft was carried away, Hylas thought he saw a dark shadow moving after it, like a stain in the Sea. He wondered if Akastos knew he was being followed; and for how much longer he would manage to escape.

Dusk fell, and Hylas ate a lonely meal of olives and cheese.

The graze on his calf from the sea-snake no longer hurt, and the wound on his arm was finally healing. It was half a Moon since the Crows had attacked. Issi felt very far away.

He couldn't sleep, so he wandered down to the water's edge and sat watching the new Moon rise. The Sea was polished obsidian, the Moon's path a trembling thread of silver.

Far out in the bay, a dark arrow sped across it.

'Spirit!' cried Hylas.

But instead of swimming closer, the dolphin kept a wary distance, and no amount of whistling and patting the waves could persuade him to approach.

It occurred to Hylas that maybe Spirit still felt bad because of that dive. 'It doesn't *matter*!' he called, even though he knew Spirit wouldn't understand. 'I know you were only trying to show me your world! I do know!'

But he was talking to the waves. Already Spirit was far away, disappearing down the silver pathway of the Moon.

The dolphin was unhappy. He'd done something wrong – again – and he didn't know how to make it right.

He'd only wanted to show the boy his beautiful Sea, but instead he'd nearly killed him. The boy had gone limp, and the dolphin had been horrified. What had he done? It had been such a relief to get him back to the shallows; but when the dolphin had tried to say sorry, the boy had kicked him.

A few times after that, the dolphin had tried to make it up, but he'd always lost courage and swum away.

His pod sensed his unhappiness and did their best to cheer him up with much nosing and rubbing of flanks; and his little sister brought him presents of seaweed and a crab. But he responded listlessly. He couldn't bring himself to play, or even to hunt.

The boy had been his friend. Even though they couldn't swim together except on the very Edge, or speak to each other in the way that dolphins can speak, they'd felt each other's feelings, and that had been enough.

The dolphin missed the boy terribly. He feared that soon the boy would go far across the Sea, as the girl had gone. And then things would never be right between them, not ever again.

Two days later, Hylas stood in the stern of the foreigners' ship and watched the Island of the Fin People receding slowly behind him.

He'd been scanning the Sea for dolphins till his eyes ached, but so far, nothing. He felt cold and hollow inside. What if Spirit didn't come?

The ship's captain came and offered him a handful of dried anchovies. Hylas took them with a nod, but couldn't bring himself to eat.

Beside him the captain studied the waves with a sailor's restless eye. He wore a belted kilt like a Keftian, but his skin was darker, and from the holes in his ears hung two tiny flying fish carved from polished bone. Hylas didn't know where he came from or where his ship was going, except that it was heading north, towards Lykonia; that was good enough for him.

The captain said something in his incomprehensible tongue, and put his bunched fingers to his lips. *Eat.* Again Hylas simply nodded, so the man shrugged and went away.

A ripple of excitement ran through the crew – and suddenly there they were, their sleek backs arching out of the waves in mysterious unison, their silver bodies arrowing through the green water. Hylas' eyes stung. The whole pod had come to see him off. Wherever he turned he saw dolphins riding the bow wave, racing the ship and effortlessly winning. Then his heart leapt. There was Spirit.

Ignoring the curious glances of the oarsmen, Hylas bent low over the side, and Spirit swerved towards him, easily keeping pace with the ship. His dark eye met Hylas', then glanced away. As if, thought Hylas, he was asking, *Do you forgive?*

Hylas tried to answer in his mind, in the dolphin way. *Nothing to forgive.* Then out loud he said, 'There's nothing to forgive! I was never angry. It's just – I can't live in your world. And you would die in mine. That's just how it is.' A lump rose in his throat. 'That's just how it *is*.'

Spirit swam closer, and Hylas heard the soft *pfft!* of dolphin breath. He reached down as far as he could, and for a heartbeat his fingers skimmed the dolphin's back and he felt the cool, smooth hide. *Will I ever see you again?*

Spirit swerved away from him and disappeared into the deep. Then he was leaping high out of the water and twisting in mid-air, smacking down hard on his side with a *thwack* that drenched Hylas from top to toe. Shaking the water from his hair, he broke into a grin. He wasn't certain, but he thought that meant yes.

To show that he understood, he tossed an anchovy over the side, and Spirit caught it and gulped it down.

You'll always be my friend, Hylas told him in his head.

Again the dark eye met his, and he felt that Spirit understood, and was happy.

But already the pod was turning away.

For a little while Spirit swam alongside the ship, then he too was turning and heading back to his pod. For the last time his glance met Hylas'. Then he arched his back, flicked up his tail – and was gone, vanishing into his deep blue world, where Hylas could never follow.

The green sail swelled, and the creaking ship rode the waves. The tears stiffened on Hylas' cheeks.

The captain came and handed him an earthenware jar. Hylas nodded his thanks, and drank. It was wine and water, mixed with honey and roast barley meal: thick and heady and strengthening. As Hylas handed back the jar, the captain pointed at the waves, then made an arching motion with his hand, put his fist to his heart, and pointed at Hylas.

'Yes,' Hylas said with a nod. 'The dolphin is my friend.'

The captain returned to the steering-paddle, and Hylas thought about what he'd said. Then he ate the rest of the anchovies, threw the last one over the side as an offering, and felt a bit better.

It came to him that maybe Pirra was right, and everything did come back to the Goddess. Many days ago on Mount Lykas, Her words – the Oracle – had been the spark that lit the tinder and caused the Crows to attack his camp, and started him on the journey that led him to the island. There he'd found Spirit; and now Spirit was back with his pod, and he and Pirra had helped make that happen. And maybe this meant that some day, he would find Issi.

The island had dwindled to a dark blur on the horizon. Against it, Hylas caught a flash of silver. He knew in his heart that it was Spirit, making one of his great twisting leaps.

Raising his hand, Hylas shouted farewell. Then he laughed – because the Sun on the water was dazzling, and he was alive and free, and anything was possible.

Then the green sails bellied and the ship reared and plunged through the sparkling foam, and he watched the Island of the Fin People sinking slowly beneath the Sea.

Author Note

The story of Hylas and Pirra takes place three and a half thousand years ago, in what we now call the Bronze Age. As you may have gathered, it happens in the land we call ancient Greece. However, the Greece of the Bronze Age was very different from the ancient Greece of marble temples and classical sculpture with which you may be familiar. The Bronze Age was long before that. It was even before the Greeks ranged their gods and goddesses into an orderly pantheon of Zeus, Hera, Hades and all the others.

We don't know as much about Bronze Age Greece as we do about what came afterwards, because its people left so few written records. However, we know something about the astonishing cultures which flourished at that time, and which we call the Mycenaeans and the Minoans. Theirs is the world of Gods and Warriors.

Here I need to say a quick word about the place names in the story. What Hylas calls Akea (or Achaea, as it's usually spelled) is the ancient name for mainland Greece; and Lykonia is my name for present-day Lakonia, in south-west Greece; but I've kept the name Mycenae unaltered, as it's so well known. Concerning Pirra's people, I've adopted the name 'Keftian' for the great Cretan civilization which we call Minoan. However, it's one of the mysteries of the ancient world that we don't actually know what the people of that civilization called themselves; depending on which book you read, they may have called themselves Keftians, or that may just have been a name given to them by the ancient Egyptians. As for the Egyptians themselves, although the name 'Egyptian' comes from the name given to them by the Greeks, I've used it in the story because, like Mycenae, it felt too awkward and artificial to change it.

In creating the world of Hylas and Pirra, I've studied the archaeology of the Aegean Bronze Age, particularly its tombs and strongholds, artefacts and weapons. But to get an idea of how people thought and what they believed, I've also drawn on the beliefs of more recent peoples who still live in traditional ways, just as I did when I wrote about the Stone Age in the Chronicles of Ancient Darkness. And even though people in Hylas' time lived mostly by farming or fishing, rather than by hunting and gathering, as they did in the Stone Age, I've no doubt that many of the skills and beliefs of those earlier hunter-gatherers would have lingered on into the Bronze Age, particularly among the poorer and more isolated people, such as Hylas himself.

Concerning the geographical setting for the story, many people believe that Bronze Age Greece was a land of scattered chieftaincies separated by great mountain ranges and forests. It's also thought to have been wetter and greener than it is today, with far more wild animals both on land and in the Sea. In creating the Island of the Goddess, I didn't have a specific Greek island in mind, but based it on my sojourns over the decades on the islands of Ithaka, Kephalonia and Alonissos. More recently, and to gain inspiration for Lykonia, I visited Lakonia, including the Acropolis at Sparta, the Eurotas river and the deserted and immensely evocative ruins of the nearby Menelaion. To get a feel for Hylas' mountain home, I explored the Langada Gorge that winds through the Taÿgetos Mountains, and stayed for several days at the top of the Langada Pass. Wild boar still haunt the forests there; one morning, I had a slightly unnerving encounter with five piglets and their watchful mother.

To experience the caves in which Hylas and Pirra hide out, I explored the extensive, watery cave system of Vlychada, on the Bay of Diros in south-west Lakonia, as well as its small but highly informative local museum. There I learnt of the dreadful fate of some of the cave's earlier inhabitants, one of whose calcified remains sparked the idea for Pirra's encounter with the Vanished Ones. To get a feel for Keftiu, I visited Crete, where the ruins at Knossos and Phaestos, as well as the museums of Iraklion and Archanes, provided much inspiration for Pirra's homeland.

Spirit is, of course, one of the most important characters in the story, and to get to know him better I swam with socialized dolphins in Florida, where one of them kindly gave me a fin-ride, as Spirit does for Hylas and Pirra. I then travelled to the mid-Atlantic islands of the Azores, where I spent days observing wild dolphins of different species: Striped, Atlantic Spotted, Common, Risso's and Spirit's own kind, the Bottlenose. It was only when I saw wild dolphins in their natural habitat that I truly appreciated the mysterious synchronicity of their swimming. Snorkelling with them gave me a powerful sense of their otherworldliness, which made it easy to imagine how Hylas feels when he sees the dolphins swimming in the phosphorescence which he calls 'the blue fire'. Above all, watching those wild dolphins gave me an imaginative insight into how Spirit experiences life in his deep blue world.

I want to thank the people – too numerous to name – who gave me invaluable guidance and assistance while I was exploring Lakonia and Crete, as well as the marine biologists in Ponta Delgada in the Azores who helped me get as close to wild dolphins as was possible without disturbing them, and generously shared their insights on dolphin biology and behaviour. I'm also extremely grateful to Todd Whitelaw, Professor of Aegean Archaeology at the Institute of Archaeology, University College London, for giving so generously of his time in answering some questions on the prehistoric Aegean. As always, I want to thank my wonderful and indefatigable agent Peter Cox for his commitment and support; and my two hugely talented editors at Puffin Books, Elv Moody and Sarah Hughes, for their boundless enthusiasm and their vivid and imaginative responses to the story of Hylas and Pirra.

Michelle Paver, 2012

Gods and Warriors is the first book in the story of Hylas and Pirra, which tells of their adventures in Akea and beyond, and of their fight to vanquish the Crows. The next book in the series will be published in autumn 2013.